MURDER ON THE RHÔNE

CAPTAIN LACEY REGENCY MYSTERIES
BOOK EIGHTEEN

ASHLEY GARDNER

JA / AG PUBLISHING

CHAPTER 1

June 1820

The tall Frenchman seemed familiar to me, though at the moment I could not place him. He halted when he caught me staring at him down the narrow street of the Presqu'île in Lyon, where I walked with my daughter on an early June morning.

The gentleman, who dressed in a simple brown suit and boots for walking, peered at me as though he might recognize me in return, and then he abruptly swung around and began striding in the other direction. Not fleeing, but moving as a man who'd remembered he needed to be elsewhere.

Curious. The gentleman rounded a corner and was lost to sight, and I tucked the incident into the back of my mind.

It would come to me where I'd seen him before. Possibly in Paris, where I'd lived during the Peace of Amiens at the beginning of this century, or in London, into which French emigres had poured at the end of the last century. Many had returned home from their exile once the Bourbon king had been restored.

Or, I might have encountered the man on a battlefield.

England and France had been at war for such a long time, it would not be unusual for me to come across a Frenchman I'd fought on a teeming field in Spain.

Spying him today meant that we'd both survived.

I turned my attention to the more important venture—shopping with Gabriella, who was determined to find the perfect ribbons to adorn her bridal gown.

She'd been ready to rush out on her own this morning from the house my wife, Donata, had leased for our sojourn, but I'd proclaimed I'd accompany her. Brewster, who'd been breakfasting in the kitchen, had popped upstairs, his mouth full of toasted bread, but I'd waved him off. Gabriella and I could navigate a street market without harm, or so I'd believed.

Now my daughter and I strolled the back lanes on this island between Lyon's two rivers. The early morning markets and shops were thronged with those who knew that if they wanted the choicest wares and foodstuffs they had to reach the vendors as soon as they opened.

Gabriella moved with purpose through the maze to a stall I'd never have found without a precise map and a few days to reconnoiter. The round-faced woman behind it beamed when she saw Gabriella.

"*Bonjour, ma petite,*" she gushed.

Gabriella responded in her friendly manner, using the polite words a young woman would with a person her senior. Gabriella spoke flawless French, having grown up in this country. I spoke it fairly well myself, though at the moment, Gabriella and the woman segued into words I'd never heard before.

Lyonnais, I told myself. A dialect of the city and its region. I didn't understand a word of it.

As the two chattered, I took in my surroundings. The air was warm, a change from London, where it had been cold and rainy when we'd departed two weeks ago, spring long in coming.

The vendors in this lane sold everything from ribbons and

laces to fat loaves of crusty bread, vegetables in bold greens, reds, and yellows, and sweet pastries glistening with honey. Voices rose as women bartered with sellers or greeted those they knew. The scents of the pastries, bread, fruit, and the heady aroma of brewing coffee drifted over me.

Because Gabriella often came to the city with her mother or stepfather, many in the market recognized her. They certainly knew Emile Devere, Gabriella's betrothed.

Donata and I had been accorded much respect since we'd arrived and moved into the hired villa on the hill. Not because Donata was the daughter of an English earl and widow of a viscount, we'd quickly learned, but because of the Deveres.

Their large family owned an ironworks on the south end of the town, just past where the Rhône and Saône rivers met. Donata and I had been given a tour of the factory when we'd arrived, and both of us had been astonished at the extent of it.

The Deveres had been running the business for nearly a century, founded by an ancestor who'd been in the employ of the great Louis the Fourteenth. Apparently the Deveres' generosity and fair practices had gained them much repute in Lyon and the surrounding countryside.

Gabriella purchased ribbons that pleased her then moved slowly among the stalls, stopping to speak with almost every vendor, who were happy to visit with their favorite young lady this morning.

Knowing from experience that Gabriella would be some time, I stepped into the tavern in which I'd been taking coffee and breakfast most days since our arrival.

I'd made the mistake of ordering a full breakfast upon my first visit, which had consisted of much meat. I'd ended up eating for hours, to the amusement of and with encouragement from the locals. I'd then gone home and napped, unable to do much of anything else for the rest of the day.

Today, I greeted the proprietor, a bulky man called Baptiste

Beaumont, with a friendly *bonjour,* and asked for coffee and with a bit of ham and bread.

I nodded to the other gentlemen in the shop's dim interior. They were here every morning and had somewhat accepted me as a regular. But only, I'd soon realized, because my daughter was marrying a Devere.

Emile had never once boasted to me how well-regarded his family was, which made me view him with a bit more respect.

I exchanged a few pleasantries with the men while I sipped my coffee, but mostly we sat in agreeable silence.

When the commotion began outside, I started up in alarm, but fortunately it came from nowhere near Gabriella. I saw from the open doorway that she still wandered the stalls, too deep among the vendors to notice the noise.

I and a few of the others followed our curiosity out of Beaumont's shop and through lanes to emerge on the main square, from which the tumult emanated.

Napoleon Bonaparte had begun the restoration of this square twenty years ago, and it was now a vast, open plaza ringed with new buildings. Once called the Place Royale and adorned with a statue of the Sun King, it was now officially Place Bonaparte, though most I spoke to still referred to it as the Place Royale. With another Louis back on the throne, it seemed safe once more to use the old name.

The din came from a throng of people chasing a woman and two sturdy male servants, all three of whom sprinted for a waiting carriage. The woman's fine frock and cloak fluttered as she ran, the mob closing in fast.

The coachman couldn't pull nearer to the lady and her protectors because another knot of people caught at the horses. The coachman stood on his box and plied his whip without mercy to those reaching for the reins, but even so, his conveyance could not move.

I and my inquisitive friends halted at the edge of the square while the horde of pursuers swept past. I saw, caught up in the mob and striving to leave it, another of the Deveres.

This was Fernand, one of Emile's uncles. Emile had three of those, all on his father's side. I'd met two thus far—Fernand and Giraud—plus Emile's father Auguste, a quiet man who spoke little English.

Fernand spoke it fairly fluently, and also German, as he sometimes went to London or Stuttgart to meet with those who sold the goods the Deveres turned out in their factory.

I stepped into the crowd, seized Fernand, and pulled him from the melee.

Fernand struggled before he recognized me, then he slumped in relief and let me tow him to safety. We caught our breaths beside a sun-drenched wall on the edge of the square, me leaning heavily on my walking stick.

"What on earth is happening?" I asked him. "Who are they chasing?"

Fernand, who stood a foot shorter than me and sported a soft belly from eating many a fine supper, rested his hands on his knees as he wheezed.

"Signora Ruggeri," he said when he could. "The most hated woman in Lyon."

"Signora?" I repeated, my brows rising.

"She is from Padua, or claims to be." Fernand straightened as his breath became steadier. "She is the mistress of the Comte Lejeune."

I had heard Donata mention the name—she seemed to know every highborn family in Lyon—but I'd never met the man.

Signora Ruggeri had by now managed to reach the carriage, but the crowd closed in as she wrenched open its door. The signora screamed as hands reached to drag her from the coach's step.

I started forward, unwilling to stand by and watch a woman be beaten to death. There was a sword inside the walking stick's sheath, which I could use to warn people out of my way.

Fernand caught my arm before I could take two steps.

"No, *mon ami.* Her coachman was a prizefighter and ferocious enough to protect her. You see?"

The coachman continued to apply his whip without remorse to the men and women surrounding him. He discouraged enough of her pursuers to allow the two muscular servants to shove the lady into the carriage and slam the door.

The servants leapt onto the back of the coach as the coachman urged his team forward, scattering those who tried to stop him. The large vehicle hurtled out of the plaza and into one of the narrow streets beyond.

Some pursued, but as the carriage gained speed, they drifted back to the square, disgruntled and muttering.

"Never lift a finger to help that woman," Fernand advised me. "Else you become the most hated *man* in Lyon."

"Good Lord, what has she done that is so horrible? All I saw was a lady trying to reach her carriage and a crowd ready to murder her."

"What *hasn't* she done?" Fernand answered, shaking his head. "Come, we will sit, and I will tell you the tale."

CHAPTER 2

Fernand and I left the square and made for the lane from which I'd emerged. A glance at the market street showed Gabriella still browsing the stalls, oblivious to the angry violence in the plaza.

We entered Beaumont's shop, where my unfinished breakfast still waited. The older men I and the others had left behind still reposed at their usual tables, as they apparently had done all through the siege of Lyon, the reprisals afterward, and Bonaparte's subsequent arrival.

I asked for a coffee for my friend, which was promptly brought. Beaumont set it down carefully before Fernand, clearly in awe that a Devere had come into his tavern.

"What has this signora done that is so heinous?" I asked once Beaumont had retreated. "Many aristocrats take mistresses, and have done since time immemorial."

Fernand enjoyed a sip of coffee, then he shook his head as he set down his cup.

"She is not simply a mistress. She has taken over his life. Comte Lejeune was never a saintly man, and if he does not dote on his wife, he at least remained quietly within his circle of friends. Until, that is, he was dazzled by Isadora Ruggeri. She arrived in Lyon this spring, and caused a sensation when she appeared at the theatre—in the audience, not on the stage. Naturally, he strove to meet her. She *is* quite beautiful." Fernand shrugged, as though this were the only excuse a gentleman needed for committing adultery.

"She beguiled him?" I asked. "So might many a lady, without enraging an entire city."

"It was a harmless affair, at first." Fernand relaxed into his story. "A flirtation that led to a rendezvous, which led to him putting her in a small house in the Presqu'île that he owns. All would have been well if Signora Ruggeri had simply been grateful for what the comte gave her, but she proved to be ambitious and greedy. She declared that the house in town was not good enough, and he must move her—immediately. So he evicted a tenant in one of his villas, a bishop, no less, and installed her there."

"Ah, I begin to see."

"That is not the end of it. The comte began to buy her ropes of jewels from around the world, the larger the stones, the better. He nearly bankrupted himself with this endeavor, or would have, had his wife not stepped in. From a powerful family herself, the comtesse was able to have the comte's men of business answer to her for any expenditure."

"Wise," I said. "Though heartbreaking for the comtesse, I'd think. My own wife would cast me out and bar the door." I imagined Donata's chill and cutting anger and took a warming sip of coffee.

"The comtesse is a good woman," Fernand said with admiration. "Valiant." He gave this praise in French, and the graying heads around us bobbed in agreement. "Hers is a very old family, with origins going back to the twelfth century, long before this region became part of France. Her husband, in contrast, is from Paris."

Snorts sounded, the people of the south derisive of those in the north, very much like those in my own country.

"Though I have compassion for the comtesse, this is not a new tale," I pointed out.

"Perhaps, but then Signora Ruggeri began appearing at the theatre and the opera in the comte's box," Fernand continued. "Arriving early enough so the comtesse would have to retreat rather than confront her in public. The signora insisted on the comte giving her precedence at all gatherings—fetes in the Place Royale, and so forth. Finally, she tried to persuade Lejeune to divorce his wife, though as a good Catholic, he never will. When she did not succeed with that, she began trying to have his two sons disinherited, I suppose with a goal to have the comte leave her as much money as possible in his will. He is, unfortunately, believing her, in spite of the comtesse's pristine reputation."

I listened to all this in growing amazement. "She certainly is audacious. I take it that sympathy lies with the comtesse?"

"Of course," Fernand said adamantly. "The signora has paid a few ruffians to protect her, but the comtesse is ours, isn't she? Though, I believe Signora Ruggeri will have others to turn to when the comte finally comes to his senses. She has made other conquests." Fernand winced. "Some too close to home."

I wasn't certain what Fernand meant by that but decided I'd ask him when there weren't so many ears turned our way.

"Perhaps the fact that she cannot appear in the street without being attacked will convince her to go elsewhere," I said.

"That is my hope." Fernand took a fortifying sip of coffee. "Then our city can return to its peace."

I agreed that this would be for the best. I continued my small breakfast, while the men around us went back to their own conversations, and Fernand turned to more neutral topics, such as his last trip to London and what he'd enjoyed there.

"Your food is terrible," he said good-naturedly. "But your ale is fine."

"Very true," I answered. "We can turn grains into any number of liquids, excellent for keeping warm in the winter."

Fernand chuckled along with me.

Presently, I glimpsed Gabriella through the doorway and excused myself to meet her. Fernand accompanied me, after sliding Beaumont coins for my meal and coffee before I could stop him.

Gabriella's face lit when she saw Fernand. She and Emile's uncle kissed each other's cheeks, Gabriella speaking comfortably with him in French and Lyonnais.

This was her home, I realized anew as the three of us started for the Pont Tilsit would take us across the Saône. No matter how often Gabriella visited England, enjoying Donata's parents' home in Oxfordshire or our house in South Audley Street, she was part of *this* place. She'd known Emile and his family for years, and the Deveres were happy to embrace her as their own.

Envy stung me, though I told myself I was ridiculous. Gabriella had spent most of her life near Lyon, and of course, she'd be connected to the city and its people far more than she ever would be to me. She'd grown up as an Auberge, who were prosperous farmers south of the city, linked to and absorbed by the Deveres when she'd become betrothed to Emile.

We passed from the narrow streets to the bridge, an arched structure that would take us over the Saône. The river was running high, as was the Rhône on the other side of the Presqu'île, spring rains and snowmelt rushing from the faraway Alps to fill it. The cathedral of Saint-Jean-Baptiste rose on the other side of the Saône, the stained glass windows of its nave facing east, toward us.

As we emerged into an open space near the bridge, I spied the Frenchman I'd seen earlier.

The tall man strolled along not far from us, heading in the opposite direction on the quay on this side of the river. He did not see me this time, intent on whatever was his destination.

"Devere," I said, interrupting his conversation with Gabriella. "Do you know that gentleman?" I gestured covertly at the man in question, not wanting to rudely point.

"Eh?" Fernand squinted across the distance. "Ah, yes, that is Colonel Moreau. Why do you ask?"

"I'm certain I've met him before, but I can't quite place him." The niggling feeling unnerved me.

"His forename is Nicolas, and he lives in Vieux Lyon," Fernand said helpfully. "Began as a lieutenant in Bonaparte's army, and rose to the rank of colonel. Well thought of, even if he favored the new regime."

I tried to recall the name, but I could not. Again, I might well have seen him during the turmoil of the war or during my time in Paris.

The man faded into the crowd along the quay, and I decided that he was a mystery for another time.

We crossed the bridge, and Fernand took his leave from us to travel south along the river, back to the factory. Gabriella and I walked to our rented home, she happy with her purchases from the market.

Rubble from Lyon's Roman past littered the slopes of the hill we climbed, nestled among the monasteries and churches there. The wealthy lived in large villas on the hill's summit, including the one Donata had procured for us.

She'd decided it would be more practical if we did not stay with or even near the Auberges, my first wife's family, though they had a rather large house on a fine patch of land south of the city. Donata had pointed out that the first wife and the second living too close was not a good idea, and I'd readily agreed.

Gabriella had asked leave to spend some nights with us, which her mother hadn't liked, but I'd of course encouraged. I didn't mind at all rising early with Gabriella when she stayed with us, walking out with her to the market streets. Her two half-sisters had come to visit from time to time, filling the echoing villa with girlish laughter.

Brewster, somehow, had heard of the altercation in the Place

Royale. He confronted me as soon as we entered the villa's inner courtyard.

"This is why I dog your steps, guv." Brewster scowled at me after Gabriella had greeted him sunnily and scurried inside. "Safe as houses, ye said. Well, houses can fall on a bloke, can't they?"

"All was well, Brewster," I assured him. "The mob wasn't after *me*. I was simply observing. Fernand Devere was the one almost caught in it."

"Not sure about that family," Brewster muttered darkly, with a quick glance at the door Gabriella had darted through. "Something wrong there."

"They are far more respectable than I feared they'd be," I said. "Highly regarded and well off, not scratching for a living."

"Brought themselves up from nothing." Brewster's tone held working-class suspicion of those who got above themselves. "Labored for the kings and queens until they opened their business to anyone who could pay."

"So did many a person who supplied things to the royals," I told him. "The palaces of old were hives of industry. Anyway, how do you know all this? You've been insisting you don't speak French."

Brewster shrugged his massive shoulders. "Words here and there, and some in this house speak a bit of English. It don't take much to get the point across." He skewered me with his annoyed glare. "Don't go wandering about town without me again. Think about keeping your daughter safe, if nothing else. What if she'd been in the square when that lot decided to strike?"

The first thing I'd done was to make certain Gabriella was nowhere near the commotion, but I didn't argue. "I take your point, Brewster. You may guard my heels from now on."

Brewster did not look any happier as he stumped back into the house and in the direction of the kitchen.

My wife was still abed, as it was not her habit to rise much before two in the afternoon. I watched Gabriella sort her purchases in the high-ceilinged sitting room—ribbons and lace and other frills, she explaining to me what she'd use each one for. I mostly had no idea what she was talking about, but I enjoyed that she wanted to share the preparations for her wedding with me.

Once a maid helped Gabriella fold the things away, she declared she'd have a nap, to rest for the long evening ahead Donata had planned.

I conceded that she had a good idea and adjourned to my own chamber. A peek into Donata's as I passed it showed her room dark and shrouded, the hangings around her bed firmly closed. I smiled as I softly shut the door, my wife's habits ever predictable.

My bedchamber was vast, its bed with brocade curtains set squarely in the middle of the room. The ceiling was a soft blue, painted with cherubs in the cheerful Rococo style. I wasn't used to such sumptuousness—our South Audley Street house was decorated with restraint—but happily, the bed was comfortable.

I drifted quickly off to sleep once I lay down, but I'd used my bad leg too much this morning. A deep ache jabbed at me, even in my full slumber.

The pain turned my dreams to the incident that had caused the injury in the first place. In the scrubby hills of northern Spain during the Peninsular War, I'd been captured and tortured for the pleasure of a group of French soldiers. One of them had crushed my knee with his boot heel, slamming into it again and again, while I couldn't halt my cries of agony.

A second face broke through the haze of dreams, and I sat straight up in the bed, gasping.

I knew full well where I'd seen the Frenchman called Colonel Moreau before. It was clear, in turn, that he'd recognized me.

CHAPTER 3

*S*leep was now out of the question. I rose and slid on my boots and coat, too agitated to summon Bartholomew, my valet, to assist me. I paced the room in the late afternoon sunshine, which further hurt my leg, but I could not calm myself.

I'd managed, I thought, to put the entire experience behind me. But then the memories would rise from nowhere, stealing my breath and drenching my body in cold sweat.

In April of 1814, shortly after the Battle of Toulouse, my commander, Colonel Brandon, sent me on a mission to report on the movements of a French company.

Unbeknownst to me, Brandon hadn't meant me to return. He'd sent me into a hillside crawling with French soldiers, a sure chance to cause my death.

I'd hidden, using all the skills I'd learned in a dozen years of campaigning, and waited for a chance to make my way back to camp. Unfortunately, I'd been discovered by a knot of French troops, who'd decided to desert and live off what booty they could capture from the nearby villages or any soldier who happened to stumble their way.

After stealing all my gear, they'd beaten me for the fun of it, their large sergeant striking my knee repeatedly with his heavy boot. They'd then strung me up by the heels from the nearest tree to bat at me with bayonets and butts of rifles, pushing me from companion to the other.

I'd been left hanging while they consumed the food and drink I'd brought with me, lighting a fire to keep themselves warm while I shivered in the cold, stripped to my small clothes.

Moreau had been there. As I dimly remembered, he'd not participated in the actual beating, but he'd not stopped the men from doing so. He'd shared in my flask of brandy and watched while the soldiers had gone through my coat and thrown my boots into the stream below their makeshift camp.

Once the men had fallen into satisfied slumber, Moreau had cut me down. He'd said not a word, hadn't offered excuses, apologies, or assistance. He'd dragged me under a stand of scrub, then abandoned me in a heap and disappeared into the night, leaving the soldiers behind.

Where he'd gone, and why, to this day I had no idea.

Not many hours later, a handful of British soldiers had come through the clearing to find the Frenchmen in a drunken stupor. There had been a short, ugly fight that had left the Frenchmen either dead or carried off as prisoners.

The British troops hadn't seen me shrouded in the bushes, and I'd been too weak to call out. I wasn't certain they'd have rescued me, in any case—they likely would have mistaken me for another French soldier and run me through to end my misery.

In end, I'd crawled away on my own, retrieving my boots from the river, and somehow got myself to a farm, where I'd been found by the children of the house. There, after I'd disposed of the French deserter who'd more or less taken the family prisoner, I'd convalesced, with the help of the children's mother, and eventually made my way back to my camp. I'd discovered Brandon's duplicity, and both of us had been sent back to England, careers over.

Moreau had obviously survived the encounter. He'd been gone when the British soldiers had found and taken his men, but he'd left me to die, regardless.

Now Moreau was in Lyon, where he lived and thrived.

What should I do? Avoid him? Confront him? Scheme to take my vengeance?

I wasn't certain I had the interest in vengeance anymore. I'd recovered, healed, continued.

Since returning from the Peninsula, I'd married a beautiful if sharp-tongued lady of the aristocracy, cultivated deep friendships, and reconnected with Gabriella. Even Brandon and I had reconciled somewhat, though he still carried the guilt of what he'd done.

Did I truly need to dredge it all up again?

I might not have to worry overmuch. My path and Colonel Moreau's had crossed by chance this morning, and possibly, they would not cross again. After all, I'd been in Lyon two weeks, and this was the first I'd seen of the man. He lived in the old city, Fernand had told me, and I spent most of my time on the island between rivers or up on this hill.

Eventually, I calmed myself enough to sit and focus on a book Grenville had lent me on the history of ancient Lyon. Then, when the shadows lengthened, I summoned Bartholomew to help me dress for my outing with Donata.

The interesting book, as well as Bartholomew's good-naturedness, never dimmed, restored me to my usual stoic self. I tucked my memories and my fury away, reminding myself again of my current good fortune.

"Have you heard of Signora Ruggeri, Bartholomew?" I asked while he brushed down my best coat.

Bartholomew had the ability to pick up languages, no matter what country he journeyed with me to, and he got on well with the staff in any house. If there was gossip about a person in this city, he'd already know it.

Bartholomew paused, a brush in each hand. "Oh, aye, there's

lively talk about *her*. There is even a joke below stairs, when someone gets above himself. *You think you're Signora Ruggeri, do you?* they say. I had to ask what it meant."

"A lady of bold reputation, I take it."

Bartholomew resumed brushing. "Says she's from Padua, though no one knows for certain where she sprang from. They admire Comtesse Lejeune, wife of the man this Italian lady is mistress of, but don't think much of the comte. He's not from these parts, you see, and most of the lands and money are hers. He owns a few properties around the town, but the old chateau on the hill comes from her family."

He finished with his usual verve, giving my sleeve a final swipe.

"You are a mine of information, Bartholomew."

"Never hurts to understand the lay of the land, does it? The staff is already in awe of her ladyship and adore Miss Gabriella."

Which was usual for whatever house we lived in. "Are they in awe of me?" I asked in curiosity.

A guffaw. "Not so much, sir."

"Know me for a soft touch, do they? Ah, well. I'd rather that than servants who fear me."

"That's not likely, is it?" Bartholomew laid his brushes neatly into their box and closed the lid. "They catch on quickly, they do, as to who they need to obey."

"My wife," I said without concern. "As it should be."

I did not have time to ask Bartholomew more about Signora Ruggeri, or even venture a question about Colonel Moreau, because Gabriella appeared in my doorway, dressed in finery, and announced it was time we were off.

———

Not until we were in the carriage, rolling through gates patrolled by large, hard-faced men to the grandest villa I'd yet seen did I learn the details of our evening outing.

"Who lives here?" I asked Donata as we followed a long drive toward a many-windowed house with two massive towers on each end. The gardens around the villa bore hedges that were trained and tamed into stiff green topiaries.

"The Comte Lejeune," Donata said. Her gray silk sleeve brushed me as she wrapped her arm through mine, the feathers of her headdress tickling my cheek. "His wife is a dear friend of my mother's."

I started at the name. Donata glanced at me quizzically, but I did not want to launch into the tale of the comte's reviled mistress while Gabriella regarded us serenely.

"It's a very old house," Donata went on, as our carriage followed the slow line of conveyances to the front door. "Built over the remains of a castle a few hundred years ago. Kept very fine though," she finished in approval.

The coach finally halted and I stepped down, then handed out my wife and daughter, not bothering to stem my pride in them.

A host of servants was on hand to welcome us into the chateau, all under the direction of a haughty majordomo. Two liveried footmen flanked the grand front door, and three more footmen inside reached for our wraps. A maid ushered Donata and Gabriella toward withdrawing rooms, and a manservant guided me to a similar one for gentlemen.

There, I found Lucius Grenville, who was staying in Lyon with Marianne, surrounded by a horde of gentlemen already enthralled by him.

"Ah, Lacey." Grenville nodded at me, while the others turned to see who merited his attention. He continued in French. "Messieurs, let me introduce you to my very good friend, Gabriel Lacey, of Norfolk, England."

The dozen gentlemen in the room looked me up and down, clearly wondering what Grenville saw in this tall man with unfashionably sunbaked skin and dark hair threaded with gray. Glances went to my walking stick, which I could not move far without, and then dismissed me as no threat. From their expressions, these gentlemen had no inkling where Norfolk lay, nor did they care.

I noted that Grenville hadn't labeled me as *Captain*, or mentioned my regiment. He was trying to be diplomatic, I gathered, not reminding those who might have been in Napoleon's army that I'd done my best to shoot them at one time.

He needn't have bothered. None of these gentlemen appeared hardened enough to have been one of Bonaparte's brilliant marshals or even his generals or colonels.

The cream of those hand-picked commanders were now lying low or sadly gone forever. These younger gentlemen, dressed in the latest stare of fashion, their hair carefully waved or curled, had likely stayed home during the long wars, hiding from passing armies.

I greeted them politely, but any interest in me quickly faded. After brisk nods and murmurs of *bonsoir*, they returned their attention to Grenville.

He was holding forth with amusing anecdotes of his travels from London, including his seasickness on the Channel crossing, which his listeners found hilarious. Grenville, a natural raconteur, exaggerated his wretchedness, including the sounds he'd made, to the alarm of the ship's captain.

His audience roared. I listened for a few minutes, then bowed and backed out of the chamber.

I had to admit admiration for the house I wandered through and agreed with Donata that it had retained its grandeur. Black-and-white marble tiles in the main hall complemented the marble columns and arches that framed the stone-balustraded staircase. I mounted the steps, ready to reach the ballroom and find a quiet corner in which to sit and watch Donata and Gabriella enjoy themselves.

At the top of the staircase, a floor of polished terra-cotta led toward tall open doors to the ballroom, where people conversed and an orchestra played. The wall opposite me held a painting of bright yellow flowers and pale orange peaches reposing in a basket, the fruit, flowers, and canted basket rendered in exquisite and lifelike detail.

I caught sight of Gabriella lingering near a carved chest at the opposite end of this hallway and quickly went to her.

"I thought you'd have stayed with Donata," I said in surprise.

Gabriella shook her head and took my offered arm. "She was deep in conversation with other ladies, and I was curious about the villa."

"Shall we explore together?" I asked.

Gabriella nodded. "It is a lovely house."

I detected a forced note and pulled her aside. "What is it? Has something happened?"

"Oh, no, Father, nothing like that," Gabriella answered, then she quieted. "Please do not think me ungracious or spoiled. I know Lady Donata persuaded her friends to include me tonight."

"You? Ungracious and spoiled?" I asked in amazement. "You do not know how to be either. Now tell me what has upset you."

Gabriella studied the intricate pattern of stones at our feet. "Nothing I can point to, exactly. But I overheard those in the withdrawing room speaking disparagingly of Emile and his family. Asking Lady Donata if she couldn't have found a better match for me. I was in the corner and do not know if they realized I was in the room or not."

My ire flared. "What did Donata say to this?"

"I do not know. I slipped out before anyone saw me."

I forced myself to tamp down my anger. "I assure you, Donata will be giving them the rough side of her tongue." I touched my fingers to Gabriella's chin, and she reluctantly raised her gaze to mine. "Emile is a fine young man, and everyone in town speaks highly of his family."

"The Deveres are in trade, and the people here tonight are aristocrats. *Their* families fled when Lyon was besieged by the Parisians." Gabriella's eyes sparkled dangerously. "Emile's grandfather was executed after Lyon's surrender, and his father and uncles nearly were as well. Emile would not even be here if the revolutionaries had succeeded. The Deveres sacrificed themselves for this city, while the fathers of these ladies and gentlemen hid themselves until it was safe to emerge."

I hadn't heard the extent of the tale, though Fernand had hinted that things had been difficult for the Deveres when Lyon had resisted the extremes of the revolution. An army had been sent to suppress them, besieging the city for months.

Executions after Lyon's surrender had taken place in the large plaza first with the guillotine then with simply shooting into crowds. The executions seemed random, with counterrevolutionaries and royalists dying alongside common workers and moderate, middle-class gentlemen.

"It is easy for those who do not suffer to judge," I said. "I'm not certain what advice to give you, Gabriella, except to remember that the Deveres are good people, and to ignore those disparaging them. It does not matter what ignorant fools think."

"Do not resort to fisticuffs, you mean?" Gabriella sent me a brittle smile. "It is difficult, sometimes."

She was very much like me, I thought with a frisson of satisfaction. "It is indeed, but we should behave better than those who toss about insults, uncaring who will be hurt by them."

"That is why I am apologizing for being ungracious," Gabriella said quickly. "I'd rather return home than stay at a ball where I am unwelcome, no matter how elegant the house."

I understood perfectly—thinking of the gentlemen who'd all but sneered at me in the withdrawing room—but I wanted to soothe her. "If the comtesse herself did not want you here, I wager even Donata would not have talked her into inviting you. The other ladies are guests, just as you are, aren't they?"

"I suppose that is true." Gabriella took my arm again. "With you by my side, Father, we will face them down."

"That's the spirit. Now, I know from experience that Donata

might be some time. Will you give me the honor of entering the ballroom with me?"

"Of course." She sent me a brave smile. "I will recover my temper, I assure you."

"Do not bother. You have no need to bow your head and apologize when an aristocratic lady insults those you care for."

"I can be civil, however," Gabriella said, her moroseness fleeing. "That is better, is it not?"

I patted her hand, and we started courageously for the ballroom.

Before we'd gone far, we were startled by a loud screeching from the lower hall.

"What on earth—?" Gabriella asked in alarm and hastened to the staircase, me behind her. Together we peered over the balustrade.

Below us, on the ground floor, several footmen were trying to prevent someone from storming into the house.

"Unhand me," a female voice in irate French came to us. "I demand you admit me, at once. Send for the comte. He will tell you."

I recognized, to my astonishment, the vibrant movements and sleek dark hair of Signora Ruggeri, the woman who'd run for her life in the town square that very morning.

CHAPTER 4

The footmen at the base of the staircase tried desperately, and aggressively, to shove Signora Ruggeri back out the open front door.

Other guests joined us at the railing, ladies and gentlemen gaping at the scene below. Some guffawed at the signora's struggles, and one woman uttered a few unflattering words about her character.

Watching Signora Ruggeri imperiously demand entrance into the house of her lover, where she clearly was not wanted, I could not help but feel some pity for her.

I could see that she wanted very much to visit the comte on her own terms—to be treated as his equal—but she never could be. The same aristocrats who looked down their noses at the Deveres had no use for a commoner mistress trying to push into their world. Her place was in the shadows or the scandal sheets, they'd remind her, not in the comte's home.

Signora Ruggeri managed to break past the footmen and gain the foyer. The majordomo grabbed her by the arms and pivoted her around. Her screeching began once more, incoherent screams of rage tinged with fear.

That fear touched my protective instincts. Fernand had

warned me against interfering, but no woman deserved to be so roughly manhandled.

I started down the stairs toward the fray. Gabriella did not call me back, which meant she understood my need to help.

I'd taken only three steps downward when the crowd above me abruptly quieted. I turned to see what had caught their attention.

Comtesse Lejeune herself swept along the upper hall and past her guests to the staircase. I'd not yet met the comtesse, but I knew it was she by the way everyone melted aside for her, regarding her with awe.

She was a thin, rather small lady, but the stately way she carried herself made up for any lack of stature. She wore her gray-touched dark hair in a plain knot, without dangling curls or other embellishments. Her simple headdress of a diamond band with a silver feather was all the more elegant for that.

She descended the staircase, her skirts brushing me as she wafted by.

I could not help following her down, worried about what the spirited signora might do when confronted by her lover's wife.

The comtesse gestured quietly at the majordomo, who loosed his hold on Signora Ruggeri and stepped away, though he kept a wary eye on her.

Signora Ruggeri became strangely subdued once released. Instead of turning her wrath on the comtesse, she waited quietly between the burly footmen as the comtesse approached.

The guests in the downstairs hall fell silent, and I felt the weight of stares above me. All held their collective breaths, anticipating the comtesse's condemnation of her husband's beautiful mistress.

Comtesse Lejeune reached the foyer. The footmen's stances became respectful as she neared them, and the majordomo stood at attention, awaiting orders.

The comtesse ignored them all and held out poised, gloved hands to the signora.

"Signora Ruggeri, welcome," she said in a clear, ringing voice. "I saw you dancing at a fete last month. So effortless and accomplished."

Signora Ruggeri gaped awkwardly at the older woman, who exuded confidence and ease. Belatedly, Signora Ruggeri attempted a curtsy.

"Your ladyship," she murmured in accented French. "You are very kind."

The contrast between the two women was acute. The comtesse wore a subdued silver gown and might have blended into the background if not for her controlled grace. The signora was dressed in a vivid shade of maroon, her bodice cut to show off a plump bosom. Diamonds glittered in her hair, no doubt a gift from the comtesse's husband. The comtesse was regal, the signora, ostentatious.

The comtesse grasped Signora Ruggeri's hands and raised her from the curtsy. "No need for such formality, my dear. I cannot think what happened to your invitation. One hires out these things, and one can only trust that the task is accomplished correctly. Let us ascend to the ballroom, which is much more comfortable than this drafty hall."

To the crowd's and Signora Ruggeri's absolute astonishment, the comtesse tucked the younger woman's hand under her arm and proceeded to guide her up the staircase.

I stood aside to let them pass, giving the comtesse as polite a bow as I could while balancing on the stairs.

The guests swarmed up behind the two women, none wanting to miss the spectacle of their beloved comtesse taking charge of her husband's hated mistress.

I climbed more slowly after them, and Gabriella met me at the top of the stairs.

"How gallant of the comtesse," she gushed, her despondency gone. "She would have been justified to have the lady arrested. The comtesse is proving that grace and manners are more to be admired than youth and fleeting beauty."

As Gabriella at the moment possessed both youth and beauty, I suppressed a smile. I agreed with her sentiment, however. The comtesse had just given us a lesson in dignity and sangfroid.

Donata glided toward us through the throng. She took my arm as she thoughtfully regarded the pair who disappeared into the crowd.

"The comtesse came to stay with us once, in Oxfordshire," she said. "I'm certain she found us rustic and provincial. But she was kind and intelligent, engaging my father in learned conversation, and never complained of endless walks in our damp garden. She was even kind to me, an ungainly young lady of fourteen, who ought to have been beneath her notice."

I could not imagine Donata ever being ungainly, but I suppose we all were at some point in our lives. Donata was now elegant at my side, and her tone held as much admiration as Gabriella's.

Donata continued. "When the new republic inflicted retribution on this city for supporting the king, the comtesse was steadfast. They declared they'd destroy all the homes of the wealthy—or anyone they perceived as wealthy—and she worked to keep those orders from being carried out. Out of the hundreds of houses that were to be burned or pulled down, a large percentage of them escaped. The comtesse had much to do with that, quietly and behind the scenes. She is quite a lady."

"She appears to be." I wanted to see more of this woman. "Shall we go in?"

The upper hall had nearly emptied, leaving us, the less interesting foreigners, alone.

Gabriella took my other arm, and we made for the ballroom. The majordomo, who'd taken his place inside its doorway announced us.

"Capitaine Gabriel Lacey, Madame Lacey, and Mademoiselle Gabriella Auberge."

No one noticed. The guests had knotted behind the

comtesse and Signora Ruggeri, trying to pretend they weren't following.

A passing footman offered champagne, which Donata and I took and Gabriella declined.

The comtesse continued to flow across the ballroom, Signora Ruggeri firmly on her arm. I could not hear at this distance what the comtesse said to her, but whenever I caught a glimpse of Signora Ruggeri's face, she looked dazed.

"Monsieur Lucius Grenville," the majordomo intoned.

Grenville stepped into the room, his suit without a wrinkle, his fashionable shoes polished, his cravat painfully white, his hair artfully arranged. Heads turned whenever Grenville entered a chamber, but tonight, the guests utterly ignored him.

"Bit of a blow to my pride," Grenville said as he joined us. He lifted a flute of champagne from the attentive footman. "But I witnessed what happened and understand why I've been upstaged."

Donata had her sharp gaze on the interesting pair. "I've seen Signora Ruggeri before, I'm certain of it. Before arriving in Lyon, I mean, but I cannot recall where. What do you think, Grenville?"

Grenville raised his quizzing glass, staring haughtily through it at the comtesse and the signora making their slow circuit of the ballroom.

"She's made no secret of the fact that she was once an actress," Grenville remarked. "Padua is near Venice. You saw her at La Fenice, perhaps? Or mayhap a theatre in Paris?"

"I was thinking more of Sadler's Wells," Donata countered.

"Ah," Grenville answered. "Not necessarily the member of a grand company."

"I am certain I've seen her in some sort of musical performance." Donata's eyes narrowed in thought. "A rather risqué one, as I recall, but quite popular at the time. People popping into and out of bedchambers, that sort of thing. A good daughter and a bad daughter, driving the squire father mad. Yes, that was it. She played the bad daughter and had the audience roaring with laughter. She danced rather well, I recall, quite athletic. Could kick her leg up over her head."

I had no idea what play she was talking about, so I concluded Donata had seen the humorous performance in the years before I'd met her.

"I believe I recall it," Grenville said. "*The Tender Foes* or some such name. I viewed it with a gaggle of extremely ill-mannered fellows who distracted me greatly from the performance. But thinking it through, I believe you are right."

"Marianne might have encountered her," Donata suggested.

"Very true." Grenville lowered his glass. "I'll wager my dear Marianne will not only know the lady's true name but have an entire dossier on what roles she played and where. She has amazing information in her head, does Marianne." He finished with pride.

The former Marianne Simmons, once my upstairs neighbor, had been an actress in the company at Drury Lane Theatre, though she'd never been a principal. She'd left the stage about a year before she'd become Mrs. Grenville, but she retained a keen interest in the theatre.

Tonight, Marianne had chosen to attend a play's performance in the lower town with former acting friends who'd taken up residence in Lyon. I envied her the more relaxed gathering, though I believed the entertainment here had already surpassed whatever Marianne was watching on the stage.

"The lady is certainly not from Padua, as she claims," Donata said. "I'd say from Manchester. In the play, she spoke with a decided accent of that area, and such things are not easily mimicked."

"An Englishwoman then." Grenville tucked his quizzing glass into his pocket as though satisfied with their conclusions. "One who has learned to pass for Italian, at least among the French."

"No wonder she looks confused at the moment," Donata observed. "She is not certain what role to assume."

Gabriella and I listened to all this without comment, both of us intrigued by their assessment.

"Forgive me, Miss Auberge," Grenville said when he found us scrutinizing them. "Witnessing scandal in the making is vastly diverting."

"So long as you are not making the scandal yourself," I said with some humor.

"Very true." Grenville nodded. "All jesting aside, I admire the comtesse. She could so easily have let her servants throw the upstart out. I'll be curious to learn of Comte Lejeune's reaction when he hears of it."

The comte himself was notably absent. I wondered if he'd anticipated such a scenario and chosen to spend the evening elsewhere.

"That will be equally as diverting," Donata said. "Unless the comte pretends to take no notice of what his ladies get up to."

"I'd be thoroughly embarrassed, if I were he," I said mildly.

"*You* would, yes, Gabriel." Donata laid her fingers on the crook of my arm. "Although, I don't believe you'd be in such a predicament in the first place."

"Of course not." I touched her gloved hand. "I have no need."

Donata looked pleased at my declaration. "We are a highly unfashionable pair, I admit. Will there be any dancing at all, do you think, Grenville? I am growing restless."

She looked to the orchestra, who waited in a balcony above for the comtesse to indicate they should resume.

The comtesse and Signora Ruggeri had reached the far end of the ballroom. The comtesse then began steering the signora back again, making certain that every person in the room greeted her.

The crowd were content to follow the comtesse and her impromptu guest, avid to learn what would happen next. Would Signora Ruggeri retreat quietly, admitting defeat this night? Or turn her advantage in gaining the house to more insolent demands?

Signora Ruggeri never had the chance to decide. A man's voice in heavily accented French abruptly arrowed through the open windows from the courtyard below.

"Isadora! You bitch. Come out of there, *now*."

After one startled moment, the guests rushed to the windows. I confess I was only steps behind them, Grenville and Donata flanking me.

I glimpsed, over ladies' feathered headdresses, a man in a black suit and half cloak planted on the stones of the courtyard before the front door. Hatless, his hair gleaming in the torchlight, he cast an enraged gaze upward, like a lover in an opera.

"Isadora!" he roared, as footmen surged around him.

Signora Ruggeri started for the window, but the comtesse held her back.

"Best not to let him goad you, my dear," she advised.

"I did not bring him here, I promise you, madame," Signora Ruggeri said in anguish. "He must have followed me. Oh, I am sorry. I am sorry."

Her accent slipped a little as she gushed in sincere regret, and I heard even in French that Donata was likely correct about the signora's origins.

The comtesse patted her hand. "Never mind. You should rest a while. My maid will take you to a quiet chamber and give you coffee while we wait for your gentleman to leave."

Signora Ruggeri's dark eyes filled with tears. "You are too kind."

"Not at all, my dear. Every guest of mine deserves courtesy. Here is my maid." The comtesse released herself from Signora Ruggeri's now clinging grip and handed her off to a mob-capped, stern-faced older woman who took charge of her. "Look after her, please, Perrault."

The guests watched Signora Ruggeri's exit with interest, then returned attention to the windows as the man outside continued to shout.

Those shouts cut off abruptly when several of the burly

guards, Brewster among them, took hold of the man and escorted him unceremoniously to the gate.

"He was once her paramour," Grenville informed us as we eased back into the ballroom. "Vincenzo Gallo, is his name. From Padua in truth, I believe."

"The scandal deepens," Donata said. She brightened as the orchestra began to play. "At last."

Grenville, scrupulously polite, held his hand out for Gabriella, as the youngest lady of our party. "Shall we take a turn, Miss Auberge?"

Gabriella shook her head, though she smiled her thanks. "I prefer not to dance, Mr. Grenville. It is kind of you to offer, but I would like to sit with my father."

"I know when I have been rebuffed, young lady." Grenville winked at her then pivoted to Donata. "My friend?"

"Delighted." Donata rested her hand lightly in his. "As we will have no further excitement this evening, let us dance and console ourselves."

They sailed out to join the forming set. I led Gabriella to a chair on the side of the ballroom as the ladies and gentlemen began to glide about.

"You have no need to sit with me," I told her. "Though I appreciate your courtesy."

Gabriella sank down beside me. "I truly prefer not to dance unless it is with Emile. Mr. Grenville is well-mannered, but rather older than me, isn't he?"

I hid my smile at her assessment, though I was vainly pleased she preferred to remain with me instead of flitting about the ballroom.

She called me *Father* as opposed to the more familiar *Papa*, which she reserved for Major Auberge.

Gabriella's acceptance of me as her true father had erased much of my wretchedness, and I didn't mind that she was more formal with me. Perhaps one day, she'd lose her reserve and we'd be as close as though we'd never been forced apart.

For now, I enjoyed spending this time with her, before she'd become Emile's wife. I'd have fewer opportunities to see her after that.

As we watched the dancing and conversed about Emile, his family, the sumptuousness of the house we were in, and the new house Gabriella would have after she wed, the drama of Signora Ruggeri and her spurned lover faded into unimportance.

I'D THOUGHT THE SCENE AT THE BALL WOULD BE THE LAST OF MY encounters with the pretended Paduan lady and her lover, Signor Gallo, but it was not to be.

The next day, I took my early walk to the Presqu'île and Beaumont's tavern to seek my breakfast. I was alone this morning—Gabriella had departed after the comtesse's soiree, Major Auberge arriving in a carriage to escort her, as arranged. Brewster, who'd insisted on accompanying me into town, had paused to slurp coffee from a vendor as we'd made our way down the hill.

As I neared the middle of the Pont Tilsit, the bridge across the river Saône, I spied a man sprawled, face upward, on its paving stones. Bending over him was my old enemy, Colonel Moreau.

The body proved to be that of Signor Gallo, who lay in a pool of brownish blood. Moreau gripped a long knife in one fist, its blade covered with same drying blood. No one else was near, the middle of the bridge empty.

Moreau heard my step and snapped his head up. He froze, wide eyes burning, his face becoming a stark shade of gray.

"No," he declared in halting English. "This, I did not do."

CHAPTER 5

I planted my walking stick squarely in front of me, liking the sound of the blade rattling inside it.

"Why should I believe you?" I answered in French.

Moreau carefully laid the knife on the cobbles and rose once more. "You have no reason to."

He *did* recognized me. I saw it in his eyes. We studied each other warily.

What did I say to a man who'd once let his soldiers torture me, and then walked away, leaving me for dead? I'd made it home by luck and sheer determination, and I saw him register shock that I now stood before him. He must have thought I was a ghost when he'd caught sight of me yesterday.

The pair of us might have stared at each other all day, had not Brewster lumbered up beside me.

"Bloody hell. What the devil have ye done *now*?"

"I didn't kill the man," I said at once.

"Nor did I." Moreau said, continuing in English. "I swear on my life, I found him here."

"Well, then ye should walk away." Brewster directed the command at both of us. "'Twill be nothing to do with ye, will it?"

Neither Moreau nor I moved. "We should summon *les gendarmes*," Moreau said reluctantly.

"I agree," I said.

Brewster's eyes widened. "You mean the police what go about in military uniforms? They'll arrest us, guv, since we're foreign. I can't be taken to a French nick. I'll never see me Em again."

I could not say that Brewster was wrong. The three of us were conveniently standing over the body of a man who'd been murdered, and police of any country were happy with an easy solution. Moreau, a well-regarded colonel, might talk his way out of it, but Brewster and I would be fair game.

"What happened?" I asked Moreau sharply. "What did you see?"

He continued to respond in English, no matter that I questioned him in French. "I saw nothing. I was walking from the square to cross the river, and found him here on the bridge. I thought the man drunk, unconscious, and I leaned over him to discover if he was well. I saw the knife and picked it up ..."

"A foolish thing to do, but it can't be helped," I said. "Where do we seek the gendarmes? We should summon them before anyone else comes."

Moreau gave me a grim nod. "I will fetch them. Wait here."

He jogged off across the bridge toward the Presqu'île, leaving us with the dead Signor Gallo.

"He's legged it." Brewster glared after Moreau's retreating figure. "We should too, guv. He's not coming back."

"I think he will, somehow."

Moreau had been stunned but not panicked, more concerned for procedure than distancing himself from the incident. He'd been this coolly efficient on the night he and his soldiers had altered my life forever.

It was too late for Brewster and me to retreat, in any case. The Pont Tilsit, named for the Treaty of Tilsit during which Napoleon and the Russian Czar had carved up Europe between them—a treaty that had not sustained, needless to say—was a major crossing of the Saône. It had been empty this soon after sunrise, but townspeople were now making for the bridge from either direction, pausing to see what was happening.

Fernand Devere was among them.

"Isn't that Signor Gallo?" he asked, aghast, when he reached me. "My God, who killed him?"

"I imagine the police will wonder that as well," I said. "But yes, it is Gallo. The paramour of Signora Ruggeri, is he not? Or former paramour, I suppose."

Fernand continued to regard the dead man in abject horror. I studied him curiously, wondering why he was so affected. Surprise and pity was natural for the poor fellow sprawled at our feet, his dark eyes staring sightlessly at the sky, but Fernand's face was tight with shock.

"Do you have any idea who could have done this?" I asked him.

Fernand whipped around to stare at me, his pupils becoming pinpricks. "No. Of course not. Why would—" He broke off as Colonel Moreau reappeared on the far side of the bridge, several men in uniform behind him. "I must go. I must—"

His last words followed him as he hastened back the way he'd come, to disappear into the narrow streets of the west bank.

The men and women who'd gathered around quickly moved aside as Moreau led the gendarmes to Gallo's body, some quietly fading into the nearby lanes.

The lead gendarme, in a dark blue coat, removed his tall hat and tucked it under his arm. His high boots over tan breeches held no dust at all, as though he spent every morning polishing them to a sheen. His hair, which held threads of gray, and was thinning over the top of his head, which I saw clearly as he bent over the body. The silver braid on one epaulet told me he was a captain, if the insignias hadn't changed since I was last in France.

He gave Gallo's body a hard once-over, noting the wound and the knife that Moreau had laid down next to him. The captain nodded at his underlings, one of whom covered the dead man's rigid limbs with a cloak, mercifully hiding his staring eyes.

The captain straightened up, shaking his head. "Signor Vincenzo Gallo. The surprise is not that he is dead but that he escaped murder for so long. He was a nuisance to many. This is the English officer who found him?"

He directed the question at Moreau, his blue eyes holding both curiosity and patience.

Moreau darted a glance at me. "I found him first," he said stiffly. "The Englishman came upon me only moments later."

The gendarme faced me, fixing his hat more securely under his arm. "I have little English," he said, forcing the words out in that language.

"*D'accord*," I answered. "I speak French fairly well."

"*Bien*," the gendarme answered, reverting to his native tongue in relief. "I have never been out of France, except during the war, and spent the whole of it in Austria, where French is widely spoken. I have often considered learning another language but have never come around to it. I am Captain Vernet, in charge of this area of Lyon. You are?"

"Captain Gabriel Lacey," I bowed. "At your service."

Vernet nodded. "I am pleased to hear it. Why are you in Lyon?"

He asked me congenially, as though a dead body did not lie at our feet. His men, a lieutenant and a sergeant, stood quietly, waiting for their captain's next command.

"My daughter is marrying a gentleman of the area," I answered. "Emile Devere."

"Ah, a Devere." Vernet sounded impressed. "My felicitations, Captain." He turned to Moreau, his nod deferential for a man of superior rank. "Colonel. Please tell me what you saw here."

"Not very much," Moreau answered without hesitation.

"Gallo lying on the bridge. Found the knife covered in blood, Gallo stabbed. I would guess murdered in the dark as he crossed the bridge last night or very early this morning."

"Followed by a cutpurse, ready to steal his money?" Vernet pondered.

"Possibly," Moreau said. "He was not a young man who took care, from what I have observed."

Vernet swung to me. "Captain? You agree?"

"Was he robbed?" I asked. "His clothing appears undisturbed."

Vernet gazed down at Gallo's fine cashmere trousers sticking out from under the cloak. "True, but a skilled pickpocket can rob a man blind without moving a thread."

"If the pickpocket was so skilled, why bother murdering him?" I asked.

The corners of Vernet's mouth quirked upward, almost a smile. "That is a question I will be asking myself. Did you see anyone else here, Captain, besides the colonel?"

"No," I had to say. "But I doubt the colonel was responsible. His actions were of a man trying to discover what had happened, not one gloating over a victim."

Moreau gave me a sideways glance. His eyes were a light shade of gray, which I remembered from that faraway day. He clearly wondered why I hadn't claimed I'd seen him kill Gallo so Vernet would have his men march him off in chains.

But I had to be fair. Moreau was guilty of supervising my torture, yes, and I'd readily accuse him of that, but I couldn't be certain that he murdered Gallo.

"Also, Colonel Moreau has no blood on him," I continued.

The blood on the stones under Gallo was dark and dried, not fresh, and the blood on the knife was the same. If Moreau had stabbed the man some time ago—long enough for his blood to dry—why wait or return to be found over the body?

Vernet made a noise of acknowledgement. "I thank you for your observations, sir. The colonel is a highly respected citizen of Lyon, and I doubt he has turned into a mad killer overnight. You, however, Captain, I do not know, so please do not leave the city until I conclude my investigation."

I made him a bow. "I am lodging in a villa on the hill. I must go to the village of Saint-Jean at the end of next week for my daughter's wedding, but otherwise, I am at your disposal."

"I am certain I can either clear your name or arrest you within that time," Vernet said with confidence.

He gestured to his men and gave them a brusque order to remove Gallo from the bridge. The lieutenant, a man in his twenties at most, repeated this command to the sergeant with impatience.

The sergeant, a thin man with a sour face, scowled at the younger lieutenant but lifted Gallo's booted legs while the lieutenant lifted the man under his arms. The two, with the body, shuffled to the island side of the bridge, then filed into a narrow street, and were gone.

Vernet slapped on his hat. "You are likely right, Colonel Moreau. Gallo walked imprudently home alone in the dark and was followed and killed for what little coins he had in his purse. He did not hide the fact that his mistress bestowed handsome gifts on him, which probably came originally from her comte lover."

"Gallo was at the Comtesse Lejeune's chateau last evening," I said as Vernet began to turn away.

Vernet swung smartly back to me. "Was he? And how do you know this, Captain?"

"I was there myself. He caused a scene at the door, before several guards, including my man here, escorted him out the gates." I indicated Brewster, who was pretending to be a stone.

"Did they?" Vernet's eyes lit with interest. "How far did you escort the gentleman?" he asked Brewster.

I translated, and Brewster scowled. "I didn't kill the bloke. What for? We dragged him to the edge of the path that led down the hill and pushed him onto it. He took to his heels right quick. Couldn't get away from us fast enough."

I relayed this to Vernet, whose eyes narrowed as he listened. Then he shrugged. "I will speak to the comte's guards. I am sure it happened as your man says."

He pretended nonchalance, but I detected the shrewdness in him. Vernet was not a man who would brush off this murder, write *by unknown cutpurse* in his report, and go home to put up his feet.

"Good day to you, Colonel. Captain." Vernet saluted each of us in turn, nodded at Brewster, then turned and walked briskly in the direction his men had taken.

People drifted out of his way, a few greeting him reluctantly when he acknowledged them.

Brewster scowled at me. "I hope you haven't landed me in it, guv. There were no need to bring up the man being at the comte's palace or me giving him a hard shove down the hill."

Moreau answered before I could. "There was need. Someone could have followed Gallo from the comte's villa and decided to end his life."

"The footmen and guards were happy to be rid of him," Brewster said. "But none followed him. They had good drink in their barracks. Decent ale. I thought all Frenchies drank wine."

"There are several fine breweries near Lyon," Moreau answered without inflection. "Captain, perhaps we can have a word?"

The hesitation in his voice told me he'd had to work himself up to the suggestion.

"Of course," I said. "There is a coffee house yonder." I pointed across the bridge in the direction of Beaumont's tavern.

"No," Moreau answered decidedly. "In the *Place*."

On a wide open ground where all could see us, he meant.

"Of course," I said, and gestured for him to lead the way.

CHAPTER 6

*M*oreau crossed the remainder of the bridge into the Presqu'île without waiting to see if I'd follow. I started after him, Brewster directly behind me.

"No need to accompany me," I told him. "You'll be wanting your breakfast, I'm certain."

"I already ate," Brewster said stubbornly. "And I'm not letting you walk off with a bloke what was just found over a dead body, knife in hand, especially a man from the Frenchie army. They were good at killing, weren't they? It's not me what will be explaining to your missus why I let you go alone."

As I could not blame him for his suspicion, I didn't argue. "Come along, then. But stand out of earshot. I have a feeling he won't want to be overheard."

"If you speak to him in French, it won't matter, will it? Don't understand a word beyond *oui* or *merci.*" He pronounced them *wee* and *mercy.*

Brewster was never as thick as he pretended to be, and I conjectured he knew more than that. But again, I did not argue as we continued on our way.

The vast square was bustling today, but with more ordinary

activities, the riotous mob from yesterday but a memory. A market did business on one end, and a contingent of ladies on a morning walk wandered across the other. Coffee houses had set out tables so gentlemen could linger as they drank, taking the fine air.

Moreau waited for me in a relatively empty patch near the middle of the square. I walked to him, and Brewster, despite his protests, did halt a discreet distance away.

As I'd observed yesterday, Moreau dressed simply, in coat, trousers, and boots meant for tramping about. His suit had obviously been tailored for him, but it was of sensible wool, not a more costly fabric. Moreau wore no hat on this warm morning, and his light brown hair stirred in the breeze.

His grey eyes held intelligence but no shame. Did he mean to tell me he knew damn well where we'd met before, perhaps threaten me to stay away from him? Or would he apologize for what had happened?

How could a man whose soldiers had nearly killed me in a most brutal fashion simply say, *I beg your pardon*?

"I did not lie to Vernet when I told him I didn't think you murdered Gallo," I said in French before he could begin. "The theory that someone followed him from the comte's home is likely the best one, and I did not see you at the comtesse's ball last night."

Moreau regarded me calmly. "I would not have been invited. I am from a family of no note, and I departed Lyon before its siege to follow a young Bonaparte when his career was rising. Was with him on the Italian peninsula and then in Egypt. The citizens of Lyon are respectful to me, but the aristocrats decidedly are not."

"Those in the comte's circle seem ready to return to the old ways," I agreed. "I spent some time in Egypt recently. Fascinating country."

"I was not there long. Your fellow Englishmen saw to that."

I inclined my head. "Indeed, the Battle of the Nile was quite a coup for Admiral Nelson. A great tragedy when he later perished."

"It was the end of our navy. And the end of the war, but we did not see it then. You recognized me," Moreau stated bluntly, his focus on me intensifying. "And remembered."

I gazed across the square to the ladies in their light summer frocks, parasols aloft to keep the sun at bay.

"Difficult *not* to remember," I said, my voice light. "The entire incident is indelibly fixed on my mind. Not to mention on my left knee." I tapped my booted leg with my walking stick.

"I believed you dead," Moreau said. "When I cut you down, I was certain you had already perished. They would not obey me, those men. Wild and drunk—deserters I was trying to herd back to camp."

"You have no need to explain yourself," I said. "It was war. We were enemies."

Moreau's expression hardened. "There is war, and then there is needless cruelty. I knew it was hopeless trying to make those soldiers obey, but I could at least let you rest with dignity. I hid you the best I could so they would not desecrate your body. I left them there, asleep and drunk, knowing I could not save them. No one ever saw them again."

"They were killed," I said. "British soldiers came upon us. They killed or captured your men but didn't see me. They probably would have gutted me by mistake, so it was a good job you *did* hide me."

Moreau's brows went up. "They did not take you back with them? Then how did you—?"

"Survive?" I sent him a mirthless smile. "As my commander likes to say, with my be-damned stubbornness. I don't have the sense to know when I'm beaten, he claims, to give up and die."

"I see." Moreau looked me up and down, his gaze unreadable once more. "I am pleased that you did not give up and die."

"My commander was not as pleased, but that is neither here nor there. If you seek forgiveness ..." I shrugged, albeit stiffly. "As I say, it was war and a long time ago. Who knows what I would have done had our positions been reversed?"

I would have given my men hell for torturing a helpless prisoner, I could say with certainty. But the French soldiers had been, as Moreau indicated, drunk and trying to desert. They might have simply shot Moreau if he'd tried harder to stop them.

"In the end, we both lived," I told him. "And here we are."

"As you say, Captain." Moreau gave me a rigid bow. "*Alors*. I will say good day to you, sir."

I bowed in return. "*Bonne journée*, Colonel."

We studied each other, both of us awkward. Moreau at last gave me a nod, and then turned and strode briskly toward the north side of the square.

"Are you going to tell me what that was about?" Brewster demanded as he approached. Not for him the silent deference of the good manservant or bodyguard.

"I met him during the war, on the Peninsula," I said. "The encounter was fairly savage, and it almost killed me. We were deciding to let bygones be bygones."

Brewster regarded me as though he doubted my sanity. "I've had plenty of savage encounters in me life, right on the streets of London. When my old enemies see me, they take another road. No bygones for us."

"The colonel and I might have been friends in other circumstances," I said. "I'd rather buy him a coffee than strike him down."

"That's why a soldier's life weren't for me. Don't want to shake hands and be friends with those trying to kill me. Don't much want no one telling me what to do either."

"The army is not for everyone," I agreed. I'd met plenty who could never adapt to the discipline that kept us alive. "Now, I've worked up an appetite. I'm returning to Beaumont's for my breakfast, if you care to join me."

I also wanted to find Fernand Devere. He'd reacted strongly to Gallo's dead body, and I had to wonder why.

Brewster said no further word as we made for the narrow lanes that led to Beaumont's wine shop.

The proprietor welcomed us with a mere lift of his brows. I'd come to know that, for Baptiste Beaumont, this was an outpouring of joy. He slammed a plate of sausages swimming in thick sauce and a hunk of bread to the table as I sat down, plunking a cup of coffee beside it.

The regulars in the cafe had heard all about the dead man and the gendarmes questioning me. They turned to me in expectant curiosity, and I had to explain what had happened as I ate. Brewster gulped coffee and kept a sharp watch on the door.

"Has anyone seen Fernand Devere?" I asked the room once I'd finished my tale. "He was on the bridge, but I lost sight of him."

Beaumont shrugged and drifted behind his counter, his effusiveness finished for the day.

"Saw him heading along the quay," a man in one corner told me. "Past the old arsenal. Probably going back to his ironworks. Seemed to be in a hurry."

"Ah." I thanked him, feigning unconcern.

Once I finished the excellent food, restoring my strength, I decided to make for the south of the city and call in at the Deveres' factory.

———

WHEN DONATA AND I HAD BEEN SHOWN AROUND THE IRONWORKS the Deveres owned, I'd expected something rather like a country blacksmith's, if a bit larger. I'd pictured a stone shelter with a few men pounding at anvils while Emile's father and uncles trundled the finished goods in horse-drawn wagons to the farmers who'd purchased them.

I had not been prepared for the scale of their operation.

We'd arrived at a large brick building with chimneys at either end that belched smoke into the cloudy sky. Several delivery vans waited in the courtyard, and a stream of workers had flowed into and out of the main foundry and the outbuildings surrounding it.

Emile, with his Uncle Fernand, had ushered us inside, giving Donata a thick woolen cloak to shield her and her gown from sparks and soot. She'd worn half-boots for this journey but had been curious enough about the workings to don the crude but sturdy boots Emile brought her to keep her own from being ruined.

The factory's interior consisted of a huge open room with men working giant bellows to stoke equally massive fires. Workers had banged on bars and poles of iron at their anvils, finishing dozens at a time. The room was open to the second floor, windows high above helping smoke to escape and not linger where the men worked.

The workers had ceased when Emile and Fernand guided us through, letting us move among them without hazard.

Today, my unexpected appearance with Brewster at my side had men glancing up from forges without ceasing their labors.

Two men poured a vat of white-hot iron into a mold, sparks bursting upward in a bright rain. The men were protected by heavy woolen suits and scarfs across their faces, but their brows and hair appeared to be permanently singed.

One man thrust a bar he'd been working into a barrel of water, steam exploding with a sharp hiss. He hoisted the bar out again and left it to cool while he walked to us, hammer in hand.

I hadn't noted this man on our previous visit. He was as large as Brewster and looked to have once been as active a fighter. His nose had been broken sometime in the past, and his cheekbone bore a large dent, scarred over with pink and white flesh. His dark hair was trimmed close, probably to keep it from the dangerous sparks, but his nearly bald head enhanced his pugilist air.

Brewster stepped slightly in front of me, taking his measure.

"I am looking for Monsieur Fernand Devere," I told the man in careful French. "Is he here?"

The man only regarded me steadily from light hazel eyes, saying nothing.

"I don't wish to disturb anyone," I continued. "I only need a quick word."

More staring, the hammer clenched tightly in his hand.

"Oi, mate," Brewster broke in, in English. "He asked you a question."

More workers had looked up and around at our conversation. Some returned to their tasks, uninterested, but others watched as though waiting for their compatriot to strike me down.

Footsteps clattered on a set of wooden stairs in the corner, and Emile, my daughter's betrothed, came into sight. His eyes widened, and he hurried the rest of the way down the stairs and over to us.

"Captain Lacey. Welcome. My apologies. We were not expecting you."

The other men relaxed as Emile rushed past them, and went back to what they'd been doing.

Emile Devere closely resembled his father and his uncles, men stamped from the same mold. He had brown hair of an unremarkable shade and eyes of nearly the same color. A round face topped a slim body that would doubtless grow harder as he aged.

Emile spoke to me in the very precise English he'd learned from Gabriella, but he was clearly uncomfortable with the language.

He was also not comfortable with me turning up out of the blue.

"Thought I'd take a chance," I answered, also in English. Donata always spoke French to Emile, wanting to put him at ease, but I could never help needling him a bit. "Is your Uncle Fernand here? I wish to speak with him."

"He is." Emile turned to the belligerent man who'd remained to watch me and Brewster in hard silence. Emile spoke to him in words unintelligible to me and gestured toward the stairs.

The man broke his intense stare and gave Emile a nod that held a hint of indulgence for the lad. He strolled to the stairs and shouted up them in the language I didn't know. An answering shout soon came to us.

"Uncle will be down presently," Emile informed me. "Can I help you with anything, sir?"

I took pity on him and switched to French. "Not at all. I suppose you heard about the tragedy in town this morning?"

"Yes, Uncle Fernand told us." Emile grew more voluble in his native tongue. "Poor man. Signor Gallo was never welcome in Lyon, but no one deserves to be killed like that, do they?"

I'd become better acquainted with Emile when he'd stayed with us in Rome last summer, and had learned that he was a kind young man, possessing true compassion. He'd not acquired the worldly toughness of his uncles and father, who I now knew had been touched by Lyon's siege and its brutal aftermath.

Emile's kindness had finally reconciled me to the fact that he'd marry my daughter—not that I could have stopped him. In theory, I had the legal ability to forbid Gabriella the marriage, but I knew that if I exercised my power as paterfamilias, the rest of my family would show their disapprobation, loudly.

In truth, I could find nothing to object to in Emile. The young man worked diligently, was respectful to his parents and family, would inherit the fruits of this business, and adored Gabriella. A father could not ask for more, I repeatedly assured myself.

"It was unfortunate," I agreed. "The gendarme did not seem to be surprised at Gallo's demise, however."

"Captain Vernet?" Emile wrinkled his forehead. "He is an astute man, I've always found, even when he feigns to be otherwise. He will no doubt discover the murderer and punish him. Ah, here is Uncle Fernand."

Fernand hesitated a step when Emile expressed his faith in Captain Vernet but then squared his shoulders and continued his approach.

The large man followed him from the stairs. Fernand barked an order at him, and the man shrugged, returning to his anvil.

"Talkative fellow, isn't he?" I asked when Fernand reached us.

Fernand glanced at the big man, who retrieved the bar he'd been working on and thrust it back into the flames of his forge.

"Do not mind Michel. He speaks only Lyonnais, and no French. He looks frightening, but he's staunch and loyal. Now, I cannot imagine that you trudged all the way here to say good morning to me." Fernand smiled tightly, his eyes holding wariness.

"It is not so far, and good exercise for me," I countered. "Perhaps we could chat in the yard?"

"Of course." Fernand gestured me to the large open doors. "It becomes noisy inside."

He let me lead the way. Though lowering clouds darkened the sky outside, the courtyard was bright after the dim interior of the factory.

Brewster followed, and so, to my dismay, did Emile.

The courtyard was not much quieter, in fact, as men busily loaded wagons in the middle of it, ready to deliver orders far and wide.

"All is well?" Fernand asked when we reached a relatively tranquil corner. "Or do the ladies have more questions about the wedding breakfast?"

Carlotta and Major Auberge were taking care of the wedding ceremony itself, but the Deveres had insisted on organizing the wedding breakfast. Carlotta and Donata were united in uneasiness about this. While the Deveres had the funds to sponsor a lavish feast, the ladies were not certain that a group of ironmongers could arrange something tasteful.

"Not today," I said. "Mercifully. I was only curious. You seemed quite upset about Gallo's murder. Beyond natural surprise and pity, I mean. I wanted to ask you why, but you departed too rapidly."

Explaining this out loud, it did sound a flimsy reason for walking a mile past the confluence to enter Fernand's place of business, uninvited. I held my ground, however, and did not apologize.

Emile studied his uncle in surprise, also interested in Fernand's answer.

Fernand flushed to the roots of his thinning hair. "Not upset. I barely knew the man. It gave me a turn, as you English say, to see him lying there. Reminded me of the old days. The executions, you know …"

He trailed off, pressing a hand to his forehead. I saw in his eyes, before he covered them, a hint of relief that he had a believable excuse to give me.

Emile regarded him in perplexity. "Are you worried because of Cousin Claude, Uncle?"

Fernand started and tried to signal Emile to silence, but the young man turned to me.

"My cousin Claude fell hard for Signora Ruggeri when she first arrived in Lyon," he explained. "Uncle Giraud—Claude's father—complained that Claude was just one more of her victims. You don't believe Cousin Claude did this murder, do you?"

CHAPTER 7

"Of course he did not," Fernand roared. Several workers, including Michel, appeared in the factory's doorway to peer out at us.

Fernand made an effort to calm himself. "Yes, Claude behaved like a fool over the signora, but that was months ago, Emile. Claude has finished with her. He'd never have murdered a man because of her."

Emile blinked. "Forgive me, Uncle. I know absolutely that Claude did no such thing, but I thought that was what you feared."

"Never." Fernand spoke stoutly, but his rapid breathing and flushed face told me otherwise.

"It is easily solved," I said. "If Claude was far from the Pont Tilsit, or indeed the entire Presqu'île, last night, then he need have no concern."

From Fernand's continued scowl, I gathered that Claude would not be so fortunate.

"I do not know where he was, but it does not matter," Fernand snapped. "A Devere would not do this."

Emile opened his mouth, perhaps to argue this point, but Fernand glared him to silence and swung on me.

"Emile and Gabriella tell me you rush about London seeking criminals to send to the gallows, Captain. We have the gendarmerie here—you do not need to interfere. Go back to your villa on the hill and await the wedding. There is no need to have Claude arrested for his imprudent passion."

Fernand balled his fists as he made this speech, which I realized were beefy and scarred, a man unafraid of labor. Fernand was on his own territory, with many to aid him, and I was an interloper.

Brewster stirred, as though ready to step between us, but I forestalled him.

"I assure you, I have no intention of spoiling the wedding," I said to Fernand. "But Claude should clear his name as soon as he can, so that he too may attend." I gave Fernand and the distressed Emile a stiff bow. "Good morning, gentlemen."

I turned, nearly colliding with Brewster, who stood close beside me. He stepped away, and we walked out of the courtyard together. The large Michel emerged to dog us until we were through the gate.

"I don't know what you were going on about," Brewster said as we reached the road. We'd spoken in French, Fernand too agitated to translate. "But Mr. Devere was ready to come at you, with his workers to back him up. Tough blokes in there. So of course, you had to go and rile them."

"Fernand fears that his nephew Claude murdered Signor Gallo," I told him as we headed northward. My leg began to ache, punishing me for not hiring a hack or cart to bring me out here.

"Does he, now? Not without reason, I take it. Else he wouldn't have shouted so loud."

"I thought the same. If there was no possibility at all, Fernand would not worry. Emile seems sanguine that his cousin is innocent, but there must be a reason Fernand is not as certain."

"He knows summat, you mean."

"He must." I scanned the dusty road and the pile of buildings of Lyon, with the gleam of wide river dividing around it. "The best way to make certain Claude is innocent is to find out where he was last night. I hear the police are quick to arrest suspects here. If we can keep Claude free, it will do much to alleviate the family's worries."

"You mean find out who really killed the man, don't you?"

I nodded. "If it comes to that."

Brewster heaved an aggrieved sigh, his gaze going heavenward. "Here we go," he muttered.

———

I MANAGED TO CONVINCE A FARMER TRUNDLING HIS GOODS TO the city to allow me a ride on the back of his cart the last half mile to Lyon. I had to give him coin and promise him a cup of wine at Beaumont's shop, but he nodded and let me repose among his crates of onions. My aching leg eased, though my eyes watered a good bit.

Brewster trudged behind the cart, a scowl on his face. He was fed up with me putting myself in danger to find the answer to puzzles, but I ignored his disapproval.

Helping clear Emile's cousin of this crime should not be too difficult, I told myself as we rocked along—unless, of course, the lad actually committed it.

I'd do what I could. I'd come to like the Deveres and did not want to see them distraught. Also, it would never do for Gabriella to begin her new life with Emile's family locked in scandal.

The carter let me off at the end of the Pont Tilsit, now free of Gallo's body and the blood he'd spilled. I returned to the wine shop for a bit of rest and a cup of earthy wine, then Brewster and I climbed the hill to the villa.

Donata had hired a house that she called *too small, but it will do* and I called a grand country mansion. The home had been built within the last century, and bore many windows and glazed doors to let in light and provide easy access to the garden. Crenelations and cupolas lined the roof, to bring to mind the medieval age of chivalry and the grand dukes that had once ruled this area.

I'd come to enjoy the place, though it had been decorated inside with a plethora of clouds, cherubs, and gilded plaster ribbons winding across the top of every room.

Donata was awake, Bartholomew informed me when I entered the echoing ground floor hall, though still in her chamber. Grenville, on the other hand, had arrived, and waited in the rear drawing room.

I joined him in that sunny chamber, the windows open to let in the cool breeze. The clouds that had gathered while I'd traveled to the ironworks had broken apart again, becoming puffy and picturesque.

"The entire city is agog with the news of this murder," Grenville told me as I thankfully took a seat on the comfortable sofa. He imbibed coffee, which Bartholomew also brought me.

"They were still speaking of it in Beaumont's wine shop," I answered. "The men there favor the cutpurse theory."

"The ideas are rather different on this hill. Anyone I encountered on my way up was avid to discuss it. Those who'd been at the comtesse's soiree are certain that Signora Ruggeri hastened down to the city last night and killed Signor Gallo. Outraged at him, they say, for nearly ruining things for her with the comte."

"Nonsense." Donata floated in, waved off Bartholomew who approached with the coffee pot, and sank down next to me. "Signora Ruggeri spent the entire night as the comtesse's guest. She is the one person in Lyon who could *not* have murdered Signor Gallo."

"Her guest?" I asked in surprise.

Donata settled her summer-light gown and nodded in gratitude when Bartholomew presented her with a glass of sherry.

"This happened after the pair of you and Gabriella departed,"

Donata said after a refreshing sip. "When the hour grew late, the comtesse declared that it would be too dangerous for Signora Ruggeri to venture home, with Gallo out there threatening her. So the comtesse put her in one of their many chambers with her own lady's maid to wait on her. Signora Ruggeri could hardly refuse. You miss much when you retire early."

I had indeed retired after Gabriella had gone home, though Grenville had departed to spend the rest of his evening with Marianne and her friends.

"Signora Ruggeri might have slipped out," Grenville suggested. "Left after the household had gone to bed, met Gallo, and then nipped back before anyone missed her."

"The chateau is well guarded," I said doubtfully. "With only the one gate. It would be difficult for her to escape notice."

"Chateaus like the comtesse's are riddled with hidden doors," Grenville said with the confidence of long experience. "Ways for tradesmen to come and go without disturbing the family. You'd be amazed at the many entrances in the cellars. A boon for thieves, if they aren't sure to lose themselves in the labyrinth of old passageways."

I wondered if Brewster had scouted these hidden entrances at the comtesse's home, and made a note to ask him.

"I can discover whether anyone saw her slipping out," Donata offered. "Though, if *I* had killed Gallo, I'd have flung the knife from the bridge and fled the city instead of creeping back into a house where I was not wanted in the first place. But who knows? From all reports, Signora Ruggeri is still at the chateau. The comte himself has retreated to his hunting lodge, Jacinthe tells me. Wise man."

Jacinthe, Donata's lady's maid, would have dutifully reported the gossip on the matter while she'd helped Donata dress.

"It is an odd business," I said with a welcome swallow of coffee.

"Comtesse Lejeune is rather fed up with them all," Donata continued. "Her husband, his lover, the lover's lover. But the comtesse will weather it. She has no choice, does she?" Her eyes tightened.

Donata had endured her first husband, Lord Breckenridge, parading his mistresses under her nose for years, and she'd had no option but to look the other way. She'd behaved wildly herself in retaliation, though her husband had never noticed. Donata had only been released from this unhappy situation by Breckenridge's sudden death.

I slid my hand to hers where it rested on her silken gown, and squeezed it. Donata sent me a quick, but grateful smile.

"The comtesse is quite a lady," Grenville said with admiration. "The comte deserves her not. On the other hand, Lejeune himself might have ended Gallo's life, perhaps seeing Gallo as a rival. Or, he might have viewed the killing as doing his beloved mistress a favor. Lejeune is old enough to recall the days when lordships could be allowed almost anything."

"True, but such a thing would be out of character for him," Donata answered. "I find him a rather lazy man, with minimal imagination. I doubt the comte would do something so dramatic, even for passion. He prefers to avoid all difficulties, which is why he took himself to the hunting lodge."

"Where is this lodge?" I asked. Even if Lejeune was too placid to stir himself, he might have sent a faithful retainer to do the deed for him.

"Near Saint-Genis-Laval." Donata named a village south of the city. "Only a few miles from the Deveres' ironworks, in fact. Close enough for someone to nip into Lyon and commit the murder, it is true."

"I went to the ironworks this morning," I said. While Donata and Grenville regarded me with surprise, I explained Fernand's odd behavior and Emile's revelation that his cousin Claude had formed an attachment to Signora Ruggeri.

"Claude," Grenville mused when I finished. "He is the dark-haired young man with the perpetually sullen expression, son of Giraud Devere, correct?"

"And a hothead, by Fernand's reaction," I answered. "It is clear that Fernand fears Claude has done something rash. Emile seemed more certain Claude would never commit such a deed, but I have not spoken to Claude himself, yet."

"When you do, I urge you to tread lightly," Donata said. "The Deveres seem to have much influence in this city, not to mention Gabriella now has a strong connection to them. I hope Claude had nothing to do with it, but be careful, even if he did."

"If Emile's cousins are in the habit of stabbing those who anger them, I'd prefer Gabriella not to be connected with the family at all," I returned.

"I agree," Donata said. "But you do tend to rush in like a bull, Gabriel. I only warn you to be discreet. Gabriella truly loves Emile, and you do not want her to shut you out for upsetting everything."

That was the last thing I wanted. I'd missed much of Gabriella's life, and I wished to miss no more.

"Gabriella is no fool," I said. "If she discovers that the Deveres are a dangerous lot, she'll hesitate about tying herself to them. But I'd prefer she did not discover this too late."

"She'd hesitate, even if it breaks her heart?" Donata argued. "I was young once and very stubborn about the man I would marry, no matter what signs I saw to the contrary. I ran headlong into my own folly, didn't I? I do believe you right about finding out whether Emile's cousin did this dreadful act—I am cautioning you about distressing your daughter."

Grenville had sat silently during this exchange. Now he laid his cup into his saucer with a soft click.

"I too have become fond of Gabriella," he said. "I am willing to help discover whether they are a family who deserve her. I also agree with Donata that we must do it quietly. I offer my services in this quest. Command me, and it shall be done."

"That would be welcome," I said in gratitude. "Perhaps you could discover whether the comte truly was at his hunting lodge all night."

"I will endeavor." Grenville nodded and lifted his cup once more.

"I will return to the comtesse," Donata said. "We should also determine Signora Ruggeri's whereabouts without doubt."

I thanked them both. Donata and Grenville were each skilled at coaxing information out of others without those they interrogated taking offense.

As for the Deveres themselves, I had to wonder why Fernand was so certain that his nephew had committed the deed, in spite of his protests to the contrary. And also why he'd been unhappy that I'd turned up at the ironworks at all.

There was something odd there, and I wanted to know what.

I MANAGED TO TURN MY THOUGHTS TO OTHER MATTERS THAT afternoon, while Grenville and Donata left to call on acquaintances and begin to poke about in their easy fashion. I pondered my encounter with Moreau, and wondered if I should speak to him again. I did want to know more about what had happened that night, to fill in the gaps I'd forgotten.

I was not certain why I wanted that piece of my past to resurface, but perhaps I'd finally be able to forgive all concerned and put it to rest.

Bartholomew interrupted as I was sitting down in the study to write to Moreau, and thrust a note at me.

"This just come, Captain. Boy was in a tearing hurry to get it to you."

In consternation I opened the paper. On it was printed a message in English.

Vernet has arrested Claude. Please help.

It was signed,

Emile Devere.

CHAPTER 8

The barracks of the gendarmerie lay off the quay on the Rhône side of the city's island, just downriver of the massive Hôtel Dieu—the city's hospital—and the Pont de la Guillotière.

The building I faced was plain and tall, with its crumbling stucco façade revealing dark bricks beneath. High windows faced the narrow street, and the stout shutters to secure the place at night were now open to the afternoon sunshine.

A young man in a stiff uniform guarded the door. When I asked if I could speak to Captain Vernet, he only gave me a sneer.

"Go home, foreigner," he said in thickly accented English.

Brewster, who'd halted at the end of the lane, exercising his usual distrust of police, turned and glowered at the young man.

I might never have been admitted to the house had not the sour-faced sergeant who'd helped carry away Gallo's body happened by.

He snarled a few words at the guard and nodded to me. "Captain?" he addressed me in French. "Why do you wish to see Captain Vernet?"

"Is it true he's arrested Claude Devere?"

The sergeant's face clouded. "*Oui,* and we've had the whole pack of Deveres threatening us. Are you here to do the same?"

"No, indeed, but I believe the lad is simply unfortunate, not guilty. Does Captain Vernet have evidence to the contrary?"

The sergeant continued to scowl at me, then I saw him conclude that such decisions did not rest with him.

"Come," he said, gesturing me in. "I will have the captain informed you are here."

The guard stood ungraciously aside as I followed the sergeant into the interior. A glance behind me showed that Brewster had vanished.

I was used to the Bow Street Magistrate's house, with its famous Runners clumping in and out, patrollers milling, and young barristers or their clerks loitering in the halls to drum up business with the accused. Those arrested in the night queued to see the magistrate, who would decide their fate.

This building reminded me of an army headquarters, with men of lower ranks darting about to serve the higher, many of the underlings with sheafs of papers in hands or tucked under arms.

Bonaparte's reforms had made record-keeping more precise, from what I understood, but such bureaucracy took time and mountains of paper. Offices with open doors showed me rows of shelves with niches for all these documents and tables piled with wooden boxes of the same.

The sergeant took me up a flight of stone steps, which were worn in the center from so many feet over the years, and to the next floor.

Here windows let in light and air, refreshing after the close bustle of the lower hall.

The sergeant paused before a plain wooden door that looked like all the others we'd passed and knocked. To a sharp, *Entre!* he pushed it open.

We stepped into an office that was small, cramped, and dingy. Its appearance thwarted the myth that officers lived lavishly at the expense of the lower ranks. Some British officers during the war had brought luxury with them, it was true, but it was family wealth, nothing provided by the army.

The military of France must be as austere, I decided. Vernet glanced up from a simple wooden desk overflowing with papers and the slim wooden boxes of the sort I'd seen downstairs. A shelf along a wall held more boxes. The walls had once been painted a soft yellow, but time and dirt had rendered them a brownish gray.

"Captain Lacey." Vernet rose politely, looking not at all put out that I'd interrupted him. "Welcome. Please, sit."

He waved at a straight-backed chair whose white paint flaked in places to show the wood's natural hue beneath. As its seat was stacked with more papers and ledger books, I had to wait for the sergeant to clear it off before I could rest upon it.

The sergeant, his tasks completed, shuffled out of the room, closing the door noisily behind him.

"How may I assist you, Captain?" Vernet asked. "Have you come to tell me something you recall about Signor Gallo's murder?"

I perched awkwardly on the rickety chair, steadying myself with my walking stick. "You have arrested Claude Devere."

"Ah." Vernet leaned back and drummed his fingers on the only bare surface on the desk. "Yes, you are connected with the Deveres, or soon will be. As I said before, my felicitations on the nuptials."

"Thank you," I answered, a trifle impatiently. "Do you have evidence against Claude? Or was he brought in because of his infatuation with Signora Ruggeri?"

"You are well informed." Vernet ran fingertips along the desk's edge and shook his head. "Since that woman came to Lyon, I have had nothing but trouble. Fights that come to weapons drawn in back streets. Duels between higher-born men—which fortunately have come to nothing. Young Claude is a good lad, as far as I can see, but even he was once brawling in the plaza with another young man who claimed to have the lady's favor."

"Did you arrest the other young man?" I asked.

"No, because he left Lyon soon afterward and has not been seen since. That was months ago. No one has noted him returning, before you ask, so I do not believe he is the culprit."

"Once Signora Ruggeri caught Comte Lejeune's eye, Claude would have given up," I pointed out. "The son of a factory owner could hardly compete with a comte."

"That son of a factory owner has more money than the comte, in spite of the chateau on the hill and the comtesse's ancient lineage."

"Did Signora Ruggeri know that?" I asked.

Vernet barked a short laugh. "She did not appear to. The signora is the sort dazzled by a title and a large house, not to mention the jewels he nearly bankrupted himself to give her."

"Small wonder there is so much anger at Signora Ruggeri," I said. "If she is beggaring the poor man, while the rest of Lyon watches."

"There are some who would not mind to see him fall," Vernet said. "Not long before the siege, Lejeune disappeared from the city with his young sons and all the family's money. He left the comtesse behind."

I thought of the redoubtable woman I'd observed last evening, cooly welcoming her husband's mistress and even offering her a bed for the night. When I'd finally been introduced to the comtesse, I'd been impressed by her equanimity. She showed true serenity, not simply a façade erected between herself and the world.

"He left her behind?" I repeated in anger. "If he was callous enough to desert his wife in a time of danger, then I cannot blame those disgusted with him."

"He claimed she refused to leave," Vernet said. "That she vowed to remain in her home, where she'd lived her entire life, and face down those who tried to pry her from it."

I recalled Bartholomew explaining that the chateau belonged to the comtesse's family. "She inherited the place?" I asked. "In England, this would be difficult."

"The wealthy can always find ways to keep property in the family," Vernet said with disapproval. "The comte inherited a villa when he came into his title, but it is small. He leases it to a man who oversees his farms. The comtesse's father bestowed *his* house on the comte and comtesse at their marriage, as the comtesse was his only child. Hers was not a titled family, but a very old one, with much power through the ages. The comte then purchased more properties with the money he married, which he either leases out or puts whatever woman has caught his eye into. The comtesse and her man of business handle the rents, however, so the comte sees little of the returns."

Fernand had told me some of this. I was glad the comtesse was wise enough not to let her husband have free rein with the money.

"The comtesse seems a formidable lady," I said in admiration. "If she truly did volunteer to remain behind, then she is much to be admired."

"I was not in Lyon during the uprisings or the siege," Vernet said. "I am from a village near Grenoble, and joined up with the army as they rode into the Hapsburg Empire. Was assigned here after the Bourbon king returned to France. The Lyonnais might squabble among themselves, but they stick together against outsiders, I will tell you."

I had already noted that. "Then they will not be happy with you arresting a Devere."

Vernet sent me a pained look. "No, indeed." He sighed. "Claude is a good lad, if a bit hot-headed at times. Unfortunately, he was seen last night, arguing with Gallo. From the witnesses who gave my men this information, this was earlier, about nine o'clock, across the Rhône, in La Guillotière. There was shouting and waving of fists before the two parted."

I did not like hearing this. "Gallo was at the comtesse's

chateau a bit after that. Must have been about half past ten, I'd say. Claude was nowhere in evidence then, and Gallo was whole and alive."

Vernet shrugged. "Nothing to say they didn't meet up again later. Young Mr. Devere is being very vague about his whereabouts."

"Perhaps I can speak to him," I offered. "I am close to being family but won't remonstrate with him like his father or uncles would. And I am not a gendarme."

Vernet regarded me for a long time, assessing me without betraying his conclusions. The drumming of fingers recommenced, then ceased altogether.

"I suppose it could do no harm," he said. "If Claude will confess all that he did last night, and we can find evidence he speaks the truth, I will send him home. However, if he truly *did* commit the crime, I cannot look the other way, no matter what his surname is."

I could see that Vernet would prefer not to have to send a Devere to trial and maybe to the guillotine. However, he was unwilling to simply turn Claude loose, no matter what the Deveres or their solicitors were threatening.

He rose, and I followed suit. I thought he'd call a lackey to take me to wherever they were holding Claude, but Vernet himself led me from the office and along the hall then down two flights of stairs to the cellar.

The underground space was damp, the river close by. Mold blackened the corners of the ceiling and stone floor.

The cells lay at the end of a corridor, beyond various storage rooms where more gendarmes worked, coats off in the humid air. Though it was far cooler down here than on the summer street, the mugginess was oppressive.

Thick doors with small, grilled windows enclosed those arrested this day. Behind one, a woman was singing at the top of her voice, the words slurred with drink.

"Madame Marais," Vernet said when I turned to the noise.

"She is in here almost every day. She will quiet down to sleep and go home later this afternoon."

At the sound of her name, Madame Marais increased her bellowing, the song becoming a ribald one about gendarme officers and their endowments.

Ignoring her, Vernet took a ring of keys from his coat pocket and unlocked the cell door opposite that of the serenading madame.

The chamber was lit only by a window high up in the wall. By that dim glow, I saw Claude Devere hunched in on himself on a stone bunk, his head in his hands. He raised that head slowly when he heard the door open, defeat in his eyes.

He blinked when he saw me then regarded Vernet in confusion. "Why is *he* here? Did my father send him?"

"Captain Lacey has come to talk, that is all," Vernet said sternly. "I advise you to be truthful with him. I will return in a quarter of an hour, Captain. The only way out is the stairs, and I have many men between here and there."

"I assure you, I have no intention of absconding with him," I answered.

"Good. I would hate to have to shoot you. A quarter hour." Vernet gave us both a warning glare then backed out of the door and closed it. Claude flinched as the key turned in the lock.

I'd met Claude Devere during our tour of the ironworks, which I now realized had been carefully orchestrated. Claude was about the same age as Emile and resembled his cousin with his brown hair and eyes, though Claude's hair was a shade darker. His face was sharper, his chin more pointed, traits he'd likely inherited from his deceased mother.

He possessed a sullenness Emile lacked, a deep burning anger at an unknown target. He'd inherit a share of the business, as would Emile and their other cousin, Camille, daughter of their uncle Julien. Claude hadn't been as eager to welcome us into the factory, his entire bearing telling me he'd attended the introduction because he'd been ordered to.

Claude gazed at me in belligerence as I seated myself on the end of his bunk and set my hat next to me. "My father sent you," he stated in French. "Or Emile did. Why?"

"On the contrary, I sent myself here." I stretched my knee, which the many flights of stairs had not helped. "I admit that Emile alerted me to your predicament."

"They believe I stabbed Vincenzo Gallo." Claude scowled at the cell's door. "As though I'd waste my time on that mountebank."

"Did you?" I asked.

"No." Claude jerked back to me, enraged. "I told you, I'd not sully my fingers with him. They showed me the knife they found next to him, but it is not my knife. The one I carry is much better, and I wouldn't have incriminated myself leaving it beside Gallo's body."

"But you might have taken someone else's, or used an old one you were rarely seen with, and left that to point another direction."

Claude glared at me. "If I was as angry as they say and struck out at Gallo's disgusting face, when would I have had time to think about stealing another man's knife beforehand? I would have thrown the weapon into the river, in any case, no matter whose knife it was. Maybe leapt in after it."

"You make very good points," I answered in as calm a tone as I could muster. "The murder was either carefully planned or committed in hot blood. It could not have been both."

"Well, I did not do either." Claude deflated. "But that gendarme captain will not believe me. He is from the mountains," he finished with derision.

"He is very capable of reasoning, I think. He will send you to trial, I'm certain, and who knows what a magistrate will believe? A way to spare yourself that is to tell me exactly where you were last night. If you can prove you were a long way from Gallo when he was meeting his attacker, then you will be cleared."

Claude's head dropped to his hands again, and he clenched

his now greasy hair with pale fingers. "I do not wish to speak of it."

"Why not?" I slid out my pocket watch and clicked it open. "I dislike to hasten you, Claude, but Vernet gave us a short time only, and at least half of that has elapsed. If you tell me the truth, I can help you."

Claude raised his head and regarded me stubbornly. "Emile has talked a great deal about you, and Gabriella does as well. She is very proud of your honor and your assistance to others."

I warmed at Gabriella's faith in me. "Exactly. Your father will be brokenhearted if you are accused and condemned."

Claude's eyes pinched, as though he hadn't thought about the consequences to his father.

"I am appealing to that honor Emile and Gabriella boast of," Claude said. "You will understand if I do not wish to dishonor another."

"Perhaps," I answered. "But will you die to preserve this other person's honor? For a crime you did not commit?"

Again Claude hesitated. "There are things you do not understand, Captain. Things I cannot tell you."

My patience thinned. "I am not asking you to betray another, Monsieur Devere. I know that you were arguing with Gallo earlier in the evening, which Vernet told me. All you must do is prove you were elsewhere in the small hours of the morning, when Gallo was being murdered. You need name no one else."

"It is not so simple." Claude was defiant but becoming more miserable as we sat there.

Had I once been this young and foolishly obstinate?

Yes, was the answer. I'd been even more of a hothead than the young man next to me, not only willing to die for my convictions but excited to do so.

"It is perfectly simple," I said. "If you were with this person you do not wish to dishonor, then you weren't killing Signor Gallo, and neither was this other person."

Claude's brows drew together. "He might be accused?"

I leaned forward to catch his words. Claude spoke rapid French, and I didn't hear every syllable. But I swore he'd said *il*, not *elle*. *He*, not *she*.

"Not if he has an alibi. Where were you, Claude?" I asked in a hard voice. "Not with a woman?"

"No." Claude flushed, and then went redder. "And not with a man, not in the way you are thinking. I was in La Guillotière. At a wine shop. The proprietor will no doubt remember me."

Vernet had said that Claude was seen arguing with Gallo in La Guillotière, the town across the Rhône. "Were you that unruly?" I asked.

"Possibly," Claude mumbled.

"Let me summarize," I said. "Last night, you argued with Gallo, say around eight in the evening, in La Guillotière, where several people saw you. Gallo left you at the argument's end, and you stayed in La Guillotière and met with someone you don't wish to mention in a wine shop. You stayed there until you went home, probably drunker than when you arrived. You don't wish to cause trouble to this other person, so you will not name him. Is that the gist?"

Claude nodded, his scowl now tinged with shame.

"Why did you not say so to Captain Vernet?" I demanded in exasperation. "Why did he have cause to arrest you at all, if you were out of the city entirely?"

"Because when he came to our home today, I would not say where I'd been. I have no reason to. I did not kill Signor Gallo."

I supposed I was that illogical at twenty. I rose, not bothering to hide my irritation. "While you waste time here, a murderer has gotten away with killing a man, no matter how unliked that man was. It is not fair to Gallo, do you not think?"

Claude stared up at me in incomprehension. "Gallo was not welcome in Lyon. Many wanted him gone."

"It would be helpful if you could follow that statement with the names of those who *did* want him out of Lyon. Perhaps one of them wanted it so much, he did not stop short of murdering him."

Something like amusement flickered across Claude's face. "Too many to mention, Captain. It would be a very long list."

I regarded him with annoyance, but inwardly, I was relieved that Claude could prove he was elsewhere. The Deveres did not need such tragedy, and neither did Gabriella.

Keys rattled in the lock, our time at an end. The door opened, Vernet himself once again acting as turnkey.

I said my farewells to Claude without admonishing him further. He'd have to sit and stew for a while, but I hoped he'd soon admit the truth of what he'd been up to.

Madame Marais across the hall had quieted somewhat, her voice fading into an incoherent humming. Vernet led me back along the line of cells and storage rooms to the stairs.

"You need not repeat the conversation to me," Vernet said as we ascended. "I heard every word. There is an open space in the corners of the cells, and I listened from the next one."

I wasn't certain how gentlemanly this was, but on the other hand, Vernet would have heard Claude explaining his innocence.

"You will release him?" I asked when we reached the ground floor.

"That remains to be seen." Vernet led me to the open front door and paused there, clearly wishing me to leave. "We will check this wine shop in La Guillotière. It would be more helpful for Claude to name the friend he was with, but who knows? The friend might have slipped away and murdered Gallo, and Claude fears to implicate him."

"If so, he would have to be a very *good* friend."

"Young men have much loyalty to one another." Vernet shrugged. "You must recall this from your army days. Good day to you, Captain. Thank you for your assistance."

It was a dismissal. I bowed to him. "Anytime I can help."

Vernet's expression told me he wasn't likely to ask for it again soon. He gave me a cordial nod and then gestured me out.

I settled my hat as I exited the building and trudged down the lane to the quay. The day had warmed, though a cool breeze wafted from the river.

I found Brewster at the entrance to the wide bridge over the Rhône, surrounded by four men, the populace of Lyon darting impatiently around them.

Brewster's new companions were the Deveres—Fernand and Emile's father, and the other two uncles, Julien and Giraud, who was Claude's father.

Fernand regarded me with a face like thunder. "What the devil are you doing here?" he demanded. "I warned you not to interfere, Captain."

CHAPTER 9

I faced the four men in both perplexity and growing uneasiness. Brewster had his hands balled, as though he had tried to stop the Deveres charging down the street to haul me, and possibly Claude, bodily from the gendarmerie.

Fernand was the most belligerent of the four. Emile's father —Auguste—looked reluctant to be part of the contingent, and Giraud was the most worried. The fourth brother, Julien, joined Fernand in hostility and glowered at me ominously.

"I have spoken to Claude," I said, as though my future in-laws had merely stopped to make conversation. "I am convinced he had nothing to do with Gallo's death, and I'm certain Captain Vernet will release him soon."

"Of course he had nothing to do with it," Julien snapped. He was of a height with Fernand, the two of them a wall of antagonism.

"This is a family matter," Fernand said. "You do not under-stand, and you will stay out of it."

Giraud, at least, seemed relieved at my pronouncement. He did not call off his brothers, however, and neither did Auguste.

"I advise you not to provoke Vernet," I said. "He might keep hold of Claude out of annoyance with you, if you try to force his release."

"Vernet is nothing." Fernand waved a dismissive hand. "He is not even of Lyon."

"He is the law, assigned here whether he, or you, like it or not," I said with taut patience. "Now, I do not wish to quarrel with you gentlemen. My advice is to let Vernet decide to release Claude and clear him of this charge. Trying to free him your-selves might indicate you believe his guilt."

"Never," Fernand growled. "This may be how things work in your country, Captain, but the gendarmes in France can imprison a man and never let him go. Vernet will regret what he has done."

I felt Brewster close beside me, his bulk obscuring the wind from the river. I knew he wanted to seize me and drag me to safety, but I stood stoically in front of the four men.

"Vernet seems a reasonable fellow," I told them. "He heard Claude's explanation of where he'd been last night, which I believe. I give you my word he will verify the story and send Claude home."

I knew I was making a promise that the arm of French law could negate. But I bound myself by my word, and any who knew me understood that.

Giraud's eyes held sadness. He was a widower, I remem-bered, and Claude was all he had.

"I am willing to wait," he said quietly to Fernand.

"I am not," Fernand said. "But I concede that the captain has a point. If we try to storm the gendarmes, we will only be arrested ourselves." He fixed me with a hard stare, letting me know that he gave in with the greatest reluctance. "I will hold you to your word."

I bowed to him. "I appreciate your trust."

Fernand stepped close to me, never minding Brewster hovering over him. "You will not fail it," he said in English. "And you will delve no further into this matter. It has nothing to do with you."

I could not promise that. I nodded, agreeing only with his first statement.

Fernand eased from me. His brothers watched the encounter anxiously, as though worried Fernand would seize me and throw me into the river. He might have done, had we been alone.

After giving me a final glare, Fernand turned on his heel and marched away, heading toward the heart of the Presqu'île. Julien followed close behind, then came Giraud, head bowed. August, Emile's father, sent me an apologetic nod but drifted after his brothers without a word.

"I agree with 'im," Brewster rumbled at me as the Devere men faded into the crowded streets. "If Frenchies want to stab each other on the bridges, it's nothing to do with you."

"I refuse to let Claude rot in a cell because of his stubbornness," I said testily. "In any case, Emile asked for my help, and I do not wish to fail him. Now." I straightened my hat. "Let us explore this place called La Guillotière. I am a bit thirsty, and a large glass would be just the thing."

Brewster glowered, but he trundled with me onto the bridge while the Rhône rushed noisily beneath us, its waters cooling the heated air.

———

NUMEROUS TAVERNS LINED THE RHÔNE ON ITS EASTERN BANK. From what I understood, La Guillotière had once been an independent village, then had been made part of Lyon, but now was somewhat autonomous again, administered collectively with a few other towns in this area. I wondered how those who lived here kept it all in order.

The main road from Lyon ran east through La Guillotière and wound toward the Swiss Confederation and the passes through the Alps to northern Italian towns. I heard a number of men we passed speaking Italian or its dialects, which made me wonder if Signor Gallo had dwelled on this bank.

Brewster relaxed a bit as we moved from wine shop to wine shop. To be congenial, we had to sample the local drink in each one, or none inside would have spoken to us. Brewster detested wine, but he managed to procure ale in almost all of the taverns, which he pronounced surprisingly tasty.

"Your French colonel chap was right," he said as he drank his fourth tankard of the afternoon. "They can make a decent brew here."

I'd managed to put thoughts of Colonel Moreau out of my head as I'd worried about Claude, but I again wondered at the chance that had brought me face to face with my enemy.

Not being a superstitious man, I decided it a coincidence, though not a very surprising one. Moreau and I had both outlasted the wars, and Britons and Frenchmen now freely traveled between our respective countries. I was bound to come across men I'd fought sooner or later.

In the fifth wine shop we entered, we finally found a trace of Claude's movements.

"*Oui*, the older Devere lad was here last night," the proprietor said, after I'd introduced myself. He hadn't opened up until I'd explained my connection to the Deveres. "In a foul temper, but didn't do much of anything but imbibe wine. More sulky than anything else." The bulbous-faced man peered at me. "You say *your* daughter is marrying young Emile? I thought he was wedding Auberge's daughter."

"Mademoiselle Auberge is actually *my* daughter," I said. "It is difficult to explain."

The proprietor gave me a wise nod. "Not so difficult. A Frenchman understands. You are English, but ..." He spread his hands.

He obviously believed I'd been Carlotta's lover in the past, and Gabriella was our illicit offspring. Perhaps he thought

Major Auberge was being very understanding in allowing me to attend Gabriella's wedding.

As divorce was ruinous, and in the eyes of Auberge's church, unthinkable, I'd agreed to let Carlotta's previous connection to me be vague. Both Auberge and I had kept quiet about the divorce, though I'd obtained one all the same, thanks to the assistance of James Denis.

I did not correct the proprietor's assumptions. "Was Claude with anyone last night? Or was he sulking by himself?"

The proprietor's grizzled brows rose. "He was with that man killed on the bridge, wasn't he? Just outside my door, arguing with him."

I carefully set down my cup. "Signor Gallo? Are you certain?"

"Mais oui." The proprietor nodded with confidence. "They were already arguing when they arrived. Not a violent quarrel, just words. Signor Gallo sneering—he was like that. Monsieur Devere said something about Comte Lejeune I could not hear, and Gallo lost his temper. He slammed himself away, and then young Claude came inside and took to his wine."

"What's he saying?" Brewster asked me impatiently.

I quickly repeated the information, and Brewster frowned. "Sounds like Claude told Gallo that his signora was heading up the hill to see the comte," he offered.

"Possibly," I said. "Though how would Claude know?"

"Mayhap the signora told him. Mayhap she didn't forget about young Claude as much as everyone claims she did."

I could imagine Claude rubbing Gallo's nose in the fact that Signora Ruggeri had confided in him what she'd planned. Gallo, growing incensed, dashed from the tavern and across the city to burst into the courtyard just as Signora Ruggeri was being led through the ballroom by the comtesse.

"Claude didn't follow him?" I switched to French to ask the proprietor.

The man shook his head. "No. Ordered another bottle and

made his way through it. Oh, shared it with his cousin, of course."

I stilled. "Cousin?"

"*Oui,* young Emile. He came in maybe a half hour after Claude arrived. They drank their way through the bottle and left together. That is, Claude drank most of it, and Emile had to help him stumble away." A smile flitted across his mouth. "Your daughter has no cause to worry. Emile is not much for being in his cups."

I tried to return the smile, but my heart hammered. Emile had never mentioned the fact that he'd been with Claude in La Guillotière last night, either when I'd spoken to him at the iron-works or in his hasty note this afternoon.

Claude had spoken about dishonoring someone by giving me his name. Had he meant Emile?

"When did they leave?" I asked.

The proprietor frowned at my question. "You'd better ask them, hadn't you?"

"It is important," I said sternly.

The man sighed. "Ten, maybe? Not late. They went that way down the lane." He pointed to the left. "Home, most like, unless they stopped at another tavern. Emile seemed anxious to get his cousin out of La Guillotière. Wise. Rich boys don't belong here after dark."

Had Emile hunted for Claude, fearing what he'd do if he found Gallo, and escorted him home? Emile hadn't told me he'd taken Claude under his wing last night, only stated that Claude couldn't have killed Gallo and never would.

Blast the lad. If he'd been with Claude, and neither had been anywhere near Gallo at the time of his murder, why hadn't Emile simply told me?

"Damnation," I said out loud.

The proprietor's scowl deepened. "What is this word?"

"What an Englishman says when he is vexed," I said in

French. "I beg your pardon." I put coins on the table for what we'd drunk, plus a few extra.

The proprietor whisked the payment into his pocket, gave us a final frown, and moved off, irritably waving at other patrons who were calling for more wine.

"He said something about our Emile, didn't he?" Brewster demanded when we emerged from the shop. The long summer day was finally waning, twilight touching the sky. "I understand some words, like *cousin*, and I heard the lad's name."

"He did." I turned my steps to the bridge and gave Brewster a truncated translation of the conversation as we went.

"This looks bad," was Brewster's pronouncement.

"I agree. Why the devil didn't either of them let on they were together?"

Brewster huffed as we hastened toward the stone bridge that crossed the Rhône. "Stands to reason, they didn't want anyone to know. Not you, not their dads, not their uncles, not the gendarmes."

"Yes," I said grimly. I halted at the pillar that marked the change from the street's pavement to the bridge's. "Why did the proprietor say they'd gone that way?" I nodded downriver. "If they were heading to their own homes, there are no more convenient bridges south of here."

"Maybe they know a better route than you do. We're not from here, are we?"

"While that is true, I think they meant to stay in La Guillotière a while longer."

"What for? Landlord said it were dangerous after dark." Brewster glanced about, not in fear but in agreement. Dangerous for people who couldn't defend themselves, he meant.

"I intend to ask them." I started across the bridge, Brewster falling into step beside me.

———

ONCE IN THE PRESQU'ÎLE, I SOUGHT A HIRED HACK AND ASKED the coachman to take me south, toward the factory and the village that housed Emile and his family.

I learned from a servant at Auguste Devere's brick and stucco home that the young master was dining tonight with the Auberges, not far down the road. Auguste himself was still with his brothers, his wife calling on friends.

I debated for a moment, then bade the coachman take me to the farm where my former wife lived with her new husband and my daughter.

CHAPTER 10

The Auberges lived in a two-story house of golden stone, which had impressed me with its size but Donata had pronounced charming. Auberge had turned farmer when he'd retired from the wars, inheriting the estate from his father and continuing to work it.

When I'd first heard about Auberge's farm, I'd pictured a medieval structure with four wings enclosing a courtyard, with pigs and chickens sharing the interior space.

In contrast, this *maison* was fairly modern, bearing tall windows with blue shutters, iron railings on balconies, and a tiled roof. The outbuildings that housed the farm's few animals lay down a hill from the house, and beyond them spread the fields where Auberge's farmhands toiled.

Carlotta had grown up on a similar estate in England, where I'd found and fallen in love with her at a ridiculously young age. I suppose Auberge's offer of a quiet life in this place had been familiar and more appealing than following me through army camps, a baby in tow.

Tonight, when I descended from the coach, Brewster climbing down behind me, I did not give myself time for old regrets.

I approached the front door, painted in a faded blue that matched the long shutters, and rapped upon it. A maidservant in black with a mobcap opened it, starting to find me on the doorstep.

"Father?" Before I could state my business and ask to speak to Emile, Gabriella came floating along the hall behind her, a smile of delighted welcome on her face. "I did not know you were coming. Is Lady Donata with you? Mr. Brewster, good evening."

So greeting us, she grasped the door the maid had kept half closed and flung it wide.

"We have just finished supping," Gabriella continued. "Dreadfully early by London hours, I know. Shall you join us for coffee? Can I bring you anything, Mr. Brewster?"

Gabriella would break my heart with her kindness, which stemmed from her natural generosity.

"Might take a stroll," Brewster said. "Fine night, ain't it? I'll leave you to it, guv."

"The path up the hill leads to a lovely view." Gabriella pointed out the door and to the right of the house. "You can see the river and the lights of Lyon."

"Very nice." Brewster regarded Gabriella with unfeigned fondness. "Give us a shout when you're done with 'im." He jabbed a thumb at me then ambled off in the direction Gabriella had indicated.

"Never mind, Marie," Gabriella said to the waiting maid. "I know you are busy this evening. I'll take my father in."

The maid curtsied with a look as indulgent as Brewster's and scuttled into the dim recesses behind the staircase. Gabriella took me by the hand and pulled me inside.

The entrance hall, paved in cool and echoing slate, was open to the next floor, with a gallery encircling above. This hall led to the public rooms on the ground floor and ended in long windows that overlooked the garden.

"Did Lady Donata not accompany you?" Gabriella asked me

with a final glance out the door to the now-empty coach. "Nothing is amiss, I hope?"

"Not at all. If you cease for one moment, I will tell you. I came to see Emile."

Gabriella's dark brows rose. "Emile? Ah, I see. He has been very worried about Claude. Not bad news, I hope?" Her voice quavered with worry.

"No, indeed. Claude by now should have been sent home, if Vernet is reasonable. But I must—"

I broke off as a middle-aged woman, a little plump, with faded, once-golden hair, hurried out of a chamber in the back of the house.

"Gabriella, who has come?" she asked in French.

She stopped short when she saw me, her skirts swirling with the momentum. She regarded me with blue eyes that had once ensnared me with their wilting entreaty but now held hard suspicion.

"Captain," Carlotta said stiffly.

I had already removed my hat, and now I bowed. "Madame Auberge. Forgive me for disturbing you. I came only to speak to Emile, as he was not at home."

"Oh." Carlotta regarded me with a mixture of bewilderment, rancor, and disdain. This was her territory, *her patch,* as Brewster would say, and I was the invader.

"It is about Claude and the murder," Gabriella said quickly. "Mama, let us go and fetch Emile. I'm certain that what the captain has to say is important."

"You go, Gabriella." Carlotta stood her ground. "Do, child."

She spoke French with some defiance, as though indicating she'd left her English origins behind her forever.

Gabriella, after a hesitant glance between us, hastened off toward the dining room, where the family must have just finished their meal.

I recalled the layout of the house from the brief call we'd

paid when we'd first arrived. Donata had taken over that visit, behaving every inch the aristocrat. The servants of the house had rushed about trying to make her comfortable, while she took in everything with her cool assessment. Carlotta had been as caught up in the servants' undertaking, determined to prove her home worthy of a great lady.

Donata confided to me later that she'd adopted the arrogant persona on purpose, so that Carlotta would be distracted and not try to create any sort of scene with me. I'd warmed that Donata had put aside her own discomfort with the situation to keep our visit amicable.

Now, there was no one in the hall except Carlotta—my first wife—and myself.

"Are you well?" I asked, falling back on rote politeness.

"As well as can be expected," Carlotta answered, still firmly in French. "Why have you come? Gabriella will stay home tonight. She has been gadding about too much of late. You took her to a soiree where a man was murdered, for heaven's sake."

The years fell away, and my impatience with Carlotta returned full force.

"He was not murdered at the soiree," I said angrily. "But on a bridge in the city. It had nothing to do with the gathering, or me."

"You are always rushing into danger," Carlotta returned. "I shudder whenever Gabriella ventures to England. She comes home with hair-raising tales of your exploits, *and* you surround yourself with villains. I have decided—she will stay in this house until the wedding and visit you no more."

I'd hoped the time apart from Carlotta would have curbed my temper, but it was not to be.

I advanced on her, my stick thumping on the slates. "She is *my* daughter. Not to mention a grown woman, able to visit whomever she pleases. Once she is Mrs. Devere, she can go where she likes."

"Perhaps, but until then, Gabriella will stay under our roof. Besides, the major and I believe it might be best if she postpones the wedding, what with this scandal of Claude's arrest. Or perhaps doesn't marry Emile at all."

Carlotta emphasized the word *major*, pointing out that her new husband outranked me.

"You'd make Gabriella miserable because Claude was imprudent?" I asked in amazement, though I lowered my voice, not wishing Gabriella and Emile to overhear. "I highly doubt that Claude committed this murder, and the gendarme captain doubts it as well."

"He was *arrested*. I'll not have my daughter associating with criminals." Carlotta's disparaging glance told me she considered me in that category.

"If you restrict her to young men who have never been rash then she will likely never marry. In any case, it was Claude who was arrested. I doubt Emile has sowed a wild oat in his life."

"Does it matter?" Carlotta snapped. "I won't have her marry into an undesirable family. Perhaps you do not understand that."

My family had been nothing to hold up one's head about, she meant. My father had been a martinet, bankrupting the estate and leaving it derelict. My cousin from Canada, who might or might not have a claim on the house—the courts would decide —now occupied it while I was kept by my second wife in homes belonging to her son.

Major Auberge, on the other hand, was the epitome of respectability, other than running off with other men's wives, of course.

I wondered abruptly if Carlotta's fear about bringing scandal upon Gabriella was tied to her guilt over abandoning me and unlawfully marrying Major Auberge. She'd had to keep up the pretense of faultless virtue, in case someone questioned the perfect life she'd built for herself.

Carlotta drew a breath to argue further, but I held up my hand to check her words. Gabriella and Emile were hastening from the back of the house, and I prayed they hadn't heard us discussing them.

Emile gave no sign of it, though Gabriella had lost some of her brightness.

"Sir?" Emile asked in English. "Did you convince Captain Vernet to release Claude?"

"Shall we walk outside and discuss this?" I answered. "As my man pointed out, it is a fine evening."

"Certainly," Emile said before Carlotta could object. "Excuse me a moment, Madame Auberge. I really have been most concerned for my cousin. Excuse me, Gabriella."

"I will walk with you," Gabriella announced. The stubborn light in her eyes, so like what saw in my own every day, indicated she'd not be deterred.

I did not argue. I did not want the pair to begin married life by keeping secrets from each other.

Carlotta was clearly not happy that Gabriella stuck by her soon-to-be husband, and I could have uncharitably stated that she had never learned the habit of it, herself.

Then again, Carlotta had remained with Auberge all these years, so perhaps it was *me* she'd felt no loyalty to, not husbands in general.

Before I could utter anything unforgivable, I strode out of the house, slapping on my hat as I stepped into the cool evening air.

The sun was just slipping behind the hills, streaking the sky and its few clouds in scarlet and gold. Fields rippled across the land to lush woods on their edge, and the fresh scent of flowers from beds around the walkway scented the air.

It was a beautiful place, full of abundance, and it was no wonder Gabriella loved it so. I was glad, in spite of my anger at Carlotta, that she'd been able to grow up in such a setting.

We strolled a little way beyond the house, taking the path Gabriella had pointed out to Brewster, which wound up a gentle hill. Of Brewster, there was no sign.

Emile, oblivious to any discomfort of my past and present colliding, regarded me in both worry and hope while he waited for me to speak.

"Vernet will no doubt release Claude," I told Emile as we walked. "He should be home soon, if he is not already." I wondered if Claude would return home by himself or if his contingent of uncles and his father would escort him.

Emile exhaled in relief. "Thank you, Captain. I was certain you'd talk sense into Vernet. I am forever grateful, and I am certain Claude is as well."

"I spoke at some length with Claude," I said.

Emile's sunny smile began to fade. "Did you? I—I thought you'd only see Vernet."

I watched Emile closely. "Captain Vernet allowed me into Claude's cell, and your cousin and I had an interesting conversation. Claude admitted that he'd been in a wine tavern earlier that night. And that he'd been seen arguing with Signor Gallo himself."

"Ah." Emile flushed. "Yes, I knew that. But Signor Gallo departed without him."

"He did." I slowed my steps, both to rest my leg and to fix Emile with a stern gaze. "I ascertained the second fact directly from the tavern keeper in La Guillotière."

Emile's uneasiness increased. "Did you?"

"Yes, the tavern keeper was very forthcoming." I continued to study Emile, while he grew more and more flustered.

Gabriella regarded us both in worry. "What are you saying, Father?"

Emile turned quickly to her. "Perhaps you should return to the house, Gabriella."

Gabriella lifted her chin with a hauteur worthy of Donata.

"No indeed. I would like to hear the entire story. Did Claude scuffle with Signor Gallo? Is that the difficulty?"

"No, nothing of that sort." I debated what to reveal, then decided that Gabriella ought to know what things Emile got up to. "The proprietor said *you* were there, Emile. With Claude. I'd like to know why you chose not to tell me this."

CHAPTER 11

*E*mile took a step back, glancing fearfully from me to Gabriella.

If he believed Gabriella would gush to me that of course Emile had nothing to hide, he was mistaken. She fixed Emile with a steely gaze and waited for him to explain.

"It had nothing to do with Signor Gallo's death," Emile said in a rush. "I assure you. I promise."

"Then why not say you were with Claude last night?" I asked in bafflement. "It might have saved him being arrested."

"Because he swore me to secrecy." Emile's face had gone beet red, rivaling the colors of the deepening sunset. "We swore to each other. None were to know what we did."

"I fail to see why," I said. "Drinking wine with your cousin in a disreputable tavern is not grounds for imprisonment. Or even much shame, though I'm certain your mother and Carlotta would disapprove. What time did you arrive at the tavern? Not long after Gallo departed, I assume."

"A bit after nine, I think," Emile said in a small voice. "Claude told me he'd argued with Signor Gallo and that the man had run off in a temper."

Gabriella nodded at me. "Signor Gallo turned up at the

comtesse's at about half past ten. But Claude must have been very worried about his encounter with Signor Gallo to keep it quiet. Or perhaps Claude met him somewhere after that?" she asked Emile.

Emile shook his head adamantly. "No, Claude never saw him again. He and I drank wine in the tavern and then departed. We were together the rest of the night and ended up at home. Neither of us saw Signor Gallo. That is the truth."

His statement and agitation rang with sincerity.

"I believe you, Emile," I said. "What I do not understand is why you did not simply state this when Claude was arrested. Or tell me in your note. You thought I'd rush to the gendarmerie and use my powers of persuasion to talk Vernet into releasing Claude, did you not? You never thought I'd speak to Claude, or that he'd break your pact and admit he spent the evening with you. Which he did not, by the way. The tavern keeper told me."

"I'm sorry, sir," Emile said in misery.

"Most of the time, I would agree that how two gentlemen spend their evenings out is their own business, but this involves a murder," I said sternly. "Both of you are acting very suspiciously, and Vernet is not completely satisfied. He will continue to pry, and so I must as well. If you confide in me, I can perhaps deflect Vernet's attentions from you."

Emile was no fool—he must see how his and Claude's attempt at secrecy did not exude innocence. I hoped that their vow of silence didn't have anything to do with clandestine visits to ladies, but I would press Emile, no matter what. Gabriella deserved to know whether she was marrying a libertine.

Gabriella remained firmly beside me. "Please tell us, Emile," she said quietly.

Emile deflated, shoulders drooping in sorrow and mortification.

"We went to Gallo's lodgings," he said in a near whisper. "We knew he would not be there, because Claude had angered him into going to the comtesse's chateau."

I heard Gabriella's intake of breath while I gaped at him.

"Why the devil did you go to his lodgings?" I demanded in amazement. "A moment—if you first made certain that Gallo would not be there, then you must have been seeking something. What?"

Emile's eyes swam with tears. "Oh, sir, please do not make me tell you."

"If you do not tell me, I will have to guess, and so will Gabriella. Were you looking for something that would discredit Gallo? And why? I thought Signora Ruggeri was finished with him. She certainly wasn't happy with him turning up at the chateau."

"She despises him now, Claude says." Emile wiped at the tears that continued forming.

"She still speaks to Claude?" I asked. "Is that how he knew she would be trying to enter the comte's home last night?"

"Yes." Emile's voice was cracked. "But no, she was not quite finished with Gallo. She aided him."

"Aided him in what way? What were you searching for, Emile?" I took the forbidding tone I'd used with my soldiers when they'd tried to hide their transgressions.

Emile sniffled but squared his shoulders. "I did not want you to know this, Gabriella, but I suppose I must be truthful. If you wish to release yourself from me once I tell you, I will understand." Emile's words belied the wretchedness that seeped through every syllable.

"Is it so very bad?" Gabriella asked him gently.

"Signor Gallo was threatening my family," Emile said, so softly I had to lean to hear him. "He said he knew what they had done and could prove it, if they didn't pay him."

"That is maddeningly vague," I said, straightening. "What are they supposed to have done?"

"I don't know." Emile flung out one hand in a dramatic gesture. "That is the truth, Captain. I have no idea. Neither does Claude. We searched Gallo's rooms top to bottom but found nothing—no papers or letters or whatever he had—that mentioned my family. Nothing of any kind. Either he lied to them or he hid the things very well."

I fell silent as I considered the implications of what Emile had confessed.

First, Gallo, rather than being simply a spurned lover and a nuisance about town, was apparently also a blackmailer. Whether he did this for a living or had seized an opportunity remained to be seen.

Second, the Deveres had a secret that they'd not wanted anyone, especially a rogue like Gallo, to discover. Claude and Emile, upon learning of Gallo's threats, had met in La Guillotière, made certain Gallo went elsewhere, and searched his rooms for the evidence in order to spare their family.

Emile's declaration that he did not know exactly what the secret was rang true. I wondered if Claude knew, but from Claude's demeanor today, I doubted it. Neither young man had understood what to look for and so had found nothing.

Whatever Gallo had known, I was certain it involved the older generation of Deveres, not the younger.

Gallo as a blackmailer explained Fernand's shock when he found Gallo dead, as well as his sudden animosity to me. If Gallo had been blackmailing the Devere brothers, Fernand would fear that the secret would come to light, especially if the gendarmes investigated his murder.

Fernand had also worried that Claude had dispatched Gallo, perhaps in a misguided attempt to protect the family honor. He might fear that one of his brothers had done the same.

My imagination went further, supposing Fernand murdered Gallo himself. He'd certainly not been happy I'd been present to find the body.

"Bloody hell," I said softly.

Emile continued to look ashamed and dejected. Gabriella left her place at my side to flow to his and take his hand.

"Poor Emile," she said with such love I had to glance down the hill to the rather splendid view. "I wish you'd have told me."

"I didn't want to burden you," Emile answered hollowly. "It is a family matter."

Gabriella leaned into him. "I will be family very soon, my love. It is a burden I will gladly help you carry."

I did not wish for Gabriella to be burdened at all, but the tender gratitude Emile turned on her told me she'd known exactly what to say to him.

To my relief, Brewster descended the path above us to interrupt the unnerving tableau.

Emile flushed and gently disentangled himself from Gabriella, but Gabriella beamed her smile at Brewster, not in the least embarrassed.

"What do you advise, sir?" Emile asked me in English with flattering trust. "I suppose I should tell all this to Captain Vernet, to prove Claude is innocent."

"Wouldn't advise it," Brewster said. "Never give up too much information to the beaks. They'll use it against you, soon as you draw your next breath. What has happened? You look terrified, lad."

"It appears that Signor Gallo was blackmailing the Deveres," Gabriella said before Emile or I could decide what to tell him. "We don't know why."

Brewsters brows rose. "Was he, now? Dangerous game, blackmail. Blokes try to blackmail His Nibs all the time, but he never responds to it. Disgusting business."

His Nibs was James Denis, a man I'd never dare to blackmail without a long, hard think about it first. I imagined anyone who tried it came to a bad end.

Emile's expression was anxious. "If we tell Captain Vernet, it might help him find the killer. Signor Gallo might have been blackmailing other people as well."

Innocent lad—he'd point Vernet directly at his own family.

"You indicated that Signora Ruggeri aided Gallo," I said. "Even after they ceased their love affair."

Emile nodded. "According to Claude. I don't know if he meant about the blackmailing."

I still believed Signora Ruggeri to be the most likely culprit in the man's murder, no matter that she'd slept at the comtesse's chateau. She might have slipped out with none the wiser, or she might have instructed her coachman, whom Fernand said was a brute, to do the deed for her.

I could not risk, however, that Vernet would draw different conclusions.

"I suggest I return with you to Gallo's rooms and try to find what has your uncles and father so concerned," I said. "Before Vernet's men find it, that is. If there is truly nothing there, then your family has little to fear."

Emile appeared to be both relieved I was taking command and alarmed by my suggestion.

"What if the gendarmes have taken over his lodgings?" he asked nervously.

"Then we will discover a way around them. Brewster will help us."

Brewster grimaced at my pronouncement but he nodded. "I know ways to keep the beaks off our scent."

"Beaks?" Emile's forehead puckered. "You keep using that word."

"Magistrates," Brewster explained. "The watch, the gendarmes, the Runners—whatever they're called. Because they stick their beaks in everywhere, right?"

Emile looked uncertain, but he nodded.

"Gabriella," I said, trying sound like a strict father. "La Guillotière will be no place for you."

Gabriella regarded me serenely. "I did not expect to accompany you. I promised *Maman* I would stay in tonight, and that is what I will do. I won't have much longer to be at home, will I?"

Emile's sudden blush made me both want to laugh and to shake him.

I turned away to keep my impulses in check. "We'd better go at once," I said. "Vernet is an astute man and possibly has turned over Gallo's place already."

"True enough," Brewster said. "But it can't hurt to have a butcher's."

I was pleased Brewster agreed. I wanted him with me, not only because he could protect Emile in La Guillotière, but because the man had an uncanny knack of turning up things that others overlooked. When I'd first met him, he'd been ransacking my house in Norfolk, where he'd found silver pieces for which the nearby villagers had been searching for years.

The four of us trudged back down the hill toward the house, Gabriella now firmly at Emile's side. Once in the drive, while our hired coach creaked forward to fetch us, Gabriella squeezed Emile's hands, kissed me goodnight, said her farewells to Brewster, and skimmed into the house.

Brewster rode on the back of the coach as we headed to Lyon, which left Emile awkwardly inside the carriage with me. He continued to apologize for not confiding in me right away, and I spent the journey trying to reassure him.

The coachman deposited us on the La Guillotière side of the Rhône. Emile led Brewster and me through narrow streets beyond the tavern in which he and Claude had met, to a crumbling building whose windows were closed with black shutters.

The last of the evening's light faded as Emile rapped on the front door.

This was wrenched open by a gnarled personage whose sex I could not determine. I saw only breeches and a tattered coat, in spite of the warm weather, and gloves on cramped fingers.

When the creature raised her head, I realized it was a woman, her grizzled hair framing a curiously plump and pretty face.

She looked Emile up and down with steel-gray eyes. "It's you again, is it?"

"Yes, Madame Jourdain," Emile said politely. "Do you mind if I go once more into Signor Gallo's rooms?"

"Why? Do ye want to let them?" Madame Jourdain spat on the pavement, too close to my boot for my liking. "Gendarmes have been all through his lodging and tell me not to rent it right away, but I can't afford to leave it empty."

"Well, no, Madame, but …"

When the woman started to shut the door, I stepped forward. "My man might be interested." I jerked a thumb at Brewster.

The woman scowled at Brewster, who scowled back, uncertain what we'd said. Finally, she gave me a curt nod and flung the door open.

"He knows the way." Madame Jourdain took a jingling key from her pocket and held it out to Emile. "Was the signor's great friend." She emphasized the last words and cackled unpleasantly.

Emile flushed, pretending to ignore her. He led the way across the hallway's very dirty tile floor and up a rickety staircase.

We ascended this all the way to the top of the house, the air growing warmer and stuffier as we went. It must be suffocating on a hot day.

The door Emile paused before looked solid enough, with an iron handle and a stout lock.

This door stood open a crack. The wood around the lock hadn't been broken, but the room had been entered, probably by someone good with a picklock.

I started to push it open, but Brewster shouldered his way past me to do it himself. The door's wood grated against the uneven floor, startling the person already inside.

We both stilled when a man abruptly straightened from an open trunk in the middle of the floor to gaze back at us.

It was Colonel Moreau, my old enemy from the wars, the man I'd supposed myself finished with.

CHAPTER 12

Moreau regarded us for a long moment, saying nothing.

The three of us might have frozen there for an age, waiting for one another to break the silence, if Emile had not popped around me to see what was happening.

"I beg your pardon, sir," Emile said to Moreau in true ingenuousness. "We did not mean to disturb you. Are you thinking of taking the rooms?"

I ended my unmoving stance. "I'm certain the colonel already has much better accommodation."

"What's he want here?" Brewster demanded of me in English. "Is that Gallo's things he's pawing through?"

"Perhaps the colonel will tell us," I said, not bothering to translate to French. I knew Moreau understood me well enough.

To Moreau's credit, he did not try to invent an excuse or an obvious lie. He quietly closed the lid of the trunk and faced us without flinching.

"I am looking for something that belongs to me."

"Oh, dear," Emile said. "Was Signor Gallo blackmailing you as well?"

Moreau stared at him, clearly uncertain how to respond.

"We have learned Gallo tried his hand at extorting money from others," I told him. "A dangerous undertaking."

Moreau flicked his gaze between me, Emile, and Brewster once more. "It is as you say," he admitted in English. "He had a letter that I should not like to be read by the wrong person. Or, at least, he claimed to have it. I've found nothing here."

"The gendarmes must have already searched," I said.

"They did but only cursorily." At my surprised expression, Moreau continued. "I was Sergeant Dubois's commanding officer for a time during the war. He told me that Vernet sent them to make a quick search, looking for obvious things, such as a sign the murderer had been here, or indication of who Gallo might have met that night."

"Good, then there might be summat to find," Brewster said. "What am I looking for?"

"Anything," I replied. "Letters, papers, ledgers, books. Who knows what information Gallo collected?"

"Right." Brewster moved past Moreau, who pivoted to keep a close eye on him. "Give me a hand, lad."

Emile had remained bewildered during the exchange, but he readily went to Brewster's side. Brewster ignored the sitting room's sparse furnishings—table and chair, plain armoire, settee with sagging cushions, and the trunk Moreau had been searching, and went to the wall nearest the single window.

There he began softly tapping the window's wooden molding and pushing at the looser bricks in the wall next to it. Emile caught on and did the same on the opposite side of the window.

Moreau watched them a moment before he turned back to me. "I cannot reveal to you what I am looking for, or show you if I find it."

"I would not expect you to," I said. "A man's private correspondence is his business."

Moreau frowned, as though wondering if I needled him, but he pressed his lips together and opened the trunk once more.

I bent over it myself, curious. Gallo's belongings were meager—a few pairs of boots, a heavy coat tucked away for summer, and trinkets he must have obtained on his travels. Moreau turned up snuffboxes with rusting hinges, a flask to hold brandy or other liqueur, and one small, paper-covered tome that proved to be a book of devotions in Italian.

Moreau opened a square wooden box he found in the bottom of the trunk and drew a sharp breath.

Inside lay jewels, small pieces like bracelets, single earrings, and thin necklaces, most made of gold and studded with glittering stones. None could match the stunning compositions I'd seen on the necks and wrists of ladies at the comtesse's soiree, but they would be costly nonetheless.

"The man was a petty thief," Moreau said in distaste.

I felt Brewster behind me, craning to peek inside the jewelry box. "Looks like he were a dipper," was his conclusion. "Those are things you can slide off a wrist or an ear while you're chatting with a lady. Nothing she'd notice gone until later, so she might think she dropped it somewhere. Nasty bloke, weren't he?"

"It seems so," I agreed. "If there was some way to identify these pieces, we could return them to the ladies in question."

Brewster gave me one of his disbelieving stares. "You plan to lay them out at your lady wife's next gathering and ask her guests to pick up which are theirs? They'd have to admit they let this Gallo cove get close enough to them to steal it. No, they'll be happier to have them stay lost, I'll wager."

"You might be right," I said with a sigh. "A pity to let him get away with it, though."

Moreau studied me with some reassessment. "It seems the man 'got away' with much, as you say."

"Which broadens the number of people who might have murdered him," I said. "A jealous husband to one of the ladies whose earring lies here? One of the ladies herself, not best pleased with him? Another man or woman whose letters he stole? Might be the whole of Lyon, or anyone who followed him from the last city he was in."

"Does it matter?" Moreau asked me, as Brewster went back to poking at the walls. "A greedy and cunning man is dead and can no longer cause trouble. Why should you worry about which of his victims killed him?"

"To prevent the wrong person from being convicted and executed for the crime," I stated. "Emile's cousin nearly went down for it , and I will do my best to keep another innocent from paying. Besides, it might have been a madman, randomly stabbing people on the Pont Tilsit. Should we not stop him, if so?"

Moreau frowned. "That is what the gendarmes are for."

"Give up trying to argue with him, mate," Brewster advised from the window. "He'll go on and on about honor and lending a hand-up to those what need it, whether they want said hand-up or not."

"Thank you, Brewster," I said in a mild tone. "Let us continue searching for what we need to find, shall we?"

Brewster shook his head, muttering under his breath.

"Ah." Emile exclaimed in satisfaction. "This one is moving."

Mortar grated as Emile jerked at a brick, debris flaking from it to the floor.

"Easy lad." Brewster brushed Emile's hands aside, wrapped his giant fingers around the brick, and gently eased it out of the wall.

Once it came free, Brewster set it carefully on the windowsill then leaned to peer into the crevice.

"Huh," he said. "Nothing."

Emile crouched to peer inside. "He is correct," he said in disappointment.

I believed them, but for some reason I had to limp to the wall and look for myself. The niche was the same depth as the window embrasure next to it, but it held nothing, not even dust or scattered mortar.

"Something *must* have been inside," I observed. "Taken out, probably recently, or it would not be so clean. But by whom? Gallo himself? The gendarmes? Or people like us, searching for the secrets he collected?"

None of the three could answer me.

Emile continued to wriggle bricks on the other side of the window, hoping for another hollow, but Brewster abandoned it and moved to the fireplace. He tested bricks there, his gloves soon covered with soot.

I opened the interior door that stood next to the armoire, and entered the bedchamber.

This room was very small, with a tiny window high in the wall, more for ventilation than light. There was only enough space here for the bed and a table beside it.

Dusk had completely faded by now, rendering the room dark. I found a candle on the bedside table, but I had no way to light it. In past days, I'd have carried a small piece of flint and a steel with me, in case I needed to strike a spark. I'd gone soft, I realized, living in homes where candles and fires were always lit for me.

I returned to the outer room, where Moreau, more practical than me, had managed to light three candles, filling the air with the rancid odor of tallow.

I took one without a word and continued my search of the bedchamber.

What I turned up was not helpful. The gendarmes had obviously rifled the bedside table, which was where Gallo had kept his small clothes and a chamber pot. The last had been emptied, mercifully, but his underthings had been tossed about and then left haphazardly in the drawer. I went through them, but found nothing tucked underneath or inside any of the clothes.

The rumpled state of the bed told me that the gendarmes had likely thrown back all the covers and searched under the straw mattress. I did the same, and even went so far as to go lower myself painfully to the floor and slide under the bed.

I found no interesting books or papers tucked under the bed's slats or behind the headboard.

I was still lying in the dust under the bed when Brewster called out.

"Found summat."

I shoved myself into the open, climbing stiffly to my feet. Emile popped inside to find me and help me stand.

"Thank you," I told him as I brushed off the coat Bartholomew would shake his head over. "Nothing in here that I can see."

"Not much here either," Brewster said as I emerged. He held out two folded papers, their creases soiled. Each had once been sealed with wax, but those seals had been broken.

Moreau tried to snatch them from Brewster's hand, but Brewster sidestepped him and opened one. The three of us crowded around to see what he unfolded.

It was a letter, written in a neat hand, but I couldn't read the words from my vantage point.

"It's foreign," Brewster announced. "But not French."

"Italian, perhaps." I held out my hand and Brewster relinquished the letter.

The language was indeed Italian, I saw, recognizing some words. I'd learned more of it during my recent journey to Rome, but I wasn't fluent.

Moreau nearly breathed down my neck as he read over my shoulder. He must have been more familiar with the language, because he soon shook his head and turned away.

"Not what I am searching for," he said. "What is the other paper?"

I slid the letter into my pocket. Vernet's men had missed it— I saw the bricks Brewster had pulled out of the back of the fireplace scattered on the hearth. I pondered whether I should turn it over to the gendarmes, but I decided I'd see what was in it first. Grenville could read and speak Italian well, though the letter might be written in a dialect neither of us knew.

Brewster had already unfolded the other paper. It was much crumpled, as though someone had scrunched it up in fury, then either they or someone else had carefully smoothed it again. Brewster frowned at it then handed it to me.

The page was blank except for two printed words, which I read out: "Lucien Potier." The name was underlined heavily, three times.

"Who's that bloke when 'e's at home?" Brewster asked.

"No idea," I said. "Emile?"

Emile shook his head. "I've never heard the name, that I recall, anyway."

Moreau was frowning, but he gave no indication that he knew the name either.

I tucked this paper into my pocket as well. "I'd like to learn more before I give these to Vernet," I said. "I'd hate to drop someone in it, if Gallo was blackmailing them for an embarrassing sin."

"Might have killed Gallo for it," Brewster reminded me.

"Possibly, but if every blackmail victim had run after Gallo and stabbed him, there would have been quite a crowd on that bridge. Let me find out if whoever these belong to are dangerous people or simply unlucky, before I consult Vernet."

Brewster found this perfectly reasonable, as did Emile.

Moreau remained more uncomfortable. I wasn't certain whether Frenchmen more readily left things to the authorities than we did in England, or if they, like Londoners, were perfectly happy to chase down a thief and haul him to a magistrate themselves.

Moreau finally gave me a nod. "It shall be as you say. If someone found what I am looking for, I'd be grateful if he returned it to me instead of reporting to the gendarmes."

"Will you now tell me what you seek?" I asked. "It might help me to know what it is if I come across it."

"I doubt you will, but very well. It is a letter, in French. Not from me or about me—I am here on behalf of a friend."

Moreau must think highly of this friend if he risked being caught searching a dead man's rooms. The fact that he decided to trust me, more or less, told me he was growing desperate enough to enlist help.

"I will bring you anything I find," I promised. "Where do you reside?"

"In the Rue Saint-Jean in Vieux Lyon," Moreau told me. "I have rooms in a house near the cathedral."

"You may send word to me at Beaumont's wine shop, where I breakfast every morning. Or find me at the villa my wife hired," I added with a self-disparaging smile. "I had the good fortune to marry a wealthy lady who wishes to travel in comfort. I at one time lived in something very like the rooms in which we stand." I glanced at the bare and mold-flecked walls.

"Our fortunes ebb and flow," Moreau said without changing expression.

I wondered if he meant *his* fortunes had also ebbed and flowed or if he made a polite observation.

"Nothing else here," Brewster said with conviction. "Found other hidden nooks and crannies, but except for those two papers, they were empty."

"Which means the gendarmes were more thorough than we thought," I said.

"They missed the box of jewels," Emile pointed out.

"They must not have thought them important," I said.

Brewster shook his head. "None's as thorough as me. What it means, guv, is that our Signor Gallo had another hiding place, one that the gendarmes won't know nothing about."

CHAPTER 13

None of us answered Brewster, but we regarded him in disquiet. My gaze went to the window and the view of the house across the back court from this. La Guillotière was a maze of streets, and many more of them filled Lyon.

"How will we find this other hiding place?" Emile finally asked.

"We will have to narrow it down," I said. "A task for another day, I think."

Moreau did not answer, and Brewster nodded glumly.

We decided to quit Gallo's lodgings and retire for the night.

I took the box of jewelry with me. I'd hand it over to Donata, who could discover which ladies had lost something to Gallo and discreetly return it. Marianne, who would know the demimonde while Donata circulated among the beau monde, could also help.

Brewster said not a word when I tucked the box under my coat, and neither did Moreau. Emile regarded me in worry, but I pointed out that the housekeeper would simply pocket the trinkets if she found them. She'd discover them sooner or later if we left them, I had no doubt.

Darkness had descended fully by the time we went down the stairs, making the going precarious. I noticed Moreau slip out when Brewster trudged along the ground floor hall to return the key to the landlady.

Moreau had never offered explanation of how he'd gained entry, but I gathered that he'd somehow entered the house unnoticed and had likely picked the lock to Gallo's rooms.

I put Emile into the coach, which had lingered at the end of the bridge at my request, and sent him back to the Auberge farm.

"Tell Gabriella everything," I advised. "But only Gabriella at this stage, please."

Emile nodded, ready to obey. Not that there was much to tell. Aside from the box of jewelry, we'd found only a few cryptic papers, which would mean nothing until Grenville translated the letter or we discovered the owner of the name on the note.

To my surprise, Moreau had waited for us while we sent off the coach. He turned and walked with us across the Pont de la Guillotière to the Presqu'île.

"We're no closer to knowing who did for Signor Gallo," Brewster said as we went, both men slowing their steps for my labored pace. "If the bloke liked to try his hand at blackmail, and he were knifed in the middle of a public bridge, then anyone in the whole city could have done it."

"On the face of it," I said. "The only way to learn the truth, I suppose, is to find someone who actually witnessed the crime." I turned to Moreau. "You were the first upon him. Did you see anyone running away? Melting into the shadows? Anyone at all?"

"I cannot be certain." Moreau frowned in thought. "The sun had risen but had not yet come over the buildings on the east side of the river. The shadows between it and the hill were long. I did not notice any furtive movements or hear footsteps hurrying away. The vendors opening their stalls a few streets over made a clamor, but on the bridge it was very still. Barely a breeze. No one approached from either end until you came across."

"Very observant," I stated.

"I was in the army a long time. Habits are difficult to shake."

"Gallo might have been lying there a while," Brewster pointed out. "Done over in the pitch dark and then left."

"The physician for the gendarmerie will know approximately how long he was there," I said. "It was not raining, and the bridge was dry, as were Gallo's clothes, so that tells us nothing. There was no dew either—it has been too warm, so the absence of it on Gallo's body is not remarkable."

"So it were a nice, warm summer night," Brewster growled. "Where does that leave us?"

"Nowhere," I admitted.

Moreau bent a sharp gaze on me. "You truly do not believe I killed him?"

"I'd have preferred it to be you," I said. "I might have felt a sense of justice if you'd been arrested for murder. But I know it was not you, for the reasons I stated to Vernet. Also, you'd not have left Gallo on the bridge. You'd have gutted him stealthily in the dark, tossed him and the knife into the river, then gone home to rid yourself of any clothes he'd bled on."

Moreau gave me a nod. "As you say."

"So why *didn't* whoever killed his bloke heave him over the side?" Brewster asked. "The river's running heavy from all the rain that happened before we came. He'd have washed down into the what-you-call-it—*confluence*. Be a long way down the Rhône before he bobbed up again."

We'd reached the plaza by that time, which while dark, had plenty of evening walkers strolling its expanse. We pressed through it and into the narrow streets on its other side to emerge onto the bridge in question.

The Pont Tilsit, made of solid stone, had lasted longer than its namesake treaty Bonaparte had broken when he'd made his fateful march into Russia. A stone balustrade, as high as my chest, guarded pedestrians and carts from tumbling into the river below.

We moved to that balustrade, and I peered over, the rush of water wafting cool air over me.

"A man, or maybe two, might have heaved Gallo's body over the side," I conceded. "But he'd need strength and time."

"A woman killed him, then," Brewster said. "Gallo were a fit bloke, hard to drag anywhere."

"Possibly." I leaned my back against the balustrade. "I can think of three reasons the killer dropped the knife and ran instead of disposing of it or the body. Either he or she heard someone coming and fled, or was horrified by what they'd done and fled, or left Gallo and the knife to incriminate the next person who came along."

"Which happened to be me," Moreau said dryly.

"If you had arrived a few minutes later, it might have been me," I answered in the same tone. "I'm certain Vernet would have been happy to arrest a foreigner and be done with it."

"Not the first time the captain's nearly been nicked," Brewster informed Moreau. "You get used to it, like."

Ignoring Brewster, I scanned the houses on the western end of the bridge, which were fairly solid buildings with plenty of windows. Anyone glancing out could have seen the culprit fleeing, though it likely had been plenty dark when the deed had been committed. The Presqu'île side also had buildings crowding the bridge, but they were further from the spot where Gallo had been killed.

"It is a beautiful place in the winter," Moreau said, following my gaze along the riverbanks. "Especially during the Fête des Lumières. We place candles on our windowsills, in honor of Holy Mary, who drove plague from the city in sixteen hundred and something." He shrugged. "People had simpler ideas then, but the tradition transforms the city every December."

I was surprised at the sentimentality that tinged Moreau's

voice, incongruous with the brusque man who'd dragged my body into the brush and tramped away, leaving me to my fate.

Forgiveness ought to emanate from me—it had been long ago, after all—but the fear, pain, rage, and helplessness of that night and the many days after still haunted me. I would not weep on the man's shoulder because he found candlelit houses in December pretty.

"I wonder if Vernet has questioned those with rooms overlooking the river," I mused.

"You ain't suggesting we do it, are ye?" Brewster asked in alarm. "It's only a week or so to your daughter's wedding, innit?"

"I was more thinking I'd suggest it to Vernet if he hasn't. Someone must have seen *something*."

"If this city is anything like London, they won't have," Brewster said darkly.

Moreau nodded. "I agree with your friend. Most people want nothing to do with the gendarmes. If they witness a crime, they might dive in to fight off the assailant, but won't want appear at anyone's trial."

"That early, who'd be peering outside anyway?" Brewster asked.

I did not press my argument, as both made good points.

"I'm off home for now," I told them. "My leg aches, and I'm certain my wife has planned several rounds of outings I must escort her to. Good evening, sir." I made a cursory bow to Moreau.

"And to you," Moreau responded.

We resumed our way across the bridge, as Moreau had indicated his lodgings were on the west bank of the Saône, in the medieval city. None of us spoke, the wind springing up to bathe us in a sudden chill.

I again parted cordially with Moreau once we'd reached the far side, the cathedral looming over us. Moreau tipped his hat and walked unhurriedly along the lane that would take him to the cathedral and beyond to his lodgings.

Brewster and I continued up the hill, I regretting giving the coach to the young and agile Emile.

"By the bye, Brewster," I said as I limped onward, each step becoming more difficult. "When we were at the comtesse's chateau, did you notice other ways in and out besides the main entrance?"

"Other ways in and out?" Brewster repeated with incredulity. "Huh. Place is a warren. Cellars with tunnels leading out into the fields, or doubling back into the house. Stands to reason—an old place like that, with all the wars what have happened around these parts. Lords and ladies want to make sure they can get things in and out while everyone is shooting at their front door, don't they?"

"Then someone could slip out of the house unnoticed?"

"Course they could, if they knew the way. It's why the comte has so many guards. I wager the local thieves know their way about."

But would Signora Ruggeri? I wondered. She might, of course, have had an accomplice to show her the way. But Signora Ruggeri never intended to spend the night in that house, at least not as the guest of the comtesse, so would she have had time to put the accomplice in place?

What the devil *had* been Signora Ruggeri's intentions? To embarrass the comte or the comtesse? To stake her claim to the comte's riches? She must know by now that the comte would never marry her unless the comtesse was deceased. Even then he'd likely hesitate because of Signora Ruggeri's origins.

Had her intentions been more sinister? Perhaps to somehow eliminate her rival?

The comtesse appeared to be a very shrewd woman, and I hoped she'd considered this possibility.

"You truly believe Gallo had another hiding place for whatever secrets he'd gathered?" I asked as we trudged on.

"He were a foreigner, weren't he?" Brewster said. "The police here get into everyone's business, so he'd never know when they were going to come in and toss the place. Or if his landlady would come snooping. She looked like a right villain herself. So Gallo hides his things where a casual search ain't going to turn up much. He likely had a good clear-out at some point, and moved whatever he kept there somewhere he thought was safer."

"But didn't have time to take away the letter and paper he'd stashed in the fireplace?" I asked. "Or perhaps he thought them secure there?"

"Could be. Or could be, if they were found, they wouldn't mean nothing. A name none of us recognized. I'm thinking the letter won't give us much clue either. Gallo left those for last, because they weren't important."

"Or they belonged to a prior inhabitant of the rooms and are nothing to do with Gallo."

"Not very likely, is it? A man like Gallo would have found all the hiding places in those chambers or maybe even made a few himself."

"What you say makes sense," I conceded. "I bow to your expertise."

"It's *great* expertise, guv. There's not a nook or cranny made for hiding things I can't find. Been doing it since I were a lad."

We spoke no more after that, I saving my breath for the climb. I let out a whuff of relief when we reached the flat space outside the villa and turned in through the gate.

The gatehouse was lit with lanterns, and they also surrounded the front door, which stood open, letting the cool air into the house. Light poured from the doorway, and I saw Matthias nip through the hall carrying a tray. Grenville must have arrived.

Bartholomew took my hat, gloves, and coat at my entrance. Brewster said his goodnights and disappeared, either to find his bed or a well-deserved pot of ale.

I bade Bartholomew carry the box of trinkets to my bedchamber and followed Matthias's trail to the salon in the back of the house that overlooked the city. Matthias was just pouring out a dark amber liquid for Grenville. Donata, also present, stood to meet me as I entered.

"There you are, Gabriel." She rose on her tiptoes to kiss me lightly on the mouth before taking my arm. "Do trickle some of that brandy into a glass for me, Matthias. I imagine the captain would also appreciate a portion."

Matthias good-naturedly filled two more goblets, which he handed around.

"No soirees tonight?" I asked Donata, who sank into a gilded chair from the reign of the fifteenth Louis. She was dressed splendidly, as always, but I'd learned to differentiate her costumes for balls, the opera, or a quiet night at home.

"A gathering with a friend later," Donata replied, taking an elegant sip from her goblet. "You are released from duty tonight. You do look tired."

"Too much walking." I put myself on a settee that was more pretty than comfortable and stretched my aching leg. "I had a coach, but gave it to Emile."

"He must have been having adventures," Donata confided to Grenville. "Depend upon it. Now you must regale us with them."

"I will." The brandy loosened my muscles nicely, and I drank deeply. "After you tell me what *you* have been up to. Did either of you discover anything interesting, today?"

"As a matter of fact, I did." Grenville looked pleased with himself. "I found the comte's hunting lodge—a rather rustic place, but I can see why he enjoys it. However, he was not enjoying it last night. He was not there, and the gamekeeper informed me he hasn't darkened its door for at least a week."

CHAPTER 14

"Then the comte lied," I said, coming alert. "Why would he claim to be at his hunting lodge when he was not?"

Donata answered without worry. "I imagine he didn't see the reason to tell anyone his business. Lejeune is the sort who believes he can do as he pleases, and no one should bother him about it. That doesn't mean he was wandering the streets of the old city in the early morning to murder a man."

"But he could have arranged a meeting with Gallo," Grenville said. "To warn him away from Signora Ruggeri, perhaps. Or to order him to leave the city entirely."

"He has underlings who would do that for him," Donata argued. "Such as his guards at the chateau, who saw Gallo summarily away, as we observed."

I withdrew the letter and paper Brewster had found in Gallo's rooms and presented them. "The comte might have had good reason to meet Gallo himself. We've discovered that Gallo was a blackmailer."

Both Donata and Grenville were gratifyingly startled. I handed the letter to Grenville and the one with the name to Donata, and explained all that had happened since I'd left the villa this afternoon.

"If Gallo was a blackmailer, that rather widens the field," Grenville said, echoing Brewster's conclusions. "An unfortunate number of people have secrets they might kill for."

"Does the comte?" I asked.

Donata handed the paper back to me. "I have no idea. He and the comtesse were never close—an arranged marriage of convenience—but she has never once hinted at a transgression so terrible he'd murder to keep it quiet. Although …" She cocked her head, a curl brushing her cheek. "Signora Ruggeri was trying to put it about that the comte's sons were not actually his heirs. Suppose it is true?"

My natural instinct to defend a lady sprang forth. "That would be the comtesse's secret, surely. Besides, she does not seem the sort to be so duplicitous."

"You say that because you like her." Donata sent me an indulgent smile. "But I was not suggesting that the comtesse put a cuckoo or two in her husband's nest. I meant that perhaps he *did* bear a child out of wedlock and has been pretending that one of his sons—or both of them—are the offspring of himself and the comtesse. To make certain the title and money stay in the family."

"It is possible, I suppose," Grenville said. "Though I hate to disparage a gentleman and a lady when they are not present to defend themselves."

Donata shrugged slim shoulders. "All aristocrats have nasty secrets in their pasts, and we should not pretend otherwise. My great-great-something grandfather did horrible things during the time of the Tudors, murdering monks and stealing their lands during the first push of anti-papacy. His son wasn't kind to those trying to restore the church under Mary either. I wager yours has done similar things, Grenville. Gabriel's forebears, on the other hand, likely defended all those in distress in their end of Norfolk."

"You speculate that only because you never met my father," I said wryly.

"Well, he did try to steal his estate, after all, so I suppose your family can join the ranks of those with desperate secrets," Donata finished, a teasing light in her eyes.

"Very well," Grenville said. "Every aristocrat in Lyon has committed shameful deeds they want hushed up, and one of them decided to murder Gallo to keep him quiet." He waved the letter I'd given him. "I will translate this and determine whether whoever wrote it wished Gallo gone."

"If Signora Ruggeri didn't murder Gallo herself," I said. "Perhaps hiring someone to kill him for her. Claude was certain that Signora Ruggeri aided Gallo—whether in discovering the secrets or helping him collect money from his victims, I'm not certain. We did find a cache of gewgaws in Gallo's rooms that Brewster reasoned he stole, but they might have been payment for his silence. I brought them home in case you can find their owners," I told Donata.

Her brows rose. "I see. You have much confidence in my success."

"I have every confidence in it," I said warmly.

"Well, I will have to have a look at the things. But, returning to Signora Ruggeri, if she benefitted from the blackmail, why would she murder Gallo?"

"Perhaps she'd had enough," I said. "If Signora Ruggeri believed she was persuading the comte to give her all she wanted, she might have wished to disentangle herself from Gallo permanently."

"It is possible," Donata said. "However, I have ascertained that she did not leave the comtesse's chateau all night. The comtesse's lady's maid, Perrault, who is rather a dragon, had charge of her. Perrault went so far as to station herself outside Signora Ruggeri's door, for her protection, she declared."

"Brewster informed me that there are plenty of tunnels in the cellars where anyone can go to and fro without notice," I said.

Donata shook her head. "The comtesse would hardly put her

in a room with a secret passage to the outside. It's the comtesse's family home, so she'd know where they all are."

I had to concede the point.

"Look here," Grenville said. "I hate to mention it, because the comtesse is such a grand lady, but she herself might have slipped from the house to meet Gallo. Argued with him on the bridge about whatever hold he thought he had over her or their family. The confrontation turned violent and the comtesse, shocked at what she'd done, dropped the knife and fled."

"Highly doubtful," Donata said at once, then she sighed. "But I suppose, by my own logic, we have to consider the possibility."

"She'd have had blood on her clothes if she stabbed him," I said, trying to remain practical. "On her gloves at the very least."

"Which the faithful Perrault would dispose of for her," Donata said unhappily. "All of her servants would lie themselves blue for her."

"Even if the comtesse proves to be the culprit, I doubt she'd face the same consequences as someone like Claude Devere," I said. "I hope I have cleared *his* name, at least."

"Poor Claude has been a foolish young man," Donata agreed. "But, yes, we must worry about whatever hold Gallo had over the Devere family. Unfortunately, it means any of *them* might have silenced him."

"I know," I said glumly. "I am cheered that we found nothing damning in Gallo's rooms, but Brewster speculates that Gallo had a better hiding place. Which we will have to hunt for in all of Lyon and possibly the small towns outside it."

"It is common knowledge the comte has bestowed a villa on Signora Ruggeri," Grenville said. "Turning out a bishop to do it. Could Gallo have forced Signora Ruggeri to hide the secrets he'd collected for him there?"

"If so, she might have made a bonfire of them by now," I said.

"Or she might keep the things," Grenville countered. "To continue where Gallo left off. If the comte tires of Signora

Ruggeri, as most men do of demanding mistresses, she might reason she'll need the funds."

"I spoke to her," Donata broke in. "Signora Ruggeri was still at the comtesse's chateau when I visited this afternoon. She said very little to me and behaved like a contrite, grateful, and pitiable young woman. I could pry no more from her. I believe *you* ought to have a word with her, Gabriel."

I'd taken a swallow of brandy, and now I coughed. "*I should?*"

"She is the sort of woman who will not confide in another woman," Donata explained. "I have nothing to offer her, you see. Gentlemen are potential benefactors, but other ladies are rivals, or else will give her nothing but censure. Signora Ruggeri is more likely to unburden herself to a man, at least to a point. She is very, very careful."

"Then Grenville ought to be her confessor," I said. "He is more what Signora Ruggeri has in mind when she thinks of a gentleman."

Grenville lifted his brows. "Why do I feel vaguely insulted?"

"She is used to men like Grenville." Donata waved my suggestion away. "She will take his measure and play him accordingly. You, she will not be so certain of, Gabriel. She will answer your questions with less prevarication."

"Again," Grenville murmured.

"I am not as sanguine as you," I said. "But I can try. I'm not certain how to arrange a meeting, however. Has she left the comtesse's by now?"

"She did." Donata nodded. "Late this afternoon. The comtesse sent her off in her own carriage. My hope is that Signora Ruggeri will understand she has been defeated and withdraw. Move on to another city, another mark."

"In which case, we need to discover if she holds the secrets of Lyon's nobility before she disappears," I said. "I dislike to think we are dwelling among people with darkness in their pasts, but neither do I approve of those trying to profit from their shame."

"What will you do if you find Gallo's cache, if one exists?" Grenville asked. "Turn it over to the gendarmes?"

"No, indeed. I will burn the letters, or whatever evidence Gallo has collected, and inform his victims that they may breathe easily again."

"They might simply believe you are the next blackmailer," Grenville said.

"I will have to be emphatic, then." I lifted my brandy and took a decided sip.

"If Signora Ruggeri is wise, she will stay indoors quietly tonight," Donata said. "I, however, shall not. As I say, I am meeting with one of my girlhood friends, then I will join Grenville, Marianne, and her rather delightful theatre cronies at Grenville's house in town. Shall you come, Gabriel?"

"No." I held up my hands. "I walked too far and spent too much time abusing my bad leg all day. I will do as you say Signora Ruggeri should and stay quietly at home."

Donata's eyes flickered in disappointment, which surprised me a bit. I'd never thought of myself as scintillating company. However, I'd be here to greet her with some enthusiasm when she returned, if I wasn't too deeply asleep.

Grenville and Donata departed not long later for their outings, and Bartholomew served me a light repast in the dining room. After that I spent time writing letters—to my cousin in Norfolk, to various friends in London, including Sir Gideon Derwent and his son, and a note to James Denis, who liked to keep an eye on me.

I'd wondered since I'd arrived if Denis had an agent in Lyon. He likely did, but that agent had so far done nothing to either contact me or impede me.

I also penned a letter to Peter, who was staying with his grandparents in Oxfordshire, along with our daughter, Anne.

Not long from now, Anne would be old enough to read letters I wrote as well. I included short missives for Donata's mother and father, and then laid down my pen, fatigue overtaking me.

Bartholomew assisted me to bed and mixed a hot drink for me, after which I knew oblivion. I'd meant to wait up for Donata, but if she ever did look in on me that night, she'd have found a snoring lump drooling on his pillow. A lovely picture for any woman.

The sound sleep did me good, however, and in the morning, I felt refreshed. I drank coffee brought to me by the ever-energetic Bartholomew, then walked down the hill with the less animated Brewster.

The usual contingent of middle-aged and older gentlemen reposed in Baptiste Beaumont's tavern. They lingered over their coffee, savoring the moment, even in silence, with friends of a lifetime.

Brewster finished his coffee quickly and went out to wander through the nearby market. I ate my breakfast more slowly, puzzling over what I'd learned yesterday.

I'd have to wait for Grenville to translate the Italian letter to find out it if enlightened us, but I could pursue other avenues in the meantime.

"Beaumont," I said to the thickset man as he brought me a second pot of coffee. "Do you know of a man called Lucien Potier?" I repeated the name we'd found on the slip of paper in Gallo's lodgings.

Beaumont stilled. He was dour in the best of times, but as I spoke, his face darkened and his hand clenched around the handle of the tarnished coffeepot until his knuckles whitened.

I became aware of the sudden hush around me. The men who'd come to accept or ignore my presence had trained their gazes on me, every one of them hostile.

"I beg your pardon," I said awkwardly. "I heard the name, and I was curious."

"Never speak it again," Beaumont growled at me. "Ever. *Do you understand?*"

He glared at me a moment longer, then he turned his back and marched through to his kitchen, taking the coffee pot with him.

CHAPTER 15

$\mathcal{I}$ cleared my throat, meeting the collective stares of the tavern's patrons. "I beg your pardon," I said again.

None were moved by my apology. One by one, they turned away, resuming their breakfast or their coffee.

I slid a local newspaper toward me and began to peruse it as I ate, but I could little concentrate on the words within, nor on the excellent meal.

The atmosphere in the congenial coffee house had become as chilly as a mausoleum, and I had no idea why.

———

NOT LONG LATER, I JOINED BREWSTER IN THE MARKET STREETS. He enjoyed his strolls through them, finding little trinkets to take home to his wife in London.

When I told him what had transpired in the coffee house, he sent me a dark look.

"Not surprised, guv. I made the mistake of saying that name to one of the vendors. Had a box thrown at me. I twigged right quick to keep my mouth shut. Whoever that bloke was, it strikes a tinder in these parts."

"Vernet might know," I said. "But perhaps not, as he is not from here. Even Colonel Moreau didn't recognize the name."

Although, I realized when I thought it through, Moreau had said nothing at all. I couldn't be certain of his knowledge or ignorance.

"Might be specific to this part of the city," Brewster suggested. "Like His Nibs is well known in certain circles."

"Possibly." Was I to encounter another notorious criminal? And would Denis assist me if I ran into trouble with him? "I'd like more information before I draw conclusions. Obviously the name alone is enough to unnerve people, which explains why it wasn't part of a letter or document."

"No need, if even saying it makes everyone chary."

I'd tucked the paper we'd found into my pocket, and now my coat felt heavy. "The Deveres might know, or Auberge."

I hoped I would not have to ask Major Auberge. He likely possessed great knowledge about the people of Lyon, but I still had difficulty sitting down and having a chat with him.

"Or, your lady wife's friend, the comtesse."

"True." Donata had no qualms about coaxing particulars from her acquaintances, which she did skillfully, without causing offense. I was rather more blunt, easily upsetting people.

Once Brewster had finished his shopping, we returned home, where I intended to plan my day more coherently. I'd fatigued myself rushing all over Lyon yesterday and would hire a coach for the entire afternoon. I'd move logically from place to place, asking my questions as discreetly as possible.

That was my intention. However, while I sat at the desk in the library, making notes, Bartholomew interrupted me.

"Young Mr. Devere is here," he said, his blue eyes troubled. Bartholomew had grown fond of Emile, and now he exuded distress. "He's very upset. I've put him in the back sitting room."

I rose in alarm. "Is Gabriella with him? Is she all right?"

"He wouldn't say. He insisted on seeing you, and he's crying."

I seized my walking stick and moved as fast as I could past Bartholomew and out of the room. All I could imagine was Gabriella hurt, ill, with Emile dispatched to tell me.

My calmer reason told me that someone would have sent a message if Gabriella had been ill, with Emile remaining with her in concern.

These thoughts barely glimmered past my panic as I tramped down the stairs, cursing my slowness.

The sitting room was a sunny chamber in the rear of the house, beneath the one in which Donata, Grenville, and I had conversed last night. This room had high ceilings and wide windows that led into the garden, a lovely place for whiling away a summer afternoon.

Emile hunched on the edge of one of the graceful sofas, his head in his hands. A goblet of brandy, untouched, sat on the table next to him.

"What is it, Emile?" I demanded as I stormed in. "What has happened?"

Emile raised a tear-stained face then unfolded to his feet, the very picture of dejection.

"Captain," he sobbed. "The wedding is cancelled."

"Cancelled?" I stared at him, uncertain I'd understood. He's said *annulé*, but I repeated the word in English. "What the devil do you mean, cancelled? Did Gabriella beg off?"

Emile blinked, surprised out of his weeping. "No, no. Gabriella is as distraught as I. At least, so I am told. I was not allowed to speak to her. No, it is my father who has declared the wedding is at an end. That you and Lady Donata should pack your things and return to England."

I was torn between relief that Gabriella was apparently safe, and astonished outrage.

"What the devil? Emile, sit down and tell me, as clearly as you can, what has happened."

Emile dropped to the sofa, his chest heaving with sobs. I thumped to him, took up the brandy, and thrust it under his nose. Emile obediently gulped down a portion then drew a breath and wiped his eyes.

"I apologize, sir," he said when he could. "I have never felt such pain before. It has robbed me of air."

"Do find enough to explain this to me. Why would your father tell you to abandon Gabriella? She could have done nothing to offend."

Emile shook his head. "No, indeed, my family adore her. But my father and Uncle Fernand informed me this morning that I must break it off with her, with her entire family. I have known Gabriella and her sisters and brothers all my life. We were raised together ..."

"Did they give a reason?" I interrupted before Emile could regress into weeping. "Was it because I visited the ironworks unexpectedly?" Fernand and his worker, Michel, had been very uncomfortable with my sudden presence. "Surely they don't believe I was stealing their factory's secrets, which I wouldn't understand even if they lined them up in front of me."

"It has to do with the name on the paper we found in Signor Gallo's lodgings." Emile took another shuddering breath. "I did not tell my family of it, as you bade me, and I saw no reason to. But Uncle Fernand heard that you had been asking about this man, this Monsieur Potier, whoever he was, and my father and uncles became enraged. They told me I must shun Gabriella and never have anything to do with you or your family again."

I listened in amazement. "Because of that, you must put aside Gabriella? Have they run completely mad?"

"I do not know." Emile scrubbed his face. "But I cannot let her go, sir. I love her. I love her deeply—"

"Yes, yes," I said hastily. As pleased as I was that Emile cared for Gabriella, I did not need him waxing on about it just now. "This is absurd. I will speak to your father."

Emile sprang up in alarm. "No, you must not. I came to beg you to take Gabriella and me to England with you. We can marry in that place in Scotland where one can wed without the banns—I fear that if we waited for those to be read, my father and uncles would find some way to come and drag me back home."

"You wish me to help you elope?" I asked in exasperation. "That is very romantic of you, Emile, but you will come to regret such a step."

"I will never regret marrying Gabriella. She is my other self."

"No, I meant that both of you will grow unhappy if you are cut off from your families. You would need to make a living, and your father expects you to take over the Devere business—every tie you have is to Lyon."

"As long as I have Gabriella, I will be strong," Emile said faintly.

I ceased trying to reason with him, knowing Emile would never understand. I warned him from experience—I'd soon realized what an utter fool I'd been for coaxing Carlotta to run away with me. I'd been young and as romantic and in love as Emile was now, and I'd only succeeded in making Carlotta miserable.

"Emile," I said firmly. "We will go to your father and uncles and explain that I meant no harm. I don't know who this be-damned fellow is, and I don't care to know if it means you and Gabriella must spend your lives in wretchedness."

Emile did not renew his argument, but I could see he did not agree. He watched with a mixture of sorrow and trepidation as I rang for Bartholomew.

I bade Bartholomew send for a carriage, which arrived in a short time. I bundled Emile inside and sat across from him, while Brewster, alerted, lumbered from the house and perched on the back of the coach.

"I must have a clear idea of the ground before I march into it," I told Emile as we wound down the hill. "What exactly did your father and uncle tell you about Monsieur Potier?"

"Nothing at all." Emile regarded me in worry. "When they revealed how angry they were, I wasn't even certain what they were talking about. Michel took me aside and said that you'd been asking questions about a certain name. I didn't understand what he meant until I recalled the paper we found yesterday and concluded you must have mentioned it to someone. Michel would say nothing more about it."

I was surprised the taciturn Michel had told him even that much.

"I asked the proprietor of my usual wine shop if he'd heard the name," I confessed. "It caused a shock. Brewster says his mention of it in the market drew a similar response, so we ceased. That is all. Word certainly spread quickly."

Emile gave me a shaky smile. "This is Lyon."

We said nothing more as the carriage rattled along the bank of the Saône. The river soon met with the larger body of the Rhône at a triangle of land south of town, beyond which lay the Devere ironworks.

Emile shrank into himself as the coach turned into the lane that led to the factory. "Are you certain we should not elope?" he asked in a small voice.

"Put that thought out of your head, please. This is my fault. Indirectly, yes, but I will put things right with your father and uncles, and all will be well."

Emile clearly did not believe this, but he said nothing more.

The carriage moved through the gate to the courtyard, and Emile and I descended, Brewster hopping to the ground behind us.

The burly Michel immediately emerged from the dim recesses of the ironworks, hammer in hand. Emile darted in front of me and began imploring him in the dialect I'd heard them use before.

Michel at least listened to Emile. He nodded at the young man, and after a glare at me and Brewster, disappeared into the factory.

Emile did not follow, standing awkwardly in the yard while

the other workers sent us curious glances as they went about their business.

We did not have to wait long before Fernand stormed from the brick building with the full contingent of Deveres behind him.

"Emile," Fernand called to his nephew. "Inside."

Emile shot a look at me, torn between bravado and obedience. Then he squared his shoulders and remained where he was. My respect for him rose, though I wasn't certain if his presence would help.

"This is a misunderstanding, Devere," I said to Fernand. "I have obviously blundered where I should not, without meaning to. I apologize for disconcerting you and will say no more about it. Gabriella has nothing to do with any of this. Please do not take out your frustrations at me on her and Emile."

I thought this a reasonable argument, but Fernand's scowl deepened. "I warned you, Captain, do you not remember? I said to you several times that you should not pry into that which does not concern you. And yet, you continue to confound us. Better that you and your lady wife depart for England and leave the rest of us alone."

I could point out that if Donata had word of this conundrum, the Deveres might find themselves at the wrong end of a lawsuit. Breaking an engagement involved complicated legalities, not simply the unhappiness of the couple involved. I hoped to resolve the problem before Donata rose for the day, but Fernand's obstinacy might impede me.

"I understand that you are angry with me," I said. "But there is no need to end the engagement that has brought happiness to so many."

Emile's father, behind his three brothers, betrayed a glint of sorrow. Claude's father, Giraud, appeared to waver, but Fernand and the fourth brother, Julien, as they had yesterday in the street, regarded me intractably.

"We want nothing more to do with you," Fernand declared.

"If Emile marries your daughter, you will expect to come here, to see her children, to remind them who they are. When we believed she was an Auberge, this did not matter. But then we discovered she had another father—an Englishman and a officer in your army. What's more, one who will try to put a claim on our family, when we owe you nothing."

I grew more and more amazed as he spoke.

When we'd first arrived in Lyon, the Deveres had been curious about me and my past relationship with Carlotta, but they'd been friendly enough.

Something had changed, something I had no inkling of. Somehow, I'd tugged at a thread that had swiftly unraveled every bit of trust between the Deveres and me.

"Now you are being ridiculous," I said before I could stop myself. "I wish you no harm at all. It is only natural that I'd want to visit my grandchildren, if any happily come along. But Emile will be the head of his family, and it will be *his* decision who visits and who does not."

"Is this a threat?" Fernand demanded, and I heard Brewster stir behind me. "That you will turn our own Emile against us, when—"

He broke off, but not because of Emile's distress or Brewster's glowers. Another man had entered the yard, his boots scraping unhurriedly in the dust.

I swung around to behold Henri Auberge, Carlotta's husband and Gabriella's stepfather, standing quietly behind me.

"Fernand," Auberge said. "Cease."

CHAPTER 16

enri Auberge was a squarely-built man, not very
tall, with graying hair and a bayonet scar high on
his left cheekbone. One would not find him remarkable in a
crowd, and yet, as he gazed steadily at the Deveres with cool
hazel eyes, they grew subdued and watchful.

When I'd first met Major Auberge, he'd told me that
Gabriella had become enamored of a young man of whom he
did not approve. I later learned that this young man was Emile
Devere, but obviously Auberge had grown to accept him.

Emile was such an innocuous lad that I assumed Auberge's
initial hesitation a father's suspicion of any gentleman who
showed interest in his daughter.

Now, I wondered whether Auberge objected not to Emile's
person but to the older generation of his family. The Deveres
were well-respected, yes, but they were also proving to be
collective bullies.

Auguste, Emile's father, pressed forward, earning himself a
scowl from Fernand.

"Henri, this is nothing to do with you." Auguste spoke calmly
but with a pleading note. "The captain, he does not understand.
He must go, before—"

"It has nothing to do with the young people either," Auberge interrupted. "Shall we punish them for what is in the dust of the past?"

"It must stay in the dust," Fernand said sharply. "*He* stirs it. I want Emile to have nothing to do with him."

"You are a fool." Major Auberge stated this flatly, and Fernand blinked. "The wedding will go forward. Captain Lacey will return to England immediately afterward, and we will say nothing more about it."

Carlotta had told me, when I'd gone to the farm seeking Emile, that she and her husband had contemplated postponing or forbidding the match altogether because of Claude's arrest. Under Auberge's steely gaze, I wondered how much of what Carlotta had said was true. Or perhaps Auberge did not like others making decisions about his family for him.

Emile's father nodded contritely. "It shall be as you say. No," he said as Fernand drew a breath to argue. "We will unmake all if we continue. Stillness is best."

"Heed your brother, Fernand," Auberge said, the stern military man in him evident. "Calm yourself, change nothing, and go back to work. Captain, with me."

Major Auberge had no business ordering me to do anything, any more than the Deveres did, but I saw sense in his decision.

I bowed formally to the Deveres and sent Emile a reassuring nod. "Good day, gentlemen," I said, striving to keep my tone neutral.

None of them responded. They watched, rigid, Emile despondent, as I turned to follow Auberge.

Brewster fell into step beside me. While he understood little French, he'd have comprehended what had happened. "Tough bloke is the major, ain't he?" Brewster whispered to me. "Put them in their place right sharpish."

I could only nod in agreement.

Auberge had drifted toward my hired coach that waited at the gate. I expected him to watch me climb into the carriage and go, but to my surprise, he ascended behind me once Brewster had helped me in. Brewster swung the door shut for us before he took his place on the back of the carriage.

I found myself facing a man I'd spent many years of my life furious at, as the carriage creaked from the yard. Auberge had reconciled himself a bit to me when he and I had hunted for a missing Gabriella in the dark quarters of London. Even so, I was not comfortable riding with him in a closed carriage.

"Will you enlighten me?" I asked as we bumped along. "I agree with you that if Fernand had remained silent I'd not have stormed here to demand what he was on about."

"No, I will not," Auberge answered. "It is none of your affair, and nothing to do with Gabriella and Emile. Please give me your word that you will pry no further."

His response stirred my curiosity even more, but it was clear I'd obtain no information from him.

"I must warn you, I first came across the name that has so many incensed in Signor Gallo's lodgings," I said. "The same Signor Gallo who was found dead on the Pont Tilsit on Thursday morning. Whatever Gallo knew, there is no telling who he passed the information to. Perhaps one of the Deveres feared it so much that *they* silenced Gallo forever."

"They did not," Auberge said. "Fernand became enraged and tried to break off the betrothal only after he heard that you had asked questions this morning. I'm certain the Deveres had nothing to do with this Italian's death."

Auberge spoke stiffly, a man reassuring himself at the same time he tried to convince me.

"You seem very certain of that."

Auberge studied me with calm assessment. "Lyon is not London. We have the gendarmerie, not your Runners. No one here likes the interference of the police, but we have learned to avoid them and live with them."

"*Someone* killed Gallo and left him on that bridge."

"Someone did, but it was not Fernand Devere. I can say this

with certainty because Fernand was at our home Wednesday night, discussing many things. He did not leave until the small hours of the morning, and walked home. He did not go into Lyon and meet this Signor Gallo."

"That you know of. He could very well have gone to find Gallo after he left you." I made a conceding gesture. "However, Fernand was shocked when he saw Gallo's body. I know he feared very much that his nephew, Claude, had committed the deed in a fit of passion. Fernand was a man more afraid than guilty."

"There you are." Auberge opened his hand.

"Then, if Fernand is innocent, and Claude is as well, why the devil is Fernand and his brothers so angry with me, now?"

Auberge's expression turned stubborn. "As I told them, the past should remain there."

"If whatever occurred in the past will make trouble for Gabriella, I want to know what it is. Or I will take her back to England and keep her far from it. She'll be safe in Oxfordshire, with my wife's family."

"There will be no trouble." Auberge spoke firmly.

I'd observed the way in which Fernand and his brothers had quickly backed down from Auberge, though they'd clearly wished to thrash me for my impertinence. Auberge had protected Gabriella from danger in all the years she'd lived with him, keeping her alive and well. When she'd at last come to London and met me, she'd fallen into peril, which had not helped reconcile me with him and Carlotta.

"I will hold you to that, Major," I said.

Auberge gave me a nod. "As you should."

He rapped on the carriage roof as it approached the gate to his farm. He climbed down when the coach halted, sending me on toward Lyon with only a steady gaze as a farewell.

———

By the time the carriage reached the heart of the city, I was hungry, tired, and angry. I bade the coachman take me across to the Presqu'île and made my way once again to Beaumont's tavern for refreshment.

I wasn't certain I'd be welcome, but I refused to retreat to our villa and bar the door. If Beaumont did not want me there, he'd tell me, and I would simply find another shop in which to assuage my healthy appetite.

Brewster walked inside with me, ready to defend me if the elderly gentlemen within made ready to push me out. No one objected when I entered, however. The regulars only silently watched me take a seat at the table that had become my usual one.

Beaumont's scowl, when he emerged from the back room, was as fierce as Fernand's had been. I thought he'd tell me to remove myself, but then he trudged to me with his dusty carafe of strong red wine.

He fetched Brewster a pot of ale and brought us a loaf of bread and the beef stew he served most days. When I thanked him, Beaumont glowered at me, then he scraped a stool to the table and sat on it, planting his elbows on the board.

"He was an evil man," Beaumont said without preliminary. "Evil. There are those who fear that uttering his name will return him to us. Which I say is nonsense." He sent his glare to the rest of the room. "He must be dead by now."

I assumed we were speaking of Lucien Potier, the man whose moniker had evoked such antagonism.

Brewster eyed Beaumont, who spoke no English, with some impatience, but he chewed his bread and held his peace.

"I am sorry to have upset everyone," I said to Beaumont. "I truly know nothing of the man."

"He came after the siege," Beaumont went on. "When we were a conquered people. He made many arrests and conducted executions. Didn't matter if a man were loyal to the king or to the republic."

"I have heard something of that unfortunate history," I said in sympathy.

"The one you asked about was the worst of the lot. Arresting, torturing, shooting in cold blood. Even his own men hated him. Most of us here lost someone to him—father, mother, sister, brother. It was more than twenty years ago, but we haven't forgotten."

"Nor should you," I said. "I do apologize. I did not mean to stir up such troubling memories."

"You didn't know," Beaumont said coldly. "I am telling you so you do not mention it again."

"What became of the fellow?" I asked. "Did someone kill him? It sounds as though he'd deserve it."

"That would have been too easy, wouldn't it? No, one day, he was simply gone. Recalled, they say. He might have faced his own execution in Paris—they were turning on each other there by then. We never heard. Bonaparte came a few years after that, and we were Lyon again."

The men in the shop had turned to listen, nodding along, some with tears gleaming in aging eyes. The atmosphere in the room was heavy, laden with past sorrow.

Fernand and his brothers would have been a young men at the time of the events Beaumont described, in their twenties. The Deveres' father had been executed by the new regime, and I wondered if Potier had been directly responsible for the death. Perhaps the Deveres blamed Potier for it, regardless.

I let out a breath. "Thank you for telling me," I said to Beaumont. "I will cease discussing him."

"*Bien.*" Beaumont started to rise, then he thrust a hand into the threadbare coat he wore every day. "The colonel stopped in after you left this morning and asked me to give you this."

He held out a neatly folded piece of cream-colored paper, which I took without question.

I thanked Beaumont, and he marched away into his kitchen.

The other inhabitants turned from me, resuming their usual repasts.

I assumed Beaumont meant Colonel Moreau, and I saw that this was true when I skimmed the note, which was short and to the point.

"Moreau wants to meet," I told Brewster.

Brewster only grunted in response. He still thought me mad for being civil to the man.

We finished our repast then rose and made for the door. I tipped my hat to the collective company. "Messieurs," I said cordially before we exited.

A few nodded back, but the rest studiously ignored me.

"Got a bit chilly in there," Brewster rumbled as we headed for the bridge that would take us to Moreau's meeting point. "You have a gift for disturbing people, don't ye?"

"You've known that for a long time," I answered without offense.

In a low voice I related what Beaumont had explained, making certain passersby did not overhear. All of Lyon would have been affected by Potier's actions and not want to be reminded of them. Gallo likely hadn't understood what a storm he'd release by bantering that name about. He'd very possibly been killed for doing so.

Brewster let out a whistle when I'd finished. "Sounds like a right evil bastard. You give some blokes a bit of power, and they enjoy making everyone's lives a misery. I've known plenty of toughs like that, but this one had his own government cheering him on."

"Or, possibly, those in charge didn't know exactly what he was doing. Hence, he was recalled."

"Good riddance." Brewster frowned as we made our way across the Pont Tilsit. "So why did Gallo have the man's name on a piece of paper? To wave it in front of people to rile them?"

"Could be someone wrote it down for him, suggesting he use

the name to gain money or favors. A dangerous idea. You saw how furious people grew when we merely mentioned it. Perhaps Gallo upset someone so much it drove them to murder."

"Why, though?" Brewster asked. "If this bloke were gone twenty and more years ago, and is probably dead himself now?"

"Yes, it is curious. I will have to find out exactly what happened to him."

Brewster sent me a look of exasperation. "Instead of leaving well enough alone as all and sundry have asked ye to do?"

"I will be discreet," I promised.

"God help us," was his enlightened response.

Moreau had directed me to the plaza in front of the cathedral. He was there when we arrived, seated on a stone bench placed so the viewer could study the beauty of the lofty building.

The colonel rose when we approached, waiting calmly. I'd noted that same calm years ago, when he'd stoically witnessed the soldiers beating me to a bloody pulp.

Moreau gave me his perfunctory bow when I reached him, and I nodded in return.

"Thank you for coming," Moreau said in his careful English, and gestured to the bench. "Please, sit. I have found out much about this Lucien Potier, and it might be useful."

CHAPTER 17

Moreau and I sat in silence a few moments together, two former military officers stiffly regarding the cathedral before us, a marvel of medieval architecture. Brewster wandered the square, pretending to be a tourist but keeping within earshot.

I began before Moreau could. "I have discovered that the name Lucien Potier is a hated one."

Moreau nodded without surprise. "Yes. It was I who informed Monsieur Beaumont to tell you why your inquiries nearly barred you from his door."

"Ah," I said. "I wondered at his change of heart."

"I learned you had spoken of it when I came to leave the message for you. Beaumont was quite angry when I mentioned you, but I explained that you were ignorant of the distress you had caused."

"Good of you." I regarded him in some surprise that he'd defended me.

"I did not know much about Potier myself," Moreau continued. "When we found the name, it was familiar, but I was uncertain until I asked a close friend about him. I had already gone off with the army before he arrived and exercised his power here. When I returned from the wars, many years later, no one in Lyon wished to speak of those events, as you have discovered. When I asked my friend, however, she told me many things." Moreau's eyes flickered as he spoke the pronoun, as though he hadn't meant to reveal that this friend was a woman.

"The same friend whose letter you seek?" I asked.

"Yes." Again the flicker. "She had an unfortunate indiscretion with a roué when she was young, which Gallo somehow had evidence of."

"Then we will continue to search for this letter," I said in understanding. "What did she tell you about Potier?"

Moreau let out a breath. "Terrible things. He was, as you English say, a villain. To understand, you must know something of Lyon's history after those in Paris overthrew the monarch. Our city remained loyal to Louis and his queen and did not agree with the new National Convention. But it was more complicated than that. Some here sided with the radicals and others did not. We were a city divided. Our governments shifted back and forth for some time, but none of those regimes lasted. The Parisians did not like our choices and our loyalties, and so we were besieged."

"By an army sent in to subdue you, yes." I had read of these things. "In the end, Lyon had to surrender."

"It was a chaotic time. As I say, I had gone by then, but my family was here and my friends, and they suffered."

"I am sorry." I found myself sympathizing for past events for the second time that day.

"Our city's very name was taken from us. Lyon was henceforth to be known as *Ville-Affranchie*. In English that would be something like *the freed city*. Our conquerors planned to raze it to the ground, beginning with the villas on the hill and working their way down. Fortunately, that did not altogether happen."

I recalled Donata telling me that Comtesse Lejeune had worked to spare the many homes that were to be destroyed.

This, while her husband had fled into the countryside to save his own skin.

"Then came the executions," Moreau continued bleakly. "Men rounded up into the plaza, soldiers shooting them with cannons. Thousands died. Apparently Potier had advised the city's commander to do these things, as the executions would be quicker and more efficient. But Potier did not stop there. He went himself to individual homes, threatening those within and telling them that they'd be spared if they handed over all their money, jewels, or whatever they had. And then, of course, after he walked off with the plunder, the family would be arrested and executed, anyway. My friend said that he sometimes asked the women of the house to make a sacrifice as well," Moreau finished in profound anger and disgust.

"Please tell me that your friend does not know this from personal experience," I said, my voice deceptively calm.

"No." Moreau shook his head. "Thankfully. Her father was taken, because he refused to comply, but he'd hidden his wife and daughters beforehand, having been forewarned. Potier had him killed, and the rest of the family fled. They lived in exile until Bonaparte restored the city and gave it back its name."

"Perhaps I should hunt this Potier down, wherever he is now," I suggested in the same mild tone. "Explain to him why he was mistaken to do what he did."

Moreau eyed me in grim agreement. "I would like to as well. But none know what became of him. One day, he departed Lyon, and everyone breathed a collective sigh of relief. The mass executions ceased soon after that."

"Recalled to Paris, Beaumont speculated," I said.

"That is most likely, but no one wanted to inquire too closely. They were all simply glad to see him gone."

"No doubt." I gazed at the soaring cathedral, with its square towers and arched windows, an edifice that had stood watch over wars, brutality, many a winter, and many a spring. "What I wonder is why Gallo had Potier's name on a slip of paper, which he hid so well only Brewster could find it."

Moreau shrugged. "Anyone in Lyon would be upset by that name."

"Or enraged enough by it to kill," I said. "Perhaps Gallo stirred up the wrong memories in the wrong person."

"Signor Gallo must not have understood what it meant," Moreau said. "My friend has cautioned me against speaking of it, though she agreed I should warn you."

I regarded him with curiosity. "She knows who I am?"

Moreau gave me a nod. "I told her how I knew you. All of it."

We studied each other for a few moments.

"And she still advised you to warn me?" I asked. "I believe I admire this lady."

"*Oui,* she is admirable."

Moreau's answer told me he was not whiling away his nights in bachelor loneliness.

I realized how little I knew about this man—whether he'd been married in the past or widowed or had children or had devoted his life to the army instead of having a family.

He must have been as young as I was when I'd followed Colonel Brandon into the army, perhaps a few years older, at most. Moreau had risen all the way to colonel in Bonaparte's army, which meant he'd been a commander of some note. He also must have been canny enough to keep his head down after Waterloo, so he could return home to quiet retirement.

Other of Bonaparte's talented leaders had been exiled or condemned by the Bourbons once Louis the Eighteenth had been restored. Field Marshal Ney, whom I'd admired for his audacity in Portugal and then for his rearguard actions in the retreat from Russia, had been arrested and executed by the monarchists soon after the war. Moreau had been fortunate to escape retribution.

"We must continue the hunt for your lady's letter," I said. "I've been speculating that if Signora Ruggeri was in league with

Gallo, he might have entrusted her with his papers and letters. I intend to find out."

Moreau peered at me in surprise. "You will continue the search? Why?"

"Because Gallo's actions should not endanger others. The secrets people keep from one another should remain hidden, not exposed for all to see. That is dangerous." I brushed my thumb over the brass head of my walking stick, which Donata had given me after another dangerous episode in my life. "Besides, the person who murdered Gallo might do so again, if they think their secret will be revealed by another."

"You believe Signora Ruggeri might herself be in danger?" Moreau asked. "If indeed she'd been assisting Gallo."

"Possibly. I've seen the formidable men she employs to keep her safe, but yes, she could be the next target."

"If she did not murder Gallo herself, or had it done."

"That, too, is a possibility," I conceded.

We again sat in silence, the cathedral quietly stalwart.

I had to admit, I felt a bit helpless. I was not in a city I knew and had no access to the people I often called upon to help me. Grenville and Donata were making their enquiries, and Bartholomew aided me with reports from gossipy servants, but I did not want to risk any of them to a person who thought nothing of stabbing a man out in the open.

I did have Brewster, but he'd once been shot trying to defend me, a situation I did not want to repeat. Having to explain his injury to Mrs. Brewster had been one of the most intimidating things I'd ever done.

"I will try to gain entrance to the villa Signora Ruggeri was given," I said, thinking of Grenville's suggestion that she might have taken Gallo's papers there. "My wife has already made her acquaintance, and she might be able to invent an excuse to get us inside. I can search, as can my man." I nodded at Brewster, who was studying the carvings on the cathedral's stone walls, hands behind his back.

"You find it necessary to employ a bodyguard?" Moreau asked me. "One who obviously was once a criminal?"

"Others believe it necessary, including Brewster himself," I said. "I am wont to plunge myself into perilous situations."

"And very good at surviving them," Moreau observed.

"Too stubborn to know when to die. As I mentioned, so said my commander when I finally returned to camp."

"One day, you must tell me this story," Moreau said. "You are a man of great resilience."

"Or amazing luck." I heaved myself to my feet. "I will send word if I find anything."

Moreau rose easily beside me. "Perhaps you can contrive for me to enter the villa as well. Another pair of hands can make the search go faster."

Two days ago, I hadn't wanted this man anywhere near me. Now I contemplated him, an able gentleman with an interest in assisting his lady, as a possible ally.

I nodded. "I will send you word. In the meantime, thank you for your information. It has been most enlightening."

We regarded each other awkwardly, two men who'd been enemies in the past but were not quite friends, uncertain how to behave in this in-between state.

"Good day, Captain." Moreau tipped his hat to me.

"Colonel." I tipped mine as well, and then we strolled from the bench and across the square in opposite directions.

Donata was awake by the time I returned, making ready for her afternoon and evening outings.

She cornered me in the dining room where I'd retreated for a brandy, tired after my eventful morning.

"Bartholomew tells me you rushed away with Emile earlier," she said without preliminary. "And that Emile was very upset. What the devil happened?"

I set down my goblet and dabbed moisture from my lips.

"His family tried to call off the wedding. But everything is well now."

Donata's mouth popped open, then a frown erased her shock. She pulled out a chair next to mine and dropped into it. "Tell me everything. Instantly."

I complied. I watched Donata's fury grow as I related the tale and then her relief at its conclusion.

"I know you can never be fond of Major Auberge, Gabriel, but he has his uses." Donata accepted a cup of coffee Bartholomew had brought for her, he lingering to listen. "Thank heaven he turned up."

"I'm certain he was looking for Emile," I said. "Fearing Emile would do something rash, as he did, begging me to take him and Gabriella to Scotland to elope."

"We can arrange something like that if it becomes necessary," Donata said with her crisp practicality. "Auberge has defused the situation for now, at least."

Grenville arrived and seated himself as I told Donata what I'd learned from Moreau and Beaumont about Potier.

"The staff in this house talk about those goings-on, on occasion," Bartholomew said as he poured coffee for Grenville. "There's not one who didn't lose a parent or grandparent or other member of their family to the retaliations. It was a bad time."

"Twenty-five odd years ago now," Grenville pointed out. "I have difficulty believing Gallo would be murdered for bringing it up."

"It depends on what he intended to do with the information," I said. "Perhaps this man, Potier, still has teeth, and Gallo threatened to betray someone who'd stood up to him all those years ago."

"Potier must be dead by now, surely," Donata said with the conviction of a woman not many years past her thirtieth.

"Either in some battle or done away with by the restored monarchy."

"I might be able to discover his fate," Grenville offered. "I have many friends in Paris, some in the upper echelons, who can find out these things."

"If they can do so without causing a stir," I warned. "No one Lyon would be happy to see the man again, or even hear about him."

"Let sleeping dogs lie. Yes, I understand." Grenville nodded and lifted his cup. "I do know how to be circumspect, my dear friend."

"You are an expert at it," Donata assured him. "Were you able to translate the letter, at all? The one found in Gallo's rooms?"

"Ah." Grenville took a sip of coffee and clicked his cup into its saucer. He reached into an inner coat pocket and withdrew the letter with its broken seal. "I've had a bit of trouble with it, because the Italian it's written in is archaic. There are words and phrases I'm hopeless to translate, and a dictionary hasn't helped me."

"May I?" Donata held out a slim hand, and Grenville passed her the letter. She unfolded it and skimmed a page. "I see what you mean. The construction is odd, but it is not a dialect." She peered more closely at the paper. "It seems to be about a business transaction, but I cannot decipher of what sort."

"No signature or greeting," Grenville said. "Either those have been removed, or they were on another sheet, now lost."

"Gallo might have kept the pages with the names," I suggested. "Hidden them elsewhere. Maybe he feared what did happen—someone would find his hiding place."

"The paper is of fine quality." Donata rubbed the sheet between her fingers. "Expensive. If it is old, as you suspect, Grenville, it has held up well. Not brittle and crumbling as cheap paper will do with age."

"The stationary of an aristocrat," Grenville concluded. "Or a very wealthy merchant, as chaps from Florence or Venice tended to be in the past."

"It could have been appropriated from an archive during Bonaparte's occupation," Donata said. "Taken as a valuable artifact rather than as a document of information."

"I have another fellow I can ask about that." Grenville took the letter Donata handed back to him and carefully slid it into his pocket. "One who collects such pieces of history."

"Of course you do," I said.

"It is the Comte Lejeune himself, as a matter of fact," Grenville said, ignoring me. "That is, If I can find the blasted man. He hasn't been to his hunting lodge but hasn't returned home either. I do hope he's all right, what with chaps going about stabbing other chaps."

Grenville's hand strayed to his abdomen, where a few years ago, a man had driven a knife into *him*. He'd been assisting me on another problem and had stepped into the path of a desperate man.

"*You* take care while you're searching for the comte," I said. "I think we'd better find him. He might be the one who killed Gallo, but then, he might be another victim."

"An appalling thought either way," Grenville said. "I don't know the comte well, and I'm not certain I like him, but I wouldn't wish him harm. In any case, the comtesse does not need a husband who either murders those who threaten him or is murdered himself."

In my opinion, the comtesse would be well rid of the man, but if he'd committed a crime, she would be caught in the shame and whatever legal retaliations the French government would take. I agreed that she did not deserve such troubles to be poured upon her.

"We will run the comte to ground," I said with confidence. "Bartholomew, can you and Matthias assist? Inquire among the servants if any know where the comte actually is, or if not, where he might go?"

"Be happy to, sir." Bartholomew brightened, always eager to join in our hunts.

"Carefully," I admonished. "Gallo upset someone, and I don't want to replicate his mistake."

"Of course." Bartholomew sounded surprised I'd doubt him.

"Excellent," Donata said. "We will have opportunity to ask Signora Ruggeri about him ourselves, tonight."

My brows rose. "Will we be entertaining her?"

"Marianne will," Grenville answered. "Or, rather, one of her actor friends is, and she will hostess for him. I suggested they invite Signora Ruggeri. It will be a gathering of actors, artists, and a few of the more respectable of the demimonde. I assured Marianne we would all attend."

———

MARIANNE'S GATHERING TOOK PLACE IN A LARGE, FAIRLY MODERN house in the Croix-Rousse, north of the old city. The area had been home to silk factories of the last century and had housed their workers. After the war, artists and their set had taken over a part of it. Marianne's crony, a retired actor from London, had renovated a townhouse, transforming it into a studio and comfortable home.

The soiree's guests came from many parts of the Continent, with a smattering from Britain. Some had owned theatres and been actor-managers, and others had made grand names for themselves in their day.

Artists were there as well, including one Antoine Berjon, whose still-life painting I'd admired on the wall of Comtesse Lejeune's chateau.

Marianne, dressed in fine gray silk, greeted guests along with the host, welcoming us with aplomb. She'd grown quite stately since she'd married Grenville, comfortable in her new role as wife of a wealthy and acclaimed gentleman.

Grenville was already surrounded, as he was a famous

arbiter of taste. Every artist and poet there wanted him to give a favorable pronouncement of their next work.

Donata nudged me as we circled the room, and surreptitiously indicated a window alcove.

Signora Ruggeri reposed there alone. She wore a more subdued ensemble than when she'd stormed the chateau, tonight's gown of glossy browns and creams, the bodice modestly cut. Dark curls framed her face, her otherwise simple coiffure adorned with a feathered headdress similar to Donata's.

She glanced past me without interest, her gaze seeking Grenville. I wondered if she sized him up as a possible new protector for when the comte finished with her. Grenville was easily the wealthiest gentleman in this room.

Donata broke from me to speak to a poet she'd once sponsored in London, taking his arm and asking in a motherly fashion how he fared. As they wandered away, I strolled to the alcove.

Signora Ruggeri blinked up at me when I halted before her, clearly not recalling me from the comtesse's soiree. Her face was lined with weariness, her eyes twitching nervously.

"May I sit?" I asked after giving her a bow. "Captain Gabriel Lacey, at your service, signora. My knee troubles me if I stand too long."

"Of course." Signora Ruggeri answered in charmingly accented English and waved a hand at the chair next to hers. "You are the husband of the viscountess, are you not?"

"I am." Donata was technically no longer a viscountess, but many people still referred to her thus, as it was a more lofty position than wife to a mere army captain. "You met her yesterday, I believe."

"I did. She was most kind."

The signora's first untruth. Donata could indeed be kind but also quite pointed. She would not have been soft and gentle with Signora Ruggeri.

"My condolences," I said. "On the loss of your friend. Signor Gallo," I finished when she stared at me blankly.

When I spoke Gallo's name, Signora Ruggeri's eyes widened, and she wrapped slim but strong fingers around my wrist.

"Oh, sir," she said, her voice trembling. "I am so very afraid."

"Of what?" I asked. "You are safe here, signora."

"Perhaps, but nowhere else." Signora Ruggeri glanced out the window behind her. "They murdered Gallo, and they will not stop until I join him." Her fingers tightened on my arm. "Captain, I fear for my very life."

CHAPTER 18

$\mathcal{S}$ignora Ruggeri's declaration was delivered with the exact tremor of a stage actress used to seducing gentlemen, but I saw true fear in her dark eyes.

Sitting in a lighted window, visible from the courtyard below, was not the best place to repose if one was worried about being harmed, I mused, but nowhere else in the room could we be private.

"Please tell me why," I said in a low but soothing tone. "Why should whoever killed Gallo fear you?"

"Because he trusted me." Signora Ruggeri darted her gaze about the room. "We had to flee Padua because of his enemies, like the Carbonari, who believed he'd betrayed them …"

She named the bands of revolutionaries who worked to drive foreign rule out of Italian provinces.

"Signora." I cut off her increasingly dramatic flow of words. "The Carbonari are fighting mostly in Naples and the Papal States these days, and I doubt they worried about one confidence man from the Veneto making his way to France." I grew stern. "And why should an English actress from Manchester pretend to be a courtesan from Padua?"

Signora Ruggeri gaped at me, then her face became a blotchy

red. "How dare you, sir?" she demanded, retaining her rehearsed accent. "Because I am woman, alone and unprotected, you accuse me—"

"My wife recognized you." I indicated Donata, who was deep in conversation with her poet, feathers in her headdress bobbing. "The play was called *The Tender Foes*, which Marianne tells me was very much derived from Sheridan's *The Rivals*, and performed at Sadler's Wells. You were excellent as the mischievous daughter, my wife said."

Signora Ruggeri stared at me, torn between denial of her deception and flattery that Donata had praised her performance. I watched her debate between the two, before she bowed her head, her shoulders drooping as though in surrender.

"You cannot imagine how difficult it is to find work." Signora Ruggeri's words were a near whisper, any accent but her native one gone. "When one isn't in a regular company and has to move from place to place. Thought I'd try my luck on the Continent, but no one wanted me here either. I had to become Signora Ruggeri." She raised her head again, her brown eyes soft with pleading. "I had no choice. To take the protection of gentlemen like Signor Gallo and then the comte was the only way I could sustain myself."

It was a touching declaration, one with some ring of truth.

"I imagine these gentlemen gave you a more comfortable living than one of an itinerant actress," I said with understanding.

Signora Ruggeri shook her head, bitterness in her voice. "You do not know. You *cannot* know. No gentleman can."

"I agree with you. I recall how much Marianne struggled before she became Mrs. Grenville. It is a difficult life for ladies who have no family to surround them."

"You are trying to be kind." Signora Ruggeri softened again, her change of emotions lightning swift. "But I am correct that you can never understand. We do whatever we must to survive.

All of us, every woman in this room, take on different personas, depending on what we need."

I glanced at Donata, her face lighting with laughter at whatever wit the poet was throwing at her.

"Except for my wife," I said fondly. "She will be the same whether in finery or a chemise."

I flushed at the last, my tongue getting the better of me, but Signora Ruggeri regarded me pityingly.

"Never believe it. Your wife might be an aristocrat, but trust me, she will change herself, depending on who she's with."

I did not agree, but I ceased arguing. Donata might have dissembled in the past, but by the time I'd met her, she'd learned to always be herself and let the world believe what they wished. I was still never certain why she'd decided to throw in her lot with me.

"I mean no censure for your choices," I said. "I only wonder how you came across Signor Gallo, and why you decided to help him in his blackmailing scheme."

Signora Ruggeri started to her feet in alarm. "You insult me, sir." The words rang out, her faux-Italian accent in place once more. "I shall have you turned out of this house."

"Sit down," I commanded, not moving.

No one in the room turned at this display, every one of them more interested in Grenville, Donata, and themselves than in a little-known actress losing her temper at the window.

Signora Ruggeri noted their indifference and plopped sullenly to the chair again.

"I truly wish to help you, signora," I said. "I agree that you are in danger, but you must be truthful with me if I am to assist."

"You'll run to the beaks." She again reverted to the speech of her native city. "To the gendarmerie. I know you're mates with them."

"Hardly that. I'm more concerned with Gallo's victims at the moment, because Captain Vernet might come across their letters, or whatever Gallo had, in the course of his investigation.

We found a few things in Gallo's rooms, but there must be more. Did he entrust them to you?"

"He did."

Her answer surprised me, but I strove not to betray my reaction. "That is good news. If you will give them to me, I can destroy the papers and save many people much trouble. If you wish to protect yourself, you will let me do so, and be free of the web Gallo wove."

"It's not that simple." Signora Ruggeri regarded me limply. "He did hide his things at the house where I stayed when I first came here, the one the comte let me use in the Presqu'île. But they ain't there now. I looked. As soon as I knew Gallo was dead, I went back to that house to find them, to destroy every paper, to ensure no one was harmed by them." Her eyes moved sideways as she spoke, telling me her intentions had not necessarily been as pure as she claimed. "But they were gone. Every single last letter and document. Vanished utterly."

———

I DID NOT NECESSARILY TAKE SIGNORA RUGGERI'S WORD FOR THE disappearance of the papers Gallo had hoarded. She was an accomplished deceiver. However, she'd spoken with frustration, so I did not dismiss her claim entirely.

I let Signora Ruggeri be after that, assuring her I had no interest in exposing her true identity—most in this room would likely already know it, in any case. I also advised her not to sit with her back to an exposed window if she feared for her life.

Startled, she allowed me to escort her to a chair on the other side of the room, where I procured a brandy for her. I then joined Marianne, who presented her friends to me. None had much interest in me beyond the fact that Donata and Grenville championed me, but they were polite.

Signora Ruggeri had not revealed to me exactly why she thought she was in danger, but if she truly had been assisting

Gallo, then she was right to be cautious. Gallo's victims might believe, as I had, that Signora Ruggeri knew where the papers lay and might make use of them herself.

Signora Ruggeri remained quietly in the corner as the soiree wound on, but I made my excuses and departed, wanting to retire after another day jaunting across Lyon.

To my surprise, Donata accompanied me home, sitting next to me in the hired coach. Grenville had remained with Marianne, ready to continue the evening's entertainments.

"The amusements of this city are soon taken in," Donata said as we rolled from the Croix-Rousse toward the river. "Especially this late in the Season. It is a fine place, but has nothing on London or Paris." She dismissed the passing scenery with a wave of her hand.

"The quiet suits me," I said.

"And sometimes suits me." Donata rested her head on my shoulder. "When we are in Oxfordshire or at the Breckenridge estate, I do keep earlier hours, as you know."

"Yes, indeed," I answered warmly.

I treasured the fleeting summer weeks we spent in the country each year, when Donata and I shared a bed most nights and took our meals together. Though she never did rise with the sun, as I preferred, we walked, dined, and conversed far more than we did in London, where we each had our own pursuits.

Donata stretched a foot in a leather shoe, her fine beaded slippers in a box held by Jacinthe, who rode with the coachman. "In fact, I believe early to bed tonight would be agreeable to me."

I was not certain what prompted her sudden intimacy—perhaps watching my tete-a-tete with Signora Ruggeri?—but I did not question it. I tipped her chin toward me, and assured her without words that a night together would also agree with me.

———

I was up early the next morning, leaving Donata to rest in the warmth of my bed. As I sipped coffee in the rear salon, windows open to admit soft summer air, I perused the correspondence that had arrived while I'd dressed.

Happily, I found a note from Gabriella. I'd written to her yesterday, in the hours between my discussion with Donata and Grenville and our jaunt to the soiree. I'd promised Gabriella that her marriage to Emile would go forward, and bade her inform me whether she and Emile were well.

Gabriella, with a pluck that filled me with pride, wrote with obvious indignation that she did not intend to let Emile's family sabotage their happiness. Whatever transgression they thought I had caused was nonsense, and she would talk sense into the older members of Emile's family if need be. I was not to worry about her, she said, as she could hold her own. She'd instructed Emile not to capitulate as well.

I smiled as I folded the letter and drew forth pen and paper to reply.

I ought to have known Gabriella would be strong-willed about this. After all, she'd defied Donata and Lady Aline Carrington, two of the most formidable women in London, when they'd tried to make a match for her, declaring she'd marry Emile instead. Likewise, Major Auberge and Carlotta had not been able to dissuade her from her choice when they'd first tried.

Gabriella had decided on Emile, and that was that.

The wedding would take place next Saturday, one week from today. If the Deveres behaved until then, all would be well.

I penned more correspondence, leaving the letters with Bartholomew to deliver. Then Brewster and I walked down the hill for our breakfast and coffee.

The wine tavern had returned to its usual tranquility, with the few men who bothered to acknowledge me nodding as I entered. Beaumont served me, Brewster went shopping, and I settled in. The misstep I'd made yesterday might never have happened.

The quiet gave me time to ponder all I'd learned so far.

Gallo, the blackmailer, had been killed, presumably to keep him quiet about whatever secrets he knew. One of his victims would be the most likely suspect.

Or, I thought with disquiet, the dear friend of one of his victims, trying to find a letter to save his lady-love embarrassment.

Signora Ruggeri had met Gallo in Padua, became his lover, and started to aid him in his schemes. His extortion might have been lucrative, and Signora Ruggeri likely had seen no reason not to profit from it.

They left Padua for whatever reason—their sources of income had dried up? Or they'd fled for their lives, as Signora Ruggeri had implied?—and decided upon Lyon. La Guillotière was home to many an Italian émigré, so why not?

Soon after their arrival, Signora Ruggeri caught the eye of Comte Lejeune, who placed her in a townhouse he owned in the Presqu'île. Signora Ruggeri told me that Gallo had hidden his papers there, which could mean he'd been a frequent visitor. The housekeeper or landlady of that abode might be a good source of information in that respect.

I speculated that Signora Ruggeri had tired of Gallo once she was firmly established with the comte, which was one reason she cajoled the comte into providing her better accommodation. She'd earned the wrath of the Lyonnais in doing so, but Gallo had retreated to La Guillotière and the unprepossessing rooms we'd searched. That landlady, Madame Jourdain, might also be worth questioning, though I'd guess Vernet had asked her all about Gallo already.

Claude Devere had been accused of murdering Gallo, and had feared that either his father or his uncles had actually done so. He and Emile had searched Gallo's rooms for whatever secret the man had held about the Deveres but found nothing.

Moreau, Brewster, and I had found little more, though we'd uncovered the name of Lucien Potier and an unusual letter in Italian.

Signora Ruggeri claimed that Gallo's papers had disappeared from the townhouse, but she might have removed them herself and spun me a tale that they'd vanished.

I hoped whoever *did* have the papers would simply burn them, though I supposed we would find out sooner or later. If others, including Colonel Moreau's lady, began to be threatened about them, we'd know the letters still existed.

I also pondered the pure rage Potier's name caused in the city, along with his abrupt disappearance. Recalled to Paris, Beaumont had speculated and Moreau had agreed was most likely.

That a man so much hated had been here one day and gone the next led me to conclusions I did not like.

I tried to put the last thoughts aside as I finished my meal, fetched Brewster, and walked home.

When I entered the villa, I was informed, to my surprise, that Grenville awaited me in the ground-floor sitting room. I'd assumed he'd be fast asleep in the house he'd let with Marianne, recovering from the lively soiree.

"The revelry is still going," Grenville explained when I asked. He reposed tiredly on a cushioned chair, stifling a yawn. "Marianne's friends are robust, I must say. I decided I needed a rest and went home only a few hours after you did. Marianne laughed at me, calling me an old man, but I thought I shouldn't embarrass her by falling asleep in a corner."

"I felt the same." I seated myself and accepted coffee from Bartholomew. "Did Signora Ruggeri remain all night as well?"

"Not at all. She departed rather early. I saw her out and into her carriage, which is driven by a ruffian I'm surprised she's not terrified of. But I suppose she pays him well. I heard her tell him to return her to her villa, as speedily as he could."

She felt safe there, I concluded. I hoped she was correct.

"Awaiting the comte?" I asked.

Grenville chortled. "As to that, I have discovered where he was the night of Gallo's death. One of Marianne's friends told me."

"Oh?" I prompted when Grenville paused, enjoying himself. "Do tell me without prevarication, if you please."

"Forgive me, my dear fellow. I have spent a night trying to match wits with those who are witty for a living, and it has made me vacuous. The comte was not at his hunting lodge, as I have said. That was the story for his wife and also for the grasping Signora Ruggeri. He was with another lady entirely. An older, more stately woman with whom he's had a continuous affair for twenty years. And interesting development, is it not?"

CHAPTER 19

*I*nteresting, indeed.

"If he is enamored of this other woman, why chase Signora Ruggeri?" I wondered in surprise. "Why cause even more strife to his family, including possibly disinheriting his sons?"

"Signora Ruggeri was in league with a blackmailer, remember," Grenville said. "Perhaps she has some hold over the comte that has nothing to do with passion."

"She is daring," I agreed. "And yet retains an air of helplessness."

"Perhaps she had Gallo murdered, after all." Grenville settled into his chair and crossed one well-tailored leg over another. "For jeopardizing her lucrative business, perhaps. He might have been aiding *her,* instead of the other way about, and became too careless. She insinuated herself into the comte's home on the night in question so she could prove she was elsewhere when Gallo was killed."

"She could not have foreseen that the comtesse would invite her to spend the night," I pointed out.

"She might have believed the comte himself would. It was Signora Ruggeri's bad luck that Lejeune chose that night to visit his more steady mistress. But her good luck that the comtesse gave her a place to stay."

"Until Vernet finds the true killer, I suppose we will never know," I said philosophically. "Signora Ruggeri might be a careful woman, who would not let a hired murder be traced back to her."

"You will wait quietly until the gendarmes arrest someone and prove his—or her—guilt?" Grenville asked in astonishment. "Has the alpine air dulled your senses?"

"We are not in the Alps," I reminded him.

"No, but they are close by. The comte's hunting lodge has a fine view of them on a clear day."

"I hope Vernet arrests the correct person, yes," I continued, ignoring his quip. "Which is why I raced to the gendarmerie when they arrested Claude Devere. But I am now more interested in protecting Gallo's victims. They should not be afraid and humiliated more than they already have been. We all have peccadillos in our pasts."

"*You* don't," Grenville said.

"Not true. For a time, I was in love with my commander's wife. Unrequited, of course. I realize now that friendship with Louisa was a much better choice."

Grenville regarded me in exasperation. "You did not seduce her and then fight a duel with Colonel Brandon. You behaved well to your first wife when she deserted you, letting her start another life with Auberge. You have helped James Denis a time or two, but never with anything blatantly illegal, that I know of, and you castigate yourself for it, regardless. No, my friend, you do not have a thing a blackmailer could hold over you. They would have to get up very early to best you, Lacey. *Very* early, as I know you are walking about even before the sun rises."

"I'd be more likely to punch a blackmailer in the nose," I agreed. "But others should not have to pay a man because he once had a mistress or cheated at cards."

"To be fair, cheating at cards can get a gentleman barred

from a club or run out of town. But I agree with you, as much as I tease you. Mistakes in a man's or lady's past should be allowed to fade, provided they are not too awful. Those who profit from people's shame are reprehensible."

"Which is why blackmail is a crime," I said. "And very likely why Gallo died."

"Murder is also a crime," Grenville reminded me. "Though I can understand why someone killed him. Very well, we'll leave it to Vernet, while you protect those Gallo blackmailed."

"I can try to protect them, anyway," I said. "I'd like to have a look inside the townhouse the comte gave Signora Ruggeri when she first arrived. Are you close enough acquaintances that you can ask the comte's permission to enter? Signora Ruggeri claims everything is gone, but I'd like to see for myself."

"Imogen Cooke."

I blinked. "Pardon?"

"Isadora Ruggeri's real name is Imogen Cooke. Marianne told me. At least, that was the name she used at Sadler's Wells." Grenville lifted his cup and saucer and took another sip of coffee. "Anyway, yes, I will ask Lejeune if you can poke around the townhouse. Or, you could simply turn up and tell the house-keeper you're thinking of leasing it for a longer sojourn in Lyon."

"I'd rather try the less deceptive method first," I said.

"You've grown positively priggish during this sojourn, Lacey." Grenville shook his head. "I will put it down to the fact that your daughter is getting married, and you are feeling in your dotage."

"*You* have a grown daughter," I reminded him. "One doing very well on the stage in London at the moment."

"She is." Grenville's pride surged. "And yes, I sometimes feel positively ancient next to her. I trust you will return to your usual, adventurous self once we reach home."

"Again becoming the man who sparks your interest." I held up my hand when Grenville began an indignant reply. "You have admitted yourself that you first welcomed me into your circle because I relieved your ennui."

"Years ago, yes. I do hope we have developed a stronger friendship than that."

"We have." I relented. "Forgive me. I am pensive, and yes, Gabriella marrying and starting her own family has me out of sorts. Things will change, and I am not entirely comfortable with that."

"I understand." Grenville returned to his coffee. "I will cease my needling and write to the comte. Also to my friends in Paris about Potier, as I promised you. After I have a good, long nap, I am afraid. Marianne's friends certainly make me feel in *my* dotage, though most of them are of an age with me."

I could not explain to Grenville what truly had me out of sorts. Gallo had known secrets, possibly dreadful ones, and someone in Lyon had been driven to murder to keep him quiet.

The uneasiness of the Deveres, the tragedies in their past, and the disappearance of the instigator of those tragedies had me on edge. I needed to discover what the Deveres had done, and I wasn't certain I wanted to find out.

———

For the next two days, as we waited for replies to Grenville's inquiries, I tried to busy myself enjoying my stay in Lyon. I strolled along the river, ate meals in fine taverns with Grenville, and visited with Gabriella as much as I could.

Once the altercation between the Deveres and Auberges had settled, Carlotta relented, and Gabriella returned to spend a few days in the villa with us, to my delight. We could again walk down to the Presqu'île in the mornings, where she could find more accoutrements for her trousseau and take coffee with me at a vendor's stand in the plaza.

She was remarkably calm for a young woman about to get

married. I remarked to her thus while we strolled the plaza one morning, arm-in-arm.

"I have no need for apprehension," Gabriella replied tranquilly. "I've known since I was a girl that I'd marry Emile. We decided when we first met, as quite young children." She smiled at the memory. "There has never been a question between us. The wedding will simply confirm what we've known all along."

Her answer pleased me, but with it came a qualm of worry. Gabriella had been so sheltered from the wide world, as had Emile, in spite of France's war, that they'd yet to experience tragedy. Gabriella had known only happiness here, which both eased my heart and made me fear for her.

I did not want to cause the disruption that ruined her serenity. But if the Deveres had killed to protect their secrets, that disruption would unfortunately come. I could only hope that my speculations were wrong.

Gabriella patted my arm. "If you fear you will never see me once I am Mrs. Devere, do not. Emile and I have already discussed things. A visit to England in the summers would be welcome, and we will arrange it. I long to see Peter and dear Anne soon—they are my brother and sister after all. And one day, we might be bringing children of our own with us."

While I liked the picture she painted, I suppressed my anticipation.

Emile and Gabriella would soon be taken up with domestic pursuits. Emile worked for his father, and Gabriella would not want to travel far when she did begin bearing children. The visits would grow fewer in number before long, perhaps ceasing altogether. It was an arduous trek from here to Oxfordshire, after all.

I kept these thoughts to myself. Gabriella shone with bright plans for her future, and I would not dim them with my pessimism.

Gabriella stayed with Donata and me for a few nights, then returned to the Auberge farm on Tuesday morning, where she would remain until the wedding day. After that, Emile and Gabriella would move into the cottage the Deveres were providing for the young couple.

Gabriella had showed us over it when we'd first arrived, a modest brick home with a lush garden just outside the village where the Devere factory lay, and within walking distance of her childhood home.

The morning Gabriella departed, Grenville wrote me, informing me he'd had a reply to one of his inquiries.

Comte LeJeune confirmed that I could indeed root around in the townhouse that Signora Ruggeri had inhabited in the Presqu'île. Whatever fiction Grenville had invented for my interest, the comte did not object to my entering the house.

The comte had even provided Grenville a key, which Grenville had sent with the letter, via Matthias. The house-keeper looked after the place that was indeed seeking a new tenant, but she was not always in. Hence, the key.

Though Grenville had asked the comte about the letter written in Italian, the comte had been reticent to respond. It was Donata, surprisingly, who supplied more information about that. She requested me, via Bartholomew, to visit her at her toilette that afternoon.

When I entered her chamber, Donata, clad in a peignoir, sat at her dressing table, while Jacinthe combed out her dark hair.

"I called on the comtesse last evening, while you and Gabriella attended the theatre." Donata winced as Jacinth pulled at a recalcitrant lock. "You both were asleep when I returned, so I had to hold my news until now. I mentioned the letter Brew-ster found in Signor Gallo's rooms, and the comtesse confirmed that it *is* old, from the sixteenth century, in fact."

"She is an expert on Italian artifacts as well?" I asked, only half concentrating on her words. My wife was a beautiful woman, and I often lost myself in studying her.

"Not necessarily, but she knew about this letter, because it belongs in her husband's collection. The letter disappeared not long after he fell under Signora Ruggeri's spell. No one is surprised at this coincidence."

Donata had my full attention now. "She stole it from him?" I asked. "It's unlikely he gave it to her. Jewels, yes. Antique letters, no. But, if she meant to sell it, then why did Gallo have it stashed in his fireplace?"

Donata regarded me through the mirror as Jacinthe began to wind her hair into a neat coil. "Neither the comtesse nor I could draw a conclusion. Signora Ruggeri and Signor Gallo might not have understood the letter's worth. Or, they realized it was valuable but that no one in Lyon would purchase it, knowing the comte's passion for Italian antiquities. They'd have to take the letter elsewhere. Either Signora Ruggeri entrusted Signor Gallo to hide it, or he took it from her, and she could not fetch it back."

"Is it that valuable?" I'd seen only old paper with writing on it.

"It is, but questionable without the sheets that were left behind. The letter is from none other than Lorenzo de' Medici. Instructions to his banker in Florence. A prosaic missive, but a treasure all the same, given its writer."

"Indeed." My awe of the letter's faded ink increased. "Why did Signora Ruggeri not steal the entire letter from the comte?"

"The comtesse isn't certain. It was a long missive, and the comte kept the sheets in two bundles. Many of his letters and things he prizes are apparently in his hunting lodge, where he can pore over them in private."

"So, Signora Ruggeri helped herself to one of the bundles when she visited the comte in his hunting lodge. Then she gave it to Gallo, who is actually Italian, to see what he could make of it." I tapped my fingers on the gilded arms of my chair. "He understood what it was worth, and he took it from her."

Jacinthe cleared her throat. She usually worked in severe silence when I came to Donata's rooms, never dreaming to speak without leave.

"Yes, Jacinthe?" Donata prompted.

"It is very likely the signora was seeking documents that would embarrass the comte," she answered in her haughty tones. "The comtesse's servants say they caught her digging through a desk when she was a guest at the chateau the other night."

Donata's brows arched. "Gracious, how rude."

Jacinthe, having delivered her information, snapped her mouth shut and glided to the wardrobe to fetch Donata's morning gown.

"Signora Ruggeri must have been more of Gallo's accomplice than she's letting on," I reflected. "Even when she was purportedly hiding from Gallo and given kind hospitality, she sought a way to bleed more money from the comte and his family. I wonder why, if the comte has been as generous to her as everyone claims."

"Because his patronage won't last, and she knows it." Donata glanced at the gown in Jacinthe's arms. "Not that one, Jacinthe. I think the cream today, as it is so warm."

"She was providing for her future," I concluded, as Jacinthe headed back to the armoire. "If Grenville is right, then the comte is already tiring of the demanding Signora Ruggeri. Her dramatic entrance at his chateau might have been a final straw."

"One can scarcely blame the woman for trying to keep her head above water, though I do not approve of her methods," Donata said. "A lady without family or a protector has very little resources against the world. Better to keep the comte paying than retreat to a workhouse, or worse."

Signora Ruggeri had said much the same to me the night of Marianne's soiree.

"*You* did well against the world," I said. Donata had lost a husband but continued to live alone in her son's house in South Audley Street, hosting lavish salons and at-homes for the haut ton.

"Hardly the same thing. Yes, that will be better," Donata said to Jacinthe, who presented a creamy gown with brown and gold embroidery on its hem. "My father is an earl who did not shut me out once my marriage went sour. And my son is a viscount. As young as Peter is, his very existence helps mine. I know of heirs who are cruel to their parents, but I am fortunate that Peter is a sweet boy."

"Even so, I know it was not easy for you."

Donata had not timidly retreated into the woodwork when her philandering husband had caused her misery, which had earned her much censure. She'd faced censure again for marrying me, hardly the sort of gentleman she should have tied Peter's fortune and eventual power to.

Jacinthe's formidable frown as she readied the gown for Donata told me she agreed with my assessment about my wife's struggles.

I vacated the chamber then, allowing Donata to finish dressing. I informed her of my intention to visit the townhouse where Signora Ruggeri had dwelled, assuring her I'd take Brewster with me.

She waved me off, and I made my way downstairs to inform Brewster I was ready to leave.

"Lacey." Grenville was just being admitted into the echoing ground-floor hall. "Before you dash away, I have more news."

I led him into the drawing room where Grenville closed the door, to my surprise. "What is it?" I asked in concern.

"I heard back from my friend in Paris—the one I wrote to about this Potier fellow. I had his reply in the post just now." Grenville slid a letter from the pocket of his frock coat. "Not only does my friend work in a ministry of the restored Bourbon reign, but he is interested in French history, especially of the revolution and the First Republic. He knew all about Potier and the unfortunate events in Lyon."

"Ah." I both wanted to discover what this gentleman had to say and dreaded it. "Did he tell you what became of Potier? Was he recalled to Paris?"

"No." Grenville's voice turned grim. "The last record of Potier shows him in Lyon. He was meant to stay here another six months and then join efforts to quell any royalist pockets in the countryside. He never returned to Paris." Grenville shared a tight gaze with me. "He was in Lyon, and then he simply disappeared."

CHAPTER 20

The information sank in as my nerves stretched taut.

I'd wanted to assume Potier had returned to Paris to whatever duties he was assigned for the rest of the war, hopefully kept in a quiet office so he might commit no more acts of savagery. Anything might have happened to the man in the last twenty-five years, including his death, but his last days would have been comfortably far from Lyon.

The fact that there was no evidence of him leaving this city chilled me.

"Not what I wished to learn," I said.

"This could very well be why Gallo was murdered, could it not?" Grenville asked. "He'd discovered that someone in Lyon killed Potier, or at the very least that Potier's death had been covered up, and threatened to reveal all."

I thought of the anger and reticence of Beaumont and the men in his wine shop, the warning Moreau had given me, and the intense reaction of the Deveres.

"Damnation," I said with feeling.

"I believe we ought to keep this to ourselves, for now," Grenville said.

Which was why he'd closed the door, shutting out even Matthias and Bartholomew.

"I agree," I said. "Though you might have stirred the pot writing to your friend about him."

"I realize that," Grenville replied glumly. "However, no one in Paris might care very much. The restored Louis isn't likely to worry about the odd disappearance of a man who caused the death of so many loyalists, twenty-five years ago."

"We can hope not."

No one had been happy with me for even mentioning the name. They'd be less happy if they knew Grenville and I had made inquiries to a government official about Potier.

If my suspicions were correct, my daughter might be marrying into a family who'd had a part in bringing about Potier's end.

On the one hand, Potier had more than deserved it, from what I understood. On the other, if inquiries from Paris *were* made, Emile could be caught in the retribution, and Gabriella's peaceful life would be ruined.

"Damn and blast," I said softly.

"Quite," Grenville replied.

———

Before Brewster and I set off for the house in the Presqu'île, I sent a note to Colonel Moreau, asking if he'd like to meet us there. He'd expressed a wish to assist in any continued search, and I would honor that.

Brewster wasn't certain I was wise, but he ceased berating me halfway down the hill, falling silent entirely as we crossed the bridge onto the island between the rivers.

The townhouse Grenville directed me to lay north of the large plaza, on a fairly quiet lane of well-appointed homes. The abode was small, with stucco peeling from its brick walls, though the shutters and door were an attractive green that complemented the snug tile roof.

As I stepped to the door and took out the key Grenville had sent me, Colonel Moreau rounded the corner of the lane and caught up to us on the step.

Before I had time to insert the key into the lock, the door was pulled open by a prim-looking woman in a plain gray gown. She seemed vaguely familiar, and I realized I must have seen her during my jaunts with Gabriella and Brewster to the markets in the square and surrounding streets. By her deepening frown, she recognized me as well. With my walking stick, uneven gait, and Brewster, I'd be difficult to forget.

"Messieurs," she said, and continued in French. "The comte told me to expect you." She swung the door wide and stepped back to admit us. Her stance might be deferential, but her gaze was in no way docile.

"*Merci*," I said. "Madame … ?"

"Martin," she replied stiffly. "Please, look through the house and give me word when you depart."

She swung the door shut once we were inside and marched toward the back of the house, disappearing through a door under the stairs.

"Warm welcome," Brewster said.

"Indeed," Moreau agreed. "Where do you suggest we begin?" He asked Brewster, not me.

Brewster gazed up the staircase that wound through the house's four floors. "At the top," he said. "Work our way down."

"We could each take a floor," I suggested.

Brewster shook his head. "I'd have to search through what you already did. You'd miss what I wouldn't."

I couldn't argue with him. "You are our commander for the day."

Brewster sent me a sour glance but mounted the staircase. Moreau followed him, and I brought up the rear.

The top story held an attic that had been divided for

servants' quarters, but no servants were obviously living there. The housekeeper might have a chamber lower in the house, or perhaps she went to her own home every night. When no one rented the place, the comte might not pay for her to live in.

The three of us quickly looked through these rooms. No mattresses rested on the bedsteads, as the straw would only grow moldy and have to be replaced when more staff moved in. The furnishings were sparse, the few armoires empty.

Brewster checked floorboards and loose bricks, as he had in Gallo's rooms, but no hidden cavities were revealed.

The next floor down held more bedchambers, again with bare bedsteads. I could only be glad Brewster wouldn't be cutting into mattresses and pillows, whose ruin I'd have to explain to the housekeeper and the comte.

Brewster did find, in a back bedroom, a large hollow behind a section of paneling. Moreau and I peered into it, but it held nothing but a few spiderwebs.

"Something was here," Moreau said. Indeed, a clean square in the dust was likely the imprint of a sturdy box, now gone.

"Signora Ruggeri told me that everything had vanished," I said as Brewster replaced the panel and moved into the next bedchamber. "It appears she was correct."

"Do not despair yet," Moreau advised me. "There is more of the house to search."

True, but I knew in my bones we'd find nothing here.

The front bedchamber, with wide windows overlooking the street, was probably where Signora Ruggeri had slept. While the bed's rails were bare, the hangings were intact—light blue silk brocade embroidered with yellow flowers. They matched the draperies at the windows, which also held soft hangings of lace.

The paneling in the room had been painted a light yellow, giving the place a sunny note. An ornately plastered fireplace adorned one wall, with deeply cushioned chairs pulled close to it.

A comfortable chamber as well as a beautiful one.

Brewster found another hiding place in here, under floorboards he pried up beneath the bed. Colonel Moreau and I shoved the heavy bedstead aside so Brewster could better access it, but the hollow below proved to be empty.

"Cleverly done," Brewster said as he dropped the boards back into place. "There's not even scratch marks on these to show they come up."

"Were the niches here before Signora Ruggeri moved in?" I wondered. "Or did she or Gallo make them?"

Brewster shrugged. "Who knows? The one in the other room's been there a long time, it looks like, probably put in when the house was built. You never know when you need to hide your valuable gear, do you? This one, though, could have been fixed by anyone since then. The boards are a bit warped from time, so are easier to lift now."

Moreau and I heaved the bedstead back into place while Brewster moved into the staircase hall and began a search there.

"Why did you send for me?" Moreau asked quietly as we put the room to rights. "Yes, I asked to assist when you searched the houses, but you did not have to do me this favor."

"Oh, the favor is not for *you*," I said, trying to put some humor into my voice. "But for your lady. If we find her letter, you can take it directly to her."

Moreau nodded, accepting my statement. "It is kind of you. I would like you to meet her."

I stilled in surprise. "You would?"

"That is, she expressed a wish to meet the captain I continually encounter. I told her I would try to arrange it."

I did not have to ponder the request long. "I would be honored."

"Then perhaps when we finish here, we can adjourn to her home. It is not far."

I raised my brows. "Her neighbors will not be shocked when she has two gentlemen callers?"

Moreau relaxed into a small smile. "The neighbors are all friends. I have been visiting Madame Paillard for many years."

"You've never thought to marry?" I asked in curiosity.

Moreau shrugged. "We might, one day. But our arrangement, it suits us."

I nodded, as though I understood, but I was even more curious about his lady now.

Brewster returned from the hall. "This floor is empty."

We moved to the one below, which held a sitting room, a writing room, and a small dining room for intimate suppers or breakfasts.

I found the house cozy, and I would be tempted to lease it myself if we planned to stay longer in Lyon, but I understood why Signora Ruggeri grew impatient with it. It was a pleasant house but nothing grand, and Madame Martin had likely not been a sympathetic retainer.

Comte Lejeune could visit his dove in this nest, but it must not have been the glamour Signora Ruggeri had hoped for when she'd ensnared an aristocrat.

Brewster searched these rooms with our assistance, but we found nothing. We descended to the ground floor, the public rooms.

"She'd hardly stow the things here, would she?" I asked as Brewster began checking walls in the large drawing room. "She'd receive guests in these chambers, not to mention the comte."

"You'd be surprised, guv. I once found an entire silver service tucked behind the wainscoting in a foyer. Only one spindly footman to guard the way into the house, and that only during the day. Some people beg to be robbed."

Shaking his head, he continued tapping on walls in the dining room, while Moreau and I went through drawers in the matching sideboards.

Not until we were in the drawing room that ran the depth of

the house did Brewster find a hollow behind paneling under a window.

"Here's summat," he announced.

He pulled out large, oblong book and laid it on a long table behind a sofa. Brewster never stood back and waited for his employers to tell him what to do—he opened the book and began to scan the pages.

It was a ledger, with neat columns of names and amounts, some marked as French francs, some as Venetian coins. A third column held single letters or symbols, which were meaningless to me.

What did have meaning was the name *Devere* printed in the middle of the page. The number next to it told me they'd given Signor Gallo two hundred francs but not what they'd received in return.

"This is a damning book," Moreau declared in hushed tones, as Brewster continued leafing through the pages. "Many prominent men of Lyon are listed here. And ladies too. I suppose some names are from other cities as well, wherever Signor Gallo traveled."

"Yes," I agreed grimly. "I have to wonder why whoever cleared out the other things did not take this."

"Could be they didn't know it was here," Brewster said. "Could be the they found all the bits and bobs but didn't realize he'd cataloged it all. Or maybe they couldn't read, and didn't know what the ledger was. Not everyone is so lucky."

"If they couldn't read the ledger, then they'd not be able to understand the letters and papers either," I pointed out. "They must not have realized the ledger was here, as you say, or they were nearly caught burgling the place and ran out of time. Madame Martin might have surprised the thief."

"Or whoever it was believed the ledger was safe enough for now." Brewster replaced the panel but left the book open on the table. "No one but an experienced thief would have found this hole. I wager Gallo and the signora received their guests in here, took the cash for their silence, and then totted up the figures without having to run upstairs for the ledger."

"Possibly." I reached to touch a page but pulled my finger back as though it would tarnish me. I closed the book instead. "The most likely person to have taken all the documents out of this house was Signora Ruggeri herself."

Moreau regarded me doubtfully. "You said she admitted that Signor Gallo stashed the papers here but they vanished. Possibly Gallo took them away again."

"She did say that." I nodded. "But we must recall that Signora Ruggeri is an accomplished liar. She might have told me the tale so that I'd not attempt to search the house. Unfortunately for her, she did not have a good measure of my stubbornness."

"Most don't," Brewster said.

"When I first saw Signora Ruggeri, she was fleeing a mob," I said, ignoring Brewster. "She'd come into the square from a street that could very well lead here. I did not note her carrying anything, but I couldn't see clearly. She might have tried to clear out the house that day, ready to take the things Gallo had left to her villa."

"Gallo weren't dead then," Brewster said. "Why couldn't it have been *him* toting the things back to his own rooms?"

I stared at the paneling Brewster had tucked into place as I pondered. Not a crack or seam betrayed the hiding place's existence.

"Perhaps once Signora Ruggeri persuaded the comte to move her to more luxurious accommodations, Gallo could no longer enter this house. Signora Ruggeri might have promised to fetch the papers for him, but, once she did, took them to her new abode instead of delivering them to Gallo's rooms in La Guillotière. Hence Gallo's fury when he followed her to the comtesse's soiree."

We'd assumed Gallo had been a spurned lover intending to

force Signora Ruggeri to return to him. But if Gallo had learned she'd stolen his lucrative business from him, he might be even more incensed. The words I'd heard him shout could have meant rage at Signora Ruggeri for moving the documents out of his reach.

"What do we do with this, guv?" Brewster gestured to the ledger.

I knew he assumed I'd want to turn the book over to Captain Vernet and the gendarmes, but I lifted it from the table. "We keep it safe. Once we find the letters and papers, we inform the people in this book that they are no longer in danger."

Moreau nodded slowly, his relief plain.

"Then you'd better let me hide it," Brewster said. "I can make sure no one ever finds the thing. If the signora tries to employ a thief herself, it won't help her none. There's no thief as good as me."

"True." I handed him the book. "I trust Brewster," I told Moreau before he could protest. "He's done me many a good turn, and he's a burglar not a blackmailer."

"Disgusting, they are," Brewster said. "I'm an honest man, me."

———

BREWSTER LET HIMSELF OUT THE FRONT DOOR WITH THE LEDGER wrapped in a sack he'd found in a cupboard in the foyer. Once he was gone, I called down the backstairs to tell Madame Martin we were going.

She followed us to the front door, never changing expression when I explained that my man had gone ahead. Madame Martin watched us depart, arms folded, and remained on the doorstep until Moreau and I had rounded the corner.

"I can understand why Signora Ruggeri asked to be moved," I muttered as we trudged through the narrow lanes.

Moreau acknowledged this with a grunted laugh.

He took me to another townhouse a few streets away that was as modest as the one we'd left, though a bit better kept. The paint looked fresh, and the wrought-iron grills on the upper windows and latches on the shutters gleamed in the sunshine. I wondered if the hardware had been made in the Deveres' factory.

The door opened before Moreau could knock, revealing a housekeeper of the same age as Madame Martin but of much sweeter disposition. She curtsied politely to Moreau and me, told us the lady of the house awaited us in the sitting room upstairs, and led us there.

We ascended past wallpaper filled with flowers, birds, and pagodas framed in moldings painted a soft ivory. Gilded tables in niches bore vases of fresh flowers or objets d'art of exquisite porcelain. A year or so ago, I'd been privileged to look over the Prince of Wales's collection, and these pieces appeared to be as fine as his.

More beautiful trinkets reposed in the sitting room, this chamber decorated in tasteful shades of blue. The walls held still-life paintings of flowers or landscapes of Lyon, rendered from the perspective of the nearby hills. I glimpsed the signature of Antoine Berjon on one of the flower still lifes.

This was a very feminine house, and I realized it must be owned by the lady who rose to meet us. She was no courtesan tucked away on a back street, but a matron who'd settled into this house long ago. I surmised that either her husband or father had willed the home to her, as France did not have the same primogeniture and inheritance laws as did England.

"Captain Lacey," Moreau said, pride entering his usually neutral voice. "May I present Madame Paillard? Madame, Captain Lacey."

"*Enchantée, Madame,*" I said with true sincerity as I made her a formal bow.

"My, such good manners," Madame Paillard responded in flawless English. "How do you do, Captain Lacey?"

Madame Paillard was small and plump, the dark hair that peeked from under a lace cap just beginning to gray. Her gown was cut to flatter her, with flowing sleeves that eschewed the now-fashionable puffs. The skirt was devoid of ornamentation, nothing to mar the elegance of the striped lavender silk.

The entire costume made the rather plain woman lovely, as did her eyes, wide and thick-lashed, of a rich shade of brown. I wagered those eyes had ensnared Moreau on a moonlit night long ago.

"I do very well, indeed," I responded. "I am honored to meet you."

"You did not tell me he was so charming, Nicolas," Madame Paillard said to Moreau. "Especially given your encounter with each other during the war. Forgiveness is a becoming trait, Captain, and one I am happy to see you have embraced. Though, if you did come here to exact your revenge on Nico, please do not do so on my sitting room carpet. It has just been cleaned."

"I would not dream of it," I said with another bow. "There are plenty of back lanes in Lyon for that."

Madame Paillard's smile widened, though Moreau blinked. I let him wonder whether I was joking.

Madame Paillard waved us to sit. I took a chair near the tall window while Moreau escorted his lady to a sofa and settled in beside her.

We spoke about polite things at first, such as my daughter's upcoming nuptials, and what I had seen of Lyon and the surrounding countryside. Madame Paillard already knew where I was staying, and that Donata was an English earl's daughter. She asked me pointed questions about Donata, without embarrassment.

I answered, also without embarrassment, while Moreau appeared to be uncomfortable with the entire conversation.

While we chatted, a maid pushed a teacart into the room. The plates surrounding the coffeepot contained sumptuous pastries that I did not refuse. One was lemon curd inside an envelope of flaky, buttery crust, with just the right balance between sweet and tart. This was followed by a torte of rich, heady chocolate.

"Your wife's son inherited his father's title and lands," Madame Paillard continued as she served up these treats once the maid departed.

"He did," I answered around bites. "Peter is a fine little chap, and growing rapidly. He'll be a man before we realize."

"And you have two daughters," Madame Paillard went on. "One with Madame Auberge and one with your viscountess. Yes, Captain, I have heard all the tittle-tattle about you and Madame Auberge in your youth." Her eyes crinkled with her smile.

I wondered if she knew the entire truth, or only the fabrication that Carlotta had never married before Auberge.

"Indeed," I said, warming as I did whenever I spoke about my offspring. "Anne, the youngest, is already out-screeching Peter, who can yell like a banshee when he's provoked."

Madame Paillard chuckled. "I have two sons myself. Quite a handful they were. Grown men now, in trade in Paris."

"My felicitations," I said as she beamed with maternal satisfaction. "Forgive me, but you seem to know much about my family. Information I have not imparted to the colonel."

"My dear captain, if I waited for Nico to report to me, I'd know nothing. Lyon is excellent for gossip, as you must have realized by now. I learned everything about you via my servants and my neighbors before the colonel even told me of your past connection. The English viscountess on the hill engendered quite a lot of excitement."

"Donata will be flattered to learn this." I set down my half-finished torte, not wanting to stuff myself gluttonously. "We did come here to give you some other news." I exchanged a glance with Moreau, and he nodded. "We found a ledger of names in the house Signora Ruggeri inhabited for a time."

"Yours was in it," Moreau said gently. "Though I saw no sign of the letter."

Madame Paillard set down her coffee cup so fiercely that droplets splashed out. "Damn her," she said, switching to French in her agitation. "And damn that paramour of hers. Murder is evil, says the Bible, but sometimes it is justified, is it not?"

CHAPTER 21

Madame Paillard's declaration rang into sudden silence.

Here was a woman would could be aggressive when need be, I decided, taking in her rapid breathing, her brown eyes flashing fire.

A placid matron, she was not.

I hoped she did not mean she'd murdered Gallo herself—in a fit of rage, perhaps encountering him on the bridge early on the morning of his death. This would fit my theory of a person killing him in fury, then fleeing in shock at what they'd done.

I saw the same idea occur to Moreau, or it might have already done so when he'd stumbled across Gallo's body.

Madame Paillard removed a thin handkerchief from her pocket and dabbed her cheeks with it. "Forgive me, gentlemen. I am a bit distressed over all this, as you can imagine."

"We will find your letter," I assured her. "We are leaving no stone unturned. I have the best thief in Christendom to help me."

Madame Paillard started, lowering the handkerchief. "Good heavens. Do you mean that large man Nico has told me about? Is my silver safe?"

"He long ago gave up that way of life." *More or less,* I added silently.

"He is welcome to all my plate if he can find my letter," she proclaimed. "Except for the largest platter in the dining room. That was given to my great *grand-mère* by Louis the Fifteenth."

When I raised my brows, uncertain whether she was serious, Madame Paillard laughed.

"She was not his official mistress, by any means. Great *grand-mère* struck the king's fancy when she visited Versailles, and she was wise enough to gain what she could from his brief infatuation. She bought this house from the proceeds of what he gave her and left it to my mother, who left it to me."

I lifted my coffee cup. "To the sagacity of your great *grand-mère.*"

"Thank you." Madame Paillard said. "I do not come from a long line of courtesans, Captain, in spite of my unfortunate *affaire* when I was younger. Just resourceful women who knew their own minds."

"Enchanting ones, as well," I said.

"He is kind," Madame Paillard said to Moreau. "Kind *and* charming. What a remarkable gentleman."

I could well understand why Moreau highly regarded her.

He'd told me that Madame Paillard's father had been killed by Potier and that she and her mother and others of her family had fled the city for a time. This house had obviously been spared the threatened destruction—perhaps because of Comtesse Lejeune's intervention.

"I am sorry for your earlier troubles," I said. "The colonel explained the heinous things Potier did."

Madame Paillard gave me a nod. "I asked him to tell you, so you would understand. No one in Lyon speaks of him, because the memories are too fresh. Twenty-five years is not so long a time.

I agreed. I had realized, as I grew older, that decades could pass in the blink of an eye.

"I will say nothing more about him," I promised. "I have no wish to be ejected from town, with my daughter's wedding approaching."

"Yes, you cannot miss that," Madame Paillard said. "Marrying a Devere will see her well cared for. They have more put by than most people know. They are worth far more than the aristocrats on the hill, but those are the times now."

"I am glad to hear it," I said. "I would not like Gabriella to live in poverty."

"She certainly will not, as long as the Deveres behave themselves. They can sometimes be a bit arrogant, knowing not many will oppose them, though Fernand keeps them reined in well."

"I think I have blundered with Fernand," I confessed. "His friendliness toward me has vanished, but I made the mistake of mentioning Monsieur Potier."

"He will come around," Madame Paillard decreed. "Once he regains his temper and realizes you spoke from ignorance."

Fernand's reaction troubled me even more in light of Grenville's revelation that Potier had never reached Paris. I had written an inquiry about Potier myself a few days ago, to a man who seemed to know everything about everyone, everywhere. Even if Denis had never heard of Potier, he had the resources to discover all information about him.

"Humble yourself to Fernand Devere," Madame Paillard suggested. "If you wish to keep the peace. He likes to rule his own world."

"I have noted that," I said. "Those in the ironworks seem devoted to him." I thought of Michel, who watched me so closely whenever I appeared.

"They are," Madame Paillard agreed. "It is one reason why they've been so successful. That and selling their wares to everyone in Lyon."

"As well as England and Stuttgart," I added. "Fernand travels much."

"He does." Madame Paillard said the words quickly, as though she no longer wanted to speak of him. "You did not finish telling me what you thought of Lyon, Captain. I am always interested in an outsider's opinion."

"I like many things about it." I realized she wanted to change the topic, and so I relayed how I enjoyed the markets and taking coffee and breakfast in Beaumont's shop. I also admired the views from our villa, and the Roman ruins so casually strewn over the Fourvière hill.

"We are proud of our history," Madame Paillard said when I'd finished. "We were a thriving civilization when Paris was only a barbarian settlement on a little island in the Seine."

"London wasn't even that," I said. "According to my friend Grenville, who is an avid historian, even our native Celts did not live in London until the Romans came."

The conversation turned to history, of which Madame Paillard knew much, and I knew a little. Colonel Moreau occasionally put in an opinion or pointed out a fact, but he was content to listen to his lady.

I recalled what he'd said to me when I'd asked why they hadn't married. *Our arrangement, it suits us.* I could see that it did.

The pair were comfortable with each other, each putting in words when the other ran out of them. They exchanged fond looks when they did.

This house was decidedly Madame Paillard's home, one she allowed Moreau to share with her when he was not in his own lodgings. She did not mention a husband, though a small painting of a man in military uniform, who was not Moreau, reposed on the mantelpiece. He could not be one of her sons, because the style of hair and uniform were ones from decades past.

In any case, Moreau was content for Madame Paillard to have her place, which he visited as he wished. They had closeness and their own lives at the same time.

I spent a pleasant afternoon in the cozy abode, finding myself glad for Moreau that he'd found such contentedness after the horrors of war. There had been far too much bleakness to go around.

When it was time to depart, I found myself reluctant to go. I was relaxed, filled with coffee and pastries, and wanted nothing more than to lean back and nap.

I bowed over Madame Paillard's hand when she rose to say her farewells, thanked her for her hospitality, and let Moreau lead me to the door.

"I wonder that you were in a hurry to become an officer," I told him as we paused on the house's doorstep. "But not surprised you wished to return home."

Moreau gave me a nod. "She had married the man arranged for her just before I left Lyon, which is why I so readily departed."

"I congratulate you on your current happiness," I said. "We all deserve such a thing."

"As you say, Captain." Moreau bowed to me, and I returned the bow with more respect. "Good afternoon."

"*Bonne journée*," I responded. I tipped my hat and stepped into the street, leaving Moreau to withdraw to the pleasantness within.

Brewster joined me as I neared the square, noticeably without the ledger. I trusted that he'd found a safe place for it, but I did not offend him by asking him where.

"I stepped into the downstairs of the lady's house while you was learning things upstairs." Brewster patted his belly. "I stayed in that kitchen any longer, I'd not have been able to fit out the door. Their cook is a dab hand."

"Indeed, I noticed."

"Where to now, guv?"

"We ought to take a brisk walk after our repast, but I more have in mind a saunter home to rest."

"Aye," Brewster agreed with a short laugh. "Below stairs all worship the mistress of the house," he reported as he fell into step beside me. "Didn't like me asking too many questions."

"She is a congenial lady," I said with sincerity. "I quite liked her."

"They didn't think much of her husband. Threw in his lot with the new regime after the siege, probably so they wouldn't kill him. Lady and the rest of her family got out of the city, but he stayed. Servants didn't like to say so, but they hinted he had a hand in some of the arrests. He died right after Bonaparte came through, but not because he was punished for his sins. He caught a fever that carried him off."

"Perhaps he *was* being punished for his sins."

"Could be." Brewster shrugged. "They're happy with that colonel, though. Say everything got cheery again when he came back from war."

"I'm glad," I said. "Peace is a fine thing."

"Never understood you gents' way of shaking hands with your enemy. I beat mine down, and they leave me be."

"But they respect you, do they not? It is much the same thing."

"Suppose." Brewster shook his head but did not press the matter.

When we reached the square, I caught sight of Captain Vernet striding through it. He likewise spied me and approached. Pedestrians drifted from his path without appearing to, opening a way between us.

"Captain," Vernet greeted me with a tip of his hat.

"Captain," I said in return, keeping to French. "A fair afternoon, is it not?"

"Bit warm for my taste," Vernet said. "I hear you have been wandering Lyon, searching rooms and houses and the like."

His tone remained pleasant, but I heard a note of irritation in it.

"I have no intention of treading on your toes, Captain," I

said, trying to sound reasonable. "I was trying to make certain you cleared young Monsieur Devere of any suspicion."

"I released him immediately," Vernet sounded annoyed that I'd not believe he did. "Claude Devere is an impetuous young man, but no killer, I think. You can cease making a case for him. I am looking elsewhere."

The way Vernet clamped his lips shut told me he was not going to tell me who he suspected of the murder now.

"I am amazed there were no witnesses to Gallo's death," I said. "It was very late—or early—so the streets might have been deserted, of course. But surely someone must have seen who killed the man. A chance glance out of a window, perhaps."

Vernet snorted a laugh. "There might have been a hundred witnesses, but none are going to come forward, are they? Look around you."

A glance showed me that the people in the square had cleared a wide circle around us, none wanting to have anything to do with the gendarmes. Brewster himself had wandered away, keeping an eye on me while ostensibly examining wares at a vendor's cart on the edge of the square.

"Gallo was an outsider," I said. "You believe that, if they pull together to protect the killer, then it must have been committed by a resident of this city, not a foreigner who followed him from La Guillotière."

"Depend upon it, the murderer was Lyonnais," Vernet said. "And I have little chance of uncovering him without the towns-people's aid. So anything you have found out, Captain Lacey, you will tell me, no?"

When I entered the dining room at the villa after returning home, I found a light meal for me on the sideboard and letters at my plate. I had no need for a repast after stuffing myself at Madame Paillard's, but I downed bread and cold meat to counteract the sweets as I read my correspondence.

One letter was from Leland Derwent, a young man I'd grown quite close to, with news of his family. His mother, unfortunately, was doing poorly, and they did not expect her to last the summer. I folded the missive away, despondent. Consumption was a devastating disease that consumed the lives of so many.

It took the youthful breeziness of the next letter, from my stepson Peter, to ease my sadness about Lady Derwent. Peter was having a splendid time in Oxfordshire with his grandparents, riding, walking, and fishing. Grandfather Pembroke carried Anne out to see the horses most days, and she was very interested in the ponies.

She'd be an avid horsewoman, I thought with a frisson of pride. I'd teach her to ride as soon as I could.

I felt a wrench of longing when I set aside Peter's letter. I missed the pair of them so.

The third letter, I'd deliberately left for last, uncertain what I wanted to learn.

Pushing aside my plate, I broke the seal on the thick paper and found James Denis's spare and slanting handwriting inside.

I made inquiries about the name you sent me, he began without preamble. *Lucien Potier began life in a village north of Paris and served a few years in the army of Louis the Sixteenth. After the more radical of the national governments took power, he joined their number, helping to round up the king and his family as well as others slated for execution.*

After Lyon's surrender in 1793, he was sent to help coordinate the quelling of that city, arresting and executing anyone considered a traitor.

He curated a list of names for arrest that covered almost every aristocrat or any person with means in and around Lyon. Some of those were forewarned by friends and managed to escape, but Potier and others had many people rounded up and dispatched, including Christian Devere, grandfather of your soon-to-be son-in-law.

Potier kept careful records, which he sent back to Paris, documenting the deaths. The names on his lists who were not aristocrats, or wealthy men, or even attempting to aid the accused, he brushed aside as necessary casualties. It was war, he claimed, and civilians sometimes got in the way.

The officers in charge did complain about his heavy-handed tactics, one sending a plea to his superiors in Paris that Potier be recalled. This officer claimed that Potier was detrimental to order rather than helping to restore it. I have noted that this officer was soon reassigned to another regiment.

The last communication from Potier was in April of 1795. He sent in his lists of those he'd executed that week along with detailed information on property and money he'd seized.

The letter also mentioned his next targets. Potier had become highly suspicious of a family's continuing treachery, even though their ringleader had already been dispatched. Potier decided they were covertly plotting their revenge, and so he would pay them a visit.

That family's name was Devere.

CHAPTER 22

I laid down the letter and sat still.

That Potier had fixed upon the Deveres did not surprise me. They were an esteemed and successful family whose forebears had once served France's monarchy.

That Potier's very last dispatch mentioned he would visit them filled me with misgivings.

Moreau had told me that Potier would personally knock on the door of those he would condemn, demanding their wealth to spare them, and then drag them off to the guillotine anyway. This had happened to Madame Paillard's family, and she'd escaped only due to the bravery of her father.

Potier had noted his plan to visit the Deveres, and shortly after that, he'd disappeared forever.

I drew a breath and returned to Denis's letter, which had more to impart.

When his superiors in Paris heard nothing more from Potier, they wrote to the commander in charge of the city. This man told them that Potier had expressed a wish to retire, and one day simply packed a bag and walked off into the hills.

An official was sent to Lyon to make an inquiry, but all in

*authority there maintained that Potier had departed of his own voli-
tion, never to return. The official wrote his report and filed it.*

*Not long later, the government in Paris changed again, Bonaparte's
career was on the rise, and Lyon was left to recover by itself. No one
cared very much what had happened to Potier, as he was never a
popular figure, even to those who employed him. It was noted that he
had retired somewhere in the south of France, and forgotten.*

Filled with uneasiness, I read the letter again. The second
perusal did not change the words, and I set down the paper
once more, my thoughts troubled.

Potier had disappeared, and the conquerors of Lyon at the
time hadn't minded that he'd gone.

I wondered if one of their number had murdered Potier,
either deliberately or during a confrontation that turned deadly.
This would make a neat ending, but if so, would people like
Beaumont and the Deveres be as zealous in their effort to quell
all mention of him?

Or perhaps, realizing that Potier had likely been killed by a
citizen of Lyon, his fellow officers had collaborated in the
coverup. Potier had been so hated that even those sent to punish
the city for its rebellion had been happy that he'd vanished.

Or else, the Lyonnais had banded together to make certain
the story that Potier walked away of his own accord was taken
as truth by the Parisian officials.

Denis had many contacts in all walks of life, including those
in governments, and I did not doubt what he wrote. I imagined
all had happened exactly as Denis put forth.

I heaved a sigh and picked up the last page of the missive,
which I had not yet read.

*I have learned of a letter in Italian that you turned up during your
investigation of a dead blackmailer, one from a collection of Comte
Lejeune. I would like to purchase said letter, as it is of interest to me,
and wish for you to negotiate its sale.*

*Speak to Comtesse Lejeune, rather than the comte, as she will be
more reasonable and accept a fair price. An agent of mine in Lyon will*

provide the cash. I will instruct you how to reach him once you have come to an agreement *with the comtesse over its purchase.*

He ended the letter as abruptly as he'd begun it, signing it simply as

Denis

I laid down the paper, rested my hands on either side of it, and sank into unquiet thoughts.

———

I spent most of the evening after I'd read Denis's letter and much of the following day in the villa's library. Heavy rain began in the morning, precluding me from tramping about Lyon. I holed myself up in the comfortable chamber as the servants and Donata readied the house for the soiree my wife had planned that night to honor Gabriella and Emile and their families.

I pondered all day, as rain battered at the library's windows, what to do next. I wasn't certain confronting the Deveres would do any good, though in my heart of hearts, I wanted to learn the truth. Gabriella deserved to know it.

The rain, fortunately, slacked off by that evening, promising good weather for the festivities.

The Auberges, with Gabriella, turned up unfashionably early, to Donata's vexation.

Bartholomew installed Carlotta and Major Auberge in the ground-floor drawing room, where they waited in discomfiture for the soiree to begin. They'd brought their next oldest daughter, Chloe, who was seventeen, already having made her debut in Lyon's society. She'd been at the villa before to visit Gabriella, and was the only Auberge besides Gabriella at her ease.

The Devere brothers, including the wives of Auguste and Julien, arrived not long later. Claude Devere and the only female cousin, Camille, came as well, both surrounding Emile, as though shielding him from the older members of the family.

Camille, the daughter of Julien, had married and moved to a village in Provençal, though she'd journeyed to Lyon with her husband for the wedding. She was a bright spot among the more dour Deveres, with a wide smile and friendly brown eyes. Her husband, a tall young man who stood behind her, clearly adored her.

The Deveres filed into the sitting room, and Auberge and Carlotta rose to greet them. I made myself scarce after saying my good evenings, letting Bartholomew and Matthias make them comfortable.

Gabriella saved any awkwardness in the situation by inviting her mother, half-sister, and Camille on a tour of the house while they waited. The younger women chattered away in excitement, and Carlotta followed them, with the expression of forbearance I well remembered.

When Grenville arrived with Marianne, he took on the task of entertaining the gentlemen in the drawing room with the ease and gallantry that only he could manage.

"You will owe him a great favor for keeping the peace with your in-laws," Marianne told me as I led her away to seek Donata. "Why on earth did they arrive so early?"

"Because the time on the invitation was for nine o'clock," I said. "Only the highborn and actors believe this means to arrive at eleven or midnight. In their defense, I'd have come at the time instructed, myself."

"Been unfashionable, you mean." Marianna patted my arm. "That has always been you, Lacey."

"Thank you." I made her a bow.

"I might have to slip away unfashionably early, as a matter of fact," Marianne said as we ascended the stairs. "Grenville has put me in an interesting condition, and I tire easily these days."

I halted on the landing to stare at her. "I beg your pardon?"

The incredulity in my voice made Marianne's smile widen. "Yes, my dear friend, I am increasing. I am certain you'll have noticed me looking wan. I'm a bit old for bearing a child, and Grenville is rather worried."

Well he ought to be. I'd nearly lost Donata and Anne both when Anne had come into the world. Only the aid of the nameless surgeon Denis had sent to help had saved them.

"Then you indeed must go early," I said. "We have plenty of rooms for you to rest in, if you feel the need to sit. Shall we go to one now?"

Marianne laughed. "Good heavens, Lacey, I am not *that* fragile. All my years on the stage have made me robust, as I keep reassuring my husband. Let us find your wife, and her maid can give me lemonade or something equally foul."

I continued with Marianne up the stairs, she with a pleased smile on her face.

I could not easily picture Marianne as a mother, but she'd surprised me in many ways since the days she'd been the desperate young woman who'd lived upstairs from me in our cheap lodging house. I quite looked forward to meeting her child.

Jacinthe admitted Marianne to Donata's inner sanctum, and closed the door more or less in my face. Donata and Marianne had formed an unlikely friendship, which unnerved me not a little. I heard their laughter rise behind the door before I turned away.

At long last, more guests streamed in downstairs, which included Comtesse Lejeune. The comte was nowhere in evidence, but the comtesse seemed perfectly serene without him.

Once the soiree had commenced, the house filled with chatter and laughter, softened by music from the string quartet Donata had installed in the upper gallery. Since the June night was warm and now dry, all windows and doors had been opened, admitting fragrant air from the garden.

While the guests congratulated Gabriella and Emile, as well

as the Devere and Auberge families, Denis's letter weighed on my mind.

It was difficult to be so near Fernand and his brothers and remain silent, but I would not confront them tonight. There was no reason to spoil the festivities and take the attention from Gabriella and Emile.

I did, however, think it only fair that Emile and Gabriella should know what unnerving tidings I had discovered.

I held my peace until late in the night, when the guests began to drift away. I invited Emile and Gabriella to stay on when the Auberges and Deveres departed, for a quieter visit with Donata and myself. I'd given Donata Denis's letter to read yesterday evening, and she'd agreed with my wish to share its contents with Gabriella and Emile.

Grenville and Marianne had departed early, as Marianne had predicted. I hadn't been able to corner Grenville privately to offer my congratulations, but by the wariness in his eyes when we said goodnight, I was certain Marianne had told him that I knew.

The house quieted, and the four of us retired to the private sitting room. Donata lounged on a sofa, her slippers sliding from her feet as she yawned. Bartholomew, in no way weary, brought us refreshing cups of tea and warm brandy.

I wasn't certain how to broach the subject with Emile and Gabriella, so I simply handed them Denis's letter.

Donata and I waited while Gabriella helped Emile through the English missive, both of them growing increasingly troubled as they read.

Emile raised his head once they'd finished. "I do not understand."

Donata answered him gently. "The gist of the matter is that Monsieur Potier mentioned in his last dispatch that he would visit your family, and then he vanished. The question is, did he ever reach them?"

"You believe my uncles had a hand in the disappearance?"

Emile asked, his voice cracking. "He must have retired, as the officials said."

"Potier was responsible for the shooting of your grandfather," I said. "Among a number of other people. I am not purporting to know exactly what happened to him, but your uncle Fernand has grown very angry with me for even inquiring about this man."

I did not remind Emile of the hostility with which I was met at the factory when I'd turned up, uninvited, even before Fernand had learned of my interest in Potier.

"Because Monsieur Potier was evil." Tears stood in Emile's eyes. "Those days are best forgotten."

Gabriella slid her hand to Emile's and squeezed it. "Father is not trying to rake up the past," she assured him. "But if someone else were to question your father and uncles about him, it is wise for us to be forewarned."

"Indeed." I warmed that Gabriella understood my intentions. "I should not like you to be caught up in events that, as you say, are best left in the past. But I feel you should know about them."

"My father could not have been involved with anything untoward," Emile said with more conviction. "He is the most peaceful of men."

His uncle Fernand was more volatile, however, and the brothers took their cues from him. All four had been fairly young men during the time in question, and Emile could not know what his father had been like then. Emile had been born after the radical government had gone, leaving Lyon to pick up its pieces.

"I am hoping that is the case," I said. "I will ask you not to mention this to your family, not yet. They are upset enough, but I did not want you to remain in ignorance."

Emile nodded, though I could see he was vastly unhappy.

"Thank you for telling us, Father," Gabriella said, her voice steady. "I agree we should not air such things with Emile's father or Uncle Fernand."

Gabriella kept hold of Emile's hand as she spoke, and I had an inkling of who would be the prop in this marriage.

I was uncertain whether the gendarmes would bother investigating the history of a hated man who'd vanished twenty-five years before. The monarchy had been restored and, as Grenville posited, an agent of the radicals who'd deposed the king would not be missed. The Deveres would likely be lauded by their neighbors for ridding the world of such a man.

And yet, the Devere brothers feared.

"Those were sad times," I said to Emile. "Violent ones, too. Very few escaped tragedy. If your uncles did act, it is under-standable."

"They would not have," Emile returned stubbornly. "I am certain you are wrong."

"I possibly am." I gave Emile a reassuring nod. "I apologize for upsetting you, but it is only fair that you know of the possibility."

Emile thrust the letter back at me. "What you have avoided saying is that you suspect Signor Gallo was blackmailing my uncles about it."

"You and Claude searched Gallo's rooms for whatever hold Gallo had over them, did you not?" I asked as I returned Denis's letter to my pocket.

"Yes, but we did not know what it was about," Emile countered. "I have come across no sign of this Potier fellow in connection with my family, or even heard mention of him."

"I have not either," Gabriella put in.

And yet, I'd seen the name *Devere* emblazoned on a page of the ledger Brewster had discovered, as well as the amount they'd given Gallo. The payment might not have been to conceal information about what had happened to Potier, but Gallo had known *something* that worried them.

"Again, I am very sorry to tell you of this." I rose, and Emile and Gabriella followed suit. Donata remained on the sofa, her eyes bright as she watched us. "I will have Brewster escort you home."

Gabriella stepped to me and enfolded me a spontaneous embrace. "Do not worry, Father." She patted my waistcoat as she released me. "You were kind to broach such a difficult subject. We will keep it to ourselves for now."

Emile said nothing, only bowing to Donata in farewell.

I saw them out, down the stairs to the front door, where Gabriella embraced me again and kissed both my cheeks. Emile clasped my hand in a very English handshake, but he wouldn't meet my gaze.

Bartholomew helped them into their light wraps for the cool of the summer night, and they departed in our hired coach, Brewster swinging to his perch behind to accompany them.

I returned to the upstairs sitting room to find Donata stretched out on the sofa, sipping a brandy. She shifted enough to allow me space to sit and put her stockinged feet into my lap.

"You believe the Deveres killed Potier, don't you?" she asked me pointedly.

"I'm not certain." I lifted the glass of brandy Bartholomew had left for me. "But yes, I think it is a good possibility. And when Gallo tried to blackmail them about it, they killed him as well."

CHAPTER 23

$\mathcal{I}$f you are correct, what will you do?" Donata's voice was quiet.

I let out a long breath. "If they took Potier's life, it was understandable. They were no doubt defending home and family."

"That is plausible," Donata agreed. "Potier turned up at their factory with his threats. Would he have been such a fool as to arrive alone? Or did his own men assist in his demise?"

"Anything is possible. Apparently, no one grieved when Potier disappeared, including his fellow officials." I took a fortifying drink of brandy. "Murdering Gallo, though, that is another matter. The war is over, and killing is against the law, even if Gallo was a criminal himself."

"As I asked, what will you do?" Donata studied me calmly, letting me reach my own conclusions.

"I truly do not know. The Deveres' past actions might have been justifiable, but how can I let my daughter live with men who strike out in violence when they are threatened?"

"You strike out, at times," Donata reminded me.

I had very definitely attacked men who'd wronged those I cared for, including one who'd endangered Gabriella.

Perhaps I should be grateful the Deveres were so protective, but Gabriella would be living in the midst of them. Subject to the same violence?

I wasn't certain how long Emile could keep silent about the matter. What would happen on the day he confronted Fernand about the Deveres' past misdeeds? What would Fernand do when he discovered Gabriella also knew?

"If I discover that Fernand or one of his brothers murdered Gallo, I will have to tell Vernet. I will be a conspirator if I do not." I swallowed more brandy. "But I will say nothing until I am very, very certain."

"Putting yourself in danger while you investigate them," Donata said in resignation.

"I see no other way. I do not want Vernet rampaging in and arresting the entire family so close to the wedding. I will at least wait until after that."

"Very kind of you." Donata's eyes held an ironic glint, but I could see she agreed with me. "But have Brewster stay close."

"Wise advice." I saluted her with my brandy. "I will, my love."

WITH GABRIELLA'S WEDDING ONLY DAYS AWAY, I HAD VERY LITTLE time to look into problems, in any case. When no Devere turned up to threaten me in the intervening time, I concluded that Emile had kept his promise to remain silent.

I had an appointment on Friday evening at the comtesse's chateau to speak to her about purchasing the de' Medici letter for Denis, which Grenville had returned to her. At eight o'clock that night, I had Barthlomew dress me in one of my best suits and duly took myself there.

Brewster, as usual, accompanied me. We walked, as the night was fine, and the chateau wasn't far.

The hill, on the other hand, had me cursing my resolve—the

comtesse lived in a higher spot than we did. By the time we reached the chateau, my knee was aching.

Brewster greeted the burly men who guarded the gates, and they hailed him as a friend. We were readily admitted, Brewster staying behind to speak to them and very likely to share more of the ale he'd admired.

Denis had given me no instructions as to the price for the letter. He was not a frugal man, but nor would he appreciate paying an exorbitant amount. Denis had indicated he believed the comtesse would strike a fair bargain, and from what I'd noted of her, he likely had the right of it.

A footman admitted me to the echoing foyer, where Signora Ruggeri had imperiously demanded admittance. Without the crowds, the large entrance hall was cool, the fading sunshine casting gentle shadows on the walls and its tapestries.

While I waited for the footman to fetch me when the comtesse was ready, I strolled the corridor that stretched across the length of the house, many tall windows giving onto the courtyard.

Plenty of artwork hung here for me to admire. In addition to more flowers and fruit by Berjon, there were excellent offerings from French, Venetian, Dutch, and Flemish artists of the past.

I'd paused before a massive painting signed by the great Ruebens, when a narrow door next to it swung open.

I stared in disbelief at the person who appeared on its threshold.

"Michel?" I gaped at the large man from the Deveres' iron-works. "What are you—?"

My words cut off as Michel's giant hands closed around the lapels of my coat. He dragged me swiftly into the passageway from which he'd sprung and slammed the door behind us.

I struggled mightily, not about to be pulled into the bowels of the house without a fight. The passageway was cramped, the space too small for me to draw the sword in my walking stick, or even to strike out with the sheath.

I ducked Michel's blows the best I could, but one landed on my abdomen, and I folded in half. I expected a kick on my bad knee, but Michel did not need to resort to underhanded methods. He very quickly had me pinned beneath his massive arm, and hauled me along with him, my feet scraping on the rough tile floor.

I couldn't draw breath to shout for help, as Michel's hold cut off my windpipe. I still clenched my walking stick, but it did little good as a weapon in my ineffectual grasp.

Not far down this passageway, Michel grated open another door. He towed me down a stone staircase, cool dankness increasing as we descended.

I recalled Brewster describing the warren of tunnels beneath the chateau. How Michel knew of them, and why he was at the chateau at all, were questions his stranglehold would not let me ask. Not that he'd understand my inquiries, as he and I spoke no common language.

Michel threw me into an inky dark room about twenty yards from the bottom of the staircase. My feet slid out from under me as I tripped into the chamber, and I landed hard on the solid floor.

By the time I could pry myself up, my bad knee in agony, Michel had slammed the door.

I heard a bolt slide across it and then his heavy footsteps retreating, leaving me alone in the darkness.

CHAPTER 24

For a long while, I leaned against the stone wall of my prison, rubbing my throbbing knee and clenching my jaw against the pain.

There was no sense wasting my breath calling out, either for help or to relieve my pique. We'd come deep into the cellars, and I doubted anyone would hear me.

I strove to let reason countermand my panic. I'd brought Brewster with me, and he'd wonder after a time where I'd got to. Brewster would have no qualms about shouldering his way in and searching the house, no matter who lived here.

Of course, Michel might somehow have rid himself of Brewster as well.

I tamped down that surge of uneasiness. Brewster would not be easily bested, and he'd raise an alarm if nothing else.

Why was Michel not at the Deveres' factory, banging on bars of iron and intimidating unexpected visitors? What had he to do with the comte? Or the comtesse?

Perhaps he'd been following me, concluding I meant to accuse the Deveres of murdering Potier long ago and Gallo more recently. He might have decided I'd come here tonight to consult with the comte or comtesse about the deaths.

Or, he'd been making a delivery to the chateau, seen me, and thought he'd take the chance to punish me for my meddling.

But he'd come from the tunnels and known exactly where to sequester me inside them.

My thoughts spun in the absolute darkness as my body began to stiffen in the cool, damp air. My suit was of light fabric for summer, but no June warmth reached into the depths of this house.

Brewster would find me, I assured myself. When I failed to emerge after a certain amount of time, he'd try to discover why. No one could deter Brewster when he decided to act.

Donata, too, would miss me. We were staying in tonight, so we could rise early for the wedding in the morning. Donata would wonder why I lingered so long at the chateau, and likely send Bartholomew to inquire. Everyone in our house knew where I'd gone.

Even so, it could be some time before a rescue. I might catch a chill or a fever in this dank place, and who knew how much air this room held?

To cease such dire musings, I began to explore my prison. I started with the door, when I found it again, pressing my gloved hands over its surface.

It was made of rough wood, with horizontal bands placed over vertical boards, tacked in place with iron bolts. The hinges were also cold iron, and the latch, which did nothing when I jiggled it, was likewise of that metal.

If the door had been more ancient, I might have been able to kick my way through any rotten boards. However, it felt solid and fairly new, meaning whoever maintained the comtesse's house had recently installed it, probably with iron fixings made by the Deveres.

Leaving the door, I groped my way along the wall beside it, going slowly and carefully. I did not want to tear my hand on a protruding nail or piece of wood and give myself a festering wound.

The wall extended from the door only about five feet. I hit a corner and turned it, encountering a tall set of standing shelves a few feet from there.

I eagerly examined these, hoping to find tools of some kind with which I could pry open the door. To my disappointment, the shelves were mostly empty. I did come across an open wooden box of what felt like rags inside, perhaps ones shoved in here and forgotten sometime in the past, but nothing more.

The wall ended not far beyond the shelves and turned again. The stones became round and smooth here, contrasting the regular bricks of the other walls. I imagined this was part of the original chateau, constructed hundreds of years ago, the brick walls later installed to divide the space into smaller rooms.

While fascinating from an architectural point of view, it was not very helpful to me at the moment. Behind these old stones was probably the hill itself, the masonry propping the cellars against the dirt beyond.

My only hope of escape, it seemed, was through the door.

I discovered a much smaller set of shelves on the old wall, this one more like a compact bookcase. On that, I found bottles. Dust puffed when I slid my hand across the glass, making me sneeze.

I removed a glove and lifted one of the bottles. It was heavy and sloshed with liquid.

I'd once used grease and flame to set fire to a door behind which I'd been trapped, but I did not want to attempt that here. The smoke would quickly fill this little space and overwhelm me.

Also, as I'd observed before, I had no way to strike a spark. An oversight I would correct, if I ever gained my freedom.

I found a cork jammed tightly into the top of the bottle. That, at least, I could deal with.

I removed the small knife I carried in my pocket. Its blade was too short and delicate to help me much with the door, but it could pry a cork from a bottle.

I worked carefully, in case I unleashed a vitriolic substance, but as soon as the cork moved, I smiled.

The odor assaulting me came not from a dangerous oil or other corrosive substance, but from the warm sweetness of wine.

Had a servant hidden the bottles for himself, meaning to fetch them another time? Or had this been a storage room for drink, this cache somehow missed when the rest of the room had been emptied?

Whatever the case, I'd broached the bottle, and it would be a shame to waste what was inside. I upended the flask and tipped the liquid into my dry mouth.

The freshness of grapes picked early in the season assailed me, the wine light, airy, and crisp. It was perhaps not the aged, mellow substance that Grenville would prefer, but it danced on my palate and nicely eased my worries.

Holding the bottle in one hand, I finished my exploration of my cell. The brick wall beyond to the wine shelf was empty, and then it turned a corner, and I was back at the door.

I leaned against the wood and took another gulp of wine. My first panic assuaged, I now pondered my situation.

Michel had most likely followed me here, perhaps vowing to keep an eye on me until I departed for England. I'd asked Emile not to speak to the family about my speculations on Potier, but he'd found a confidante in Michel previously, and possibly had again.

How, though, had Michel gained entrance to the chateau? He'd been lurking behind the door in the gallery, lying in wait to pull me through. He might have found his way up through the tunnels, but from Brewster's report, the entire place was not only a labyrinth but well guarded.

Of course, Michel could be a frequent visitor to the chateau, delivering goods for the Deveres, who likely had provided the ironworks for this very stout door. In that case, the guards would know Michel and have no worry about admitting him.

The comtesse and her family must have a long association with the Deveres, perhaps one stretching back decades.

Ideas clicked together in my head, aided by this excellent wine.

Easing my fears and was only one reason I'd opened the bottle. I took another sip, savoring, then I bent down and poured the rest of the liquid out through the crack beneath the door.

Brewster might already by hunting me. If he found a puddle of wine outside one of the doors in the cellar, he'd insist on investigating the room behind it. My action would narrow down his search and save him some time.

Now to wait.

My leg ached, the cold not helping. I limped back to the wine shelf and took up a second bottle. I slid down the wall until I rested on the floor and pried out the cork.

This bottle, I used to warm myself and ease the pain in my leg.

Again, I found a refreshing, cool wine, which held the faint taste of apples. I breathed in autumn air, the scents of harvest, a cooling wind across sun-dappled vineyards.

I drank half the bottle before I made myself cease. I knew from experience on the Peninsula that nodding off in a cold, damp place could be dangerous. A person's body might chill until it couldn't warm again, even if the temperature wasn't all that frigid.

I poured the second half of that bottle under the door, then leaned my head against the wall.

Had Michel killed Gallo? To defend the Devere brothers? I could well imagine it.

However, Michel would likely be wise enough, and strong enough, to toss the man's body into the river, instead of leaving Gallo to be found by the first person over the bridge.

Michel could not have assisted in the murder of Potier—that had been twenty-five years ago, and he must have been a wee lad then. But he might have known about the murder if he'd worked for the Deveres, or even if he'd lived near the ironworks.

No matter Michel's role in either killing, he was very protective of the Deveres. He might do anything for them.

I did doze off, and woke, sneezing. The settling dust from the bottles hung in the air.

At the same time I heard, blessedly, Brewster's voice.

"Bloody hell, get that door open," he was bellowing. "Toot sweet—you understand me? *Allez*."

Another voice rumbled behind Brewster's broken French, one smoother and more patient. I also heard growls from what must be the comte's guards, and then something slammed onto the door's latch.

"Carefully," I yelled, my word slurring. "I can't move out of the way."

More bangs on the door latch, the thing solid. The Deveres' ironsmiths did good work.

At last, wood splintered from the frame, and the door sagged open. I flinched from the lantern light that spilled into my dark prison, and flung up my hand to shield my eyes.

"Guv!" Brewster's strong grip hauled me from the cold floor and into an equally cold, but now bright passageway.

Brewster heaved me up against a wall and started patting my chest and sides, while a burly man flashed an open lantern at me. Behind two more guards, another man hovered in the shadows, keeping to the circle of darkness beyond.

"Cease battering me, Brewster." I tried to push away his hands. "I'm fine. Just cold. I need coffee and a hot bath."

"There's blood all over the floor out here," Brewster said. "Yours?"

I started to laugh, and Brewster drew back, wrinkling his nose at my breath.

"It's wine, my friend," I managed. "He locked me in a forgotten wine cellar."

"Drunk, are ye?" Brewster peered at me. "Who d'ye mean by *he?*"

"Michel," I said, or tried to say. "Who is *your* friend?" I waved at the shadowy man behind him.

"Bring him," the man instructed. His voice was a familiar one, which made me laugh again. "Clean him up and make sure he's sensible enough to talk to the comtesse. She wishes him to vouch for me."

My laughter increased. "*Bonjour,* sir. What brings the careful Mr. Denis all the way from London to the dusty cellars of a French chateau?"

CHAPTER 25

*B*rewster half-carried me to a sumptuous bedroom one of the comtesse's bland-faced footmen led us to. There, Brewster sobered me up with hot coffee and by dunking my head into a wide basin of water.

The footman remained to assist, keeping his pristine gloves far from my grimy body.

I tried to ask questions as Brewster scrubbed my face and peeled my damp and dusty clothes from me, down to my smalls.

"How did you find me?" I managed around soakings. "Why was Michel roaming the comtesse's cellars? And what is *he* doing here?"

"I made the lot of them scour the place when one of them footmen tells me the comtesse was tired of waiting for ye." Brewster finished toweling off my face and handed me a comb. "Only *you* could find trouble in house you're a guest in. As to the other two questions: I don't know, and I don't know."

"Thank you, anyway." I tugged at my unruly hair, which the mirror showed contained more threads of gray. Or maybe it was the dust. "I feared I'd be too far gone by the time you reached me."

"Gave me turn, when I went down that hall and found a

huge red stain outside the door. Thought someone had gutted you proper."

"Worth the waste, then. Very good wine, I must say."

I smoothed my hair the best I could, then let the footman ease me into a clean suit he'd found for me, likely belonging to the comte.

The cut of was a style from a few years ago, but material was fine, with no wear in it. The comte had probably donned this suit once and then set it aside. The coat and trousers were too small for me, but I squeezed myself into them, as I had no choice.

"Glad you enjoyed yourself," Brewster growled at me. "If you can walk on your own, then His Nibs and her ladyship are waiting for you."

"I am much better, thank you." The fresh coffee and the very hot water Brewster had dunked my head into made my skin tingle with warmth. "You are a good nursemaid."

"I've brought plenty of drunk sots back to life, is all. Now, let's get on."

Brewster insisted on leading me from the chamber to the meeting, not trusting me not to lose myself again. We left the footman gingerly tidying up my clothes, and trudged through the tiled hall to the staircase I'd so admired on my first visit.

We ascended past the floor where the ballroom lay, emerging into another wide hallway with large windows. The long twilight lingered without, the sky a violet blue.

A corridor hung with tapestries led us to a paneled door painted in pale gray. When I tapped politely, another footmen ushered us into a comfortable room.

This was obviously a private chamber, featuring a desk strewn with papers, a bookcase of well-worn books, soft rugs on the floor, and a gilded teacart presided over by a dour-faced maid. From the woman's hard-eyed glance I me, I concluded this was Perrault, the comtesse's lady's maid and guard dog.

The comtesse rose from a sofa near the teacart, and James

Denis, a tall, youngish man with dark hair and blue eyes, likewise stood from where he'd reposed near the window.

"Captain Lacey." The comtesse swept forward, her plump hands outstretched. "You have been treated abominably, and an apology seems a thin offering for the poor hospitality shown you. I could not believe my ears when Perrault told me what Michel had done."

I took the comtesse's offered hands and glanced at the lady's maid, who moodily poured thick coffee into a tiny porcelain cup. The comtesse spoke in English, so I wasn't certain how much the maid had understood.

"*She* told you?" I asked, nonplussed. "How did she know?"

"From Michel." The comtesse sounded as though this should be no surprise. "He is her nephew. He confessed to Perrault that he had waylaid you. She was appalled, and fetched me at once."

The comtesse kissed me on both cheeks then released me and waved me to a chair.

From the way Perrault glowered at me as I sank to a gilt chair from the reign of Louis the Fifteenth, I concluded she was only appalled Michel hadn't taken care of me more permanently.

Denis said not a word during this exchange, and he re-seated himself in silence as the comtesse resumed her place.

"I do not know what Michel feared from me," I said, enjoying the chair's cushions cradling my stiff limbs. "I hope Perrault assured him I meant no harm to you, or to anyone."

"He was unhappy with your inquiries about Lucien Potier," Denis interjected in his straightforward manner. "When he saw you arrive, he thought you'd discovered the truth and had come to discuss things with the comtesse. He intended to leave you in that room until he consulted with his employers as to what to do with you."

Perrault handed me a cup of fragrant coffee and thrust another at Denis, her lips pinching. Denis took the coffee with a quiet word of thanks, and Perrault turned her back on him. I believed I'd finally found a person he could not intimidate.

"Then I am right?" I asked unhappily. "The Deveres did kill him?"

The comtesse regarded me with vast sadness.

"Madame." Perrault abandoned the coffee and went to her. "No, you must not," she said in French, then continued admonishing her in dialect until the comtesse held up her hand to stop Perrault's flow of words.

"No, Captain," the comtesse said, her words tinged with both sorrow and defiance. "*I* killed Monsieur Potier."

I froze, my cup in its saucer tilting dangerously in my hand. "Are you certain?" I asked, wondering if she shielded someone

"Of course I am. I'm not ashamed of my deed." The comtesse laid her hands in her silk-clad lap, while Denis watched her with sharp attention. "I was a young woman when Lyon rebelled and was besieged. I'd been married to the comte about seven years by then, and I had two growing sons. My husband took our boys to safety and begged me to go with him, but this was my home. I would not leave it."

She confirmed Grenville's and Donata's findings about the comte, though I did not soften much to him. Sending his sons out of harm's way I understood very well. Abandoning his wife to danger, I did not.

"From what I have learned, Potier would visit those he planned to arrest," I said, my voice gentling. "Did he come here?"

"He did. With soldiers who battered down the gate, killing one of our guards." The comtesse's face creased with sorrow and anger. "The man had worked here since he'd been a boy, grown up here. And Potier's soldiers cut him down like he was of no importance. Potier broke open the front door and trod his dirty boots on my floors. He expected me to hide in a cupboard, which he'd no doubt have been happy to rip open, but no. I faced him on the stairs."

I could well imagine the comtesse, her dignity in place, standing above Potier and his soldiers, daring them to advance any further. She must have been a very beautiful woman then, with her comeliness, though grayer now, still intact.

I turned to Denis. "Your letter indicated that the last place Potier planned to go was the Deveres' ironworks."

"He did pay them a call," the comtesse answered before Denis could speak. "Potier declared that if they'd admit I forced them to aid me in resisting the reprisals, he'd spare them. They would sign a paper to that effect, and they would be free. The Devere boys, bless them, refused to betray me. Their father had been executed months before, and they were already shattered, but they defied him. And so Potier came here to force me to confess that I fueled the resistance. Of course I confessed it. I did not hide my intentions to stop the horrors he and his cronies inflicted upon us."

"He struck her down," Perrault said in French, old rage flowing through her words. "He slapped my mistress like she was a peasant, and she fell. I was not having that."

"My dear Perrault, if you had succeeded in reaching him, you would have been killed on the spot." The comtesse turned a smile on her maid, one that held great fondness. "I had not been so foolish as to emerge from my chamber unarmed. I had a loaded pistol with me—a dueling pistol, which belonged to my husband. With it, I shot Potier dead. That menace would terrorize my city no longer."

CHAPTER 26

The comtesse held us with a long gaze once she'd made her declaration, then she wilted, drawing a shaky breath. Perrault sank beside her worriedly.

Denis was the first to break the silence. "You are very brave, comtesse." He lifted his cup in salute.

"Very foolish." The comtesse laughed, her cheeks pink. "I expected to feel bullets enter my body immediately after that, or blades, or both. The soldiers who'd been behind Potier on the stairs took aim at me, but then, one by one, they lowered their weapons. Without a word, they turned and walked away. They left the house, quit the grounds, and I never saw them again."

"They abandoned him here?" I asked incredulously.

"They did." The comtesse took a tight sip of coffee that Perrault pressed on her. "I hadn't realized how reluctantly the soldiers served him. One of them said something to me before he went, but the pistol shot still rang in my ears, and I have no idea what. But he looked satisfied."

I nodded in understanding. "What did you do then?"

The comtesse sighed. "Perrault took the pistol from me, as I couldn't seem to let it go. Potier didn't die instantly. He raised his head and glared at me and probably cursed me, but I still could hear nothing. We had to wait a few minutes …" Her lips trembled, and she pressed them tightly together.

I held my silence a moment before I made my next observation, giving her time to compose herself. "Michel has been very unfriendly to me, even before I learned anything about Potier."

The comtesse handed her cup back to Perrault. "Michel is very protective of us, and also of the Deveres. They have been good to him."

"You asked them for help with Potier," I said with conviction.

The comtesse nodded. "Perrault suggested it. Michel was just a boy at the time, but he ran errands for the Deveres and did odd jobs in the ironworks. Perrault sent for him. No one noticed a small boy running about, and he used the tunnels to enter the house. I would not let him into the hall where Potier lay, but sent him back with a message. Fernand and Giraud came. They were young men at the time, Giraud just starting his own family. They asked me no questions, only took Potier's body away."

To the ironworks, I assumed, where a body could be burned to ash in one of their great forges.

"Perrault and some of my guards cleaned up the stairs …" The comtesse faltered.

"You must speak no more of it, Madame," Perrault instructed. "Your visitors can depart." She sent a warning glare at the pair of us.

"No, no." The comtesse waved away the shock of years gone by and took the coffee from her maid once more. "Mr. Denis has come all the way from England for a business transaction, and it would be rude to turn him away. I know you will scold Michel for his part in dredging up the past, but what's done is done. Do not be too hard on the boy."

I was not as forgiving as the comtesse, but I realized the futility of showing Michel my disapprobation.

Perrault turned on us. "You will not tell the gendarmes."

Denis lifted his brows. "Tell them what? A tale of a courageous woman defending her home during the war? Besides, where is the evidence of this shooting? The witnesses? It might have been the soldiers themselves who shot Potier, or he could have come to grief entirely by accident. Who is to say?"

The comtesse had refused to desert her city in times of danger, had stood up to defend it, and had won the hearts of her fellow Lyonnais. I, like Denis, could only admire her.

"He has the right of it," I said. "You have nothing to fear from us, Madame. Please stress this to Michel." I rubbed my injured knee, my smile rueful.

"Again, I apologize," the comtesse said quickly, though she regarded us with gratitude. "He was rash to act without ascertaining your purpose."

"It is of no moment." I gave the comtesse a respectful nod and took a sip of the full-bodied coffee. "May I ask, without causing offense—was Signor Gallo blackmailing you over the matter?"

The fact that the comtesse was responsible for Potier's death explained why Gallo had the paper with Potier's name on it hidden with the valuable letter stolen from this household.

I wondered if Signora Ruggeri had seen the uneasiness that mention of Potier's name caused while she pursued the comte's affections, and passed that information to Gallo, along with the stolen missive.

"He was." The comtesse nodded. "I am not certain how much he knew, but Signora Ruggeri even tried to demand some of the payment when I gave her sanctuary, if you please. She said she was afraid of Gallo, and that he'd never share the money with her, so could I simply hand her the payment while she was here? As you English say, *cheek*."

"Did you pay him? Or her?" I asked.

"I did not. It was clear neither of them understood exactly what it was all about, and no one they spoke to of it would tell them. It is an episode in our past that no one in Lyon wishes to discuss with outsiders."

So I had discovered. I also did not recall seeing Comtesse Lejeune's name on the pages of the ledger I'd studied. She had manage to stymy Gallo and Signora Ruggeri, which must have puzzled them.

The Deveres, on the other hand, obviously had worried that Gallo might blab to the wrong person, who might conduct a thorough investigation. I wasn't certain whether the Deveres feared someone uncovering their part in the crime or were only protecting the comtesse.

If the comtesse hadn't been concerned about Gallo's knowledge, then she'd have had no reason to murder him. I comforted myself with this thought, but it still left me with the question of who *had* killed him.

One of the comtesse's retainers? Fearing what Gallo knew? I could easily imagine the fierce Perrault going after him.

However, these were matters I did not wish to pursue at the moment. If one of the comtesse's guards or Perrault had killed Gallo, or asked someone like Michel to do it, then the gendarmes would become involved, and there would be a trial for murder. The comtesse would face scandal, and whoever had killed for her would not escape punishment.

I cleared my throat. "Thank you for telling me, comtesse. I am honored by your confidence, which I will keep. Now, I believe we are here to speak of the sale of the de' Medici letter. I will vouch for Mr. Denis. He pays a fair price and never breaks his word."

———

AN HOUR OR SO LATER, I RODE BACK TO OUR VILLA WITH DENIS IN the lavish coach he'd hired for his sojourn. He'd taken a house nearby and offered to return me on his way.

"Why *did* you come to France?" I was finally able to ask him as we were bumping along the dark road from the comtesse's chateau. "Did you not trust me to negotiate for the letter, or did you have other business in the area?"

"I was too impatient to wait." Denis's gaze moved to our reflections in the dark window as though embarrassed to admit such a thing. "My agent informed me you were making a nuisance of yourself in Lyon, stirring up bad memories. I also feared that someone would steal the letter again. Lejeune appears to be feckless."

"He has not proved to be the wisest man in creation, no," I said. "I have to wonder why the comtesse bothered to marry him."

"I imagine it was a business arrangement between the families. Such marriages often degenerate into a mere understanding, with each party living a separate life."

"Great wisdom from a man who has never married," I remarked in a mild tone.

Denis regarded me with his blank-faced patience. "Many come to me for assistance in acquiring objects or money from a husband or wife, because the other relinquishes nothing. I have seen plenty in this situation, which comes of property owners forcing a bad match, with flawed intentions."

"I see. And those who make love matches never come to grief?"

"Of course they do. Marriage should be entered into carefully or not at all."

I agreed with him, but his cool detachment rankled. "Marriage is a risk, yes, but it can come with great rewards. I now have a beautiful wife of high intelligence, equally beautiful daughters, and a fine stepson."

Denis did not change expression. "If you thoroughly believed that marriage was worth any price, you would not be watching the family your daughter is marrying into so closely. You have now learned that they assisted in covering up a murder, disposing of Potier's body for the comtesse."

"Twenty-five years ago," I pointed out. "In pressing circumstances."

"Yet, they were ruthless enough to do it. They also might have murdered this blackmailer, Gallo."

"I know," I said unhappily. "Though I still contend that if one of the Deveres or Michel had killed Gallo, they would have not done so in such a public place. Or, they'd have had the sense to send the body and weapon into the river."

Denis lifted his shoulders in a faint shrug. "You will not know why it happened in this way until you discover who killed him."

"Do I want to discover the truth?" I asked, half to myself.

"You will not be able to let the thing rest until you do. No matter that it would be far better to leave it alone."

I'd come to accept Denis as a man of honor, even if his honor was not exactly the same as my concept of it. I'd even begun to see him as a friend, of a sort, but that did not mean his criticisms of myself and my character were welcome.

"Have you seen much of Lady in the past months?" I asked with feigned innocuousness, naming a woman Denis had seemed fascinated with when I'd introduced them.

It was too dark to discern his reaction, but Denis's voice turned cool. "I have. I will say no more than that, so do not bother to ask."

I hid a smile, then fell silent for the remainder of the short journey home.

———

THE NEXT DAY DAWNED BRIGHT AND WARM, AUSPICIOUS WEATHER for Gabriella's celebration.

Because we approached the longest day of the year, it was fully light in the very early hour Donata and I and Brewster departed for the village. I'd worried that my wife, unused to rising before one in the afternoon, wouldn't wake in time, but no. Donata had been flitting around the house when I'd dragged myself from bed, and now she beamed at me from the opposite seat in the small carriage.

"Such a lovely morning," she chirped. "Perfect weather for it."

"You are vibrant." I held the strap above the window as the coach wound down the steep hill toward the river. "Especially for so early a start."

"Weddings are exciting." Donata regarded me from under a small-brimmed, feathered hat. "And Gabriella will be settled at last. I was uncertain of Emile at first, but he has proved to be a dear lad."

"Exciting?" I asked doubtfully.

"Of course. I admit, it is easier to be lively when *attending* a wedding. One is spared the dreadful trepidations one has about one's own."

My brows rose. "Did you have dreadful trepidations about ours?"

Donata's smile widened, warming her eyes. "We had a small and intimate ceremony in my mother's garden. Hardly the same thing."

I noticed she did not actually answer the question, but I decided not to pursue it. I'd not experienced any worry at my first wedding. I'd been giddy. I should have let that feeling be a warning.

My wedding to Donata, however, had also seen me in a happy state, so I supposed I simply enjoyed the act of marrying.

We spoke little until the coachman halted in the village near the Auberge's home.

Gabriella and Emile would first attend a civil ceremony in the *mairie*, the town hall, which would legally make them man and wife in the eyes of France. Another statute Bonaparte had put into place.

Carlotta and Auberge had gone with them to this ceremony, along with the Deveres. We were among the throng that filled the square outside the hall, waiting for the couple to emerge.

When they did, we greeted them with cheers. Gabriella beamed a shy smile at the attention, but Emile glanced around with head high, his pride obvious. His face was quite red, as was his cousin Claude's—I imagined the older Claude had lubricated Emile thoroughly the night before.

The other cousin, Camille, walked at Gabriella's side, as though confirming she'd bolster her new cousin-in-law against the mostly male Deveres.

The couple turned and made for the church at the end of the road. The Auberge and Devere families fell in behind them, and Donata and I followed with the crowd, who cheered, waved handkerchiefs, and generally made a ruckus. Villagers left their houses to shout their encouragement or join in the procession.

Donata laughed as we walked along. "Much more enjoyable than my staid entrance to St. George's, Hanover Square."

Indeed, the entire town had turned out to rejoice with the couple.

We reached the church, a medieval pile with massive stained glass windows, which must have stood here for four hundred years at the very least. This was a Catholic church, and I'd been raised to be very dourly Church of England. My father certainly would have disapproved of me entering this building—loudly.

Nothing dire happened as Donata and I passed under the pointed arch of the doorway, its jamb lined with serene angels chasing away frolicking devils.

The church's interior was cool, light flooding through windows of the nave and the clerestory above the main floor. The polished tiles beneath our feet lent more coolness on this warm morning.

In keeping with its ancient lineage, the church had little seating, though enclosed pews of the wealthy stood near the front. Benches had been provided so that the elderly and enfeebled— which I assumed included me—could sit during the ceremony.

Music began to blast as Gabriella and Emile entered, the tall pipes of the organ pumping out mighty strains. I spied the organist, he and the instrument small in a corner, pounding away at the keys.

We shuffled into place, the multitude leaving space for the couple. The altar had been draped in green hangings, which contrasted nicely with the bundles of white flowers placed on shelves around the altar and fastened with green ribbon to the columns of the aisles.

Major Auberge took Gabriella's arm, while Emile disappeared with Claude via a side aisle, presumably to wait for her at the altar.

There had been some debate as to whether Major Auberge or I would escort Gabriella to Emile. I was her true father, I was always quick to point out, but I had to concede that Auberge had raised her, and raised her well.

Carlotta had not wanted me to do anything at all but stand in the back and observe, if that, but Auberge had acknowledged that this would not help relations between us.

Grenville, always an arbiter, had come up with a solution to suit everyone. Auberge would escort Gabriella, but I would follow them and stand with Auberge while he handed her over to Emile.

Grenville himself arrived as we were arranging ourselves, with Marianne on his arm. To my surprise, Colonel Moreau also entered. A few moments after he had nodded at me and drifted toward the left side of the church, Madame Paillard glided in. She adjusted her gloves without meeting anyone's gazes and managed to end up at Moreau's side.

When the organist finished his prelude and started with softer strains, those attending straightened in anticipation. As I took my place behind Auberge and Gabriella, I noted, out of the corner of my eye, Denis slipping in to stand at the very back of the crowd. Brewster followed him, remaining near the church's open doorway.

The priest of this church stepped out before the altar, clad in rich green robes and holding his book of office. Gabriella's two half-sisters, who today were her giggling, excited bridesmaids, led the way, then Auberge and Gabriella surged forward, me behind them.

At the altar steps, Auberge released Gabriella's hand. Emile, his face less vermillion now, reached for it.

Gabriella broke from both of them to slide past Auberge and embrace me in a crush of silk and white ribbons.

"Thank you, Father," she whispered, and kissed my cheek.

My heart swelled as I squeezed her in return, my eyes wet when I released her.

She embraced Auberge as well, then returned to Emile, who sent her a smile of so much love that my eyes stung again.

I barely saw or comprehended the start of the ceremony, and could only stand behind Auberge, hoping I didn't disturb anyone with my sobs.

A warm touch quieted me. Donata had come, sliding her hand through the crook of my arm. I gazed down at her and saw understanding in her eyes, as well as both the pain and happiness that she shared with me.

And so, my daughter was married. The ceremony was long, with a sermon based around the Wedding at Cana, followed by the eucharist. I was happy for Donata to tow me to one of the benches before an hour was out.

I rose again when Emile and Gabriella took their vows and then knelt before a statue of the patron saint of this village.

I watched my daughter cross herself easily, in unison with Emile, but then, she'd been raised in this church. She'd have learned by heart the gestures and responses of the Catholic faith.

I remembered Auberge telling me several years ago that when Gabriella had been a girl, she'd refused to say rosaries, because she'd wanted to worship the "English God" of her mother. Both Carlotta and Gabriella had adapted, it seemed, as Carlotta now crossed herself as well. My father would have had apoplexy, but Gabriella was far beyond his reach.

When the priest gave the final blessing, the watchers again erupted into cheers. Flower tossing and more handkerchief waving accompanied the happy bride and groom out into the summer morning.

The Devere brothers followed the pair, all of them as red-eyed and unsteady as Emile and Claude had been. Auguste, Emile's father, nodded at me, but the others only gave me chilly stares before they marched out.

I slowly exited the church, my heart hammering with many emotions. Donata had faded from me to easily fall into conversation with Madame Paillard, who responded with equal aplomb. Marianne joined them, leaving Grenville to escort me out.

"Cheer up," he advised. "We'll sit through the wedding breakfast and then down plenty of brandy at your villa this afternoon."

I agreed this would be a welcome respite at the end of a strenuous morning.

The procession wound along the road and out of the village, making for the Auberge's farm, where the guests and couple of honor would celebrate. While the Deveres had organized the feast, Carlotta had insisted it not take place in a factory.

We were halfway along this route when Captain Vernet of the gendarmes stepped from the side of the road and halted in front of me. He wore his military uniform, but he was alone, without his sergeant or lieutenant.

"Captain Lacey," he addressed me, without either affability or hostility. "Signora Ruggeri has disappeared, and I have information that it was you who caused this to happen."

CHAPTER 27

I stared at Captain Vernet in bewilderment, barely understanding his words.

"Steady," Grenville said to Vernet. "What do you mean by disappeared, exactly, and who is accusing him?"

"Signora Ruggeri was on her way to visit the captain," Vernet said without tension. "Late last night, Captain Lacey bade her to meet him at the house in the Presqu'île in which she used to reside. The servants confirm she departed her villa, but the house in the city is empty, though we did find signs of a struggle there." He fixed me with a sharp gaze.

"I have been nowhere near that house in the last few days," I said in bewilderment.

"Question her coachman," Grenville told Vernet. "I hear he is a protective brute. Certainly he must know where she alighted. Or has he disappeared too?"

"She did not take her coach," Vernet said. "The housekeeper says she bundled up when she left, and wore boots, as though she meant to tramp about. The coachman was surprised to hear she had gone and is very unhappy. Both he and Comte Lejeune insisted on me arresting you."

I finally cleared my thoughts. "Yesterday evening, I paid a

visit to Comtesse Lejeune at her chateau. I was there until after dark, when I returned to my own house and remained there until this morning. Then, I departed for the village we just left, to attend my daughter's wedding. My wife and servants will attest to that. I never summoned Signora Ruggeri, and this is the first I am learning of the matter."

I thought that would be the end of this strange occurrence, but Vernet produced a folded paper from his pocket.

"Here is your missive, which the housekeeper says arrived around midnight. We found it in her dressing room." He handed it to me, the words on it in English.

I have the Italian letter, the note said, *which I have discovered is worth much. I am happy to give it to you for a small share in the profit from its sale. Let us meet at once, in the house where you resided in the Presqu'île. Gabriel Lacey, Capt.*

I gazed at the paper, dumbfounded. "I never wrote this. The handwriting is far neater than anything I can produce. And why would I offer to give Signora Ruggeri the letter? It belongs in Lejeune's collection."

"And I have purchased it." Denis had approached, his step so quiet I'd not noted him. "The comtesse still has the letter, and I will call on her to retrieve it before I leave Lyon."

He spoke in fluent French, and Vernet's scowl grew fiercer as Denis offered this information.

"Then where did this summons come from?" Vernet demanded, snatching the note back from me. "I know you are a man of your word, Captain, but forgive me if I wish to verify your story before I accept it. *You,* I do not know at all." Vernet turned his glare on Denis.

Denis gave him a frosty nod. "By all means, do question it. Captain Lacey was in my presence last evening, until half past nine, when I left him on the doorstep of his hired home. I know he did not leave it until he set off for the wedding." Brewster would have informed him if I had, or perhaps Denis had put others in place in the house to watch over me.

Vernet tucked the message away. "Whether you sent for her or not, the question remains, what has happened to Signora Ruggeri?"

"She might have fled the city," Denis suggested in his cool tones. "Using the letter as a ruse and deflecting attention to Captain Lacey."

"Because she assisted Gallo in his blackmailing?" Vernet asked. "Yes, I do know about that, Captain, so do not look startled. She and Gallo were fleecing half of Lyon, including Comte Lejeune himself. She could very well have fled, but she left everything she had behind. The coachman, who has served her since she departed England, was left behind as well. He is certain she is in danger."

"Then, we had better find the blasted woman," I said, my temper rising. "Both to assure her safety and to clear my name, if the comte is putting about that I've abducted her. Though why the devil I would is baffling."

"Because you knew of her past and threatened to expose her," Vernet said without much conviction. "She told the comte she feared you."

"It is hardly logical she would answer a summons from Lacey if she was afraid of him, then," Grenville pointed out. "The man spoke to her only once that I know of."

At Marianne's soiree. I'd told Signora Ruggeri that I and my friends knew who she really was, and she'd seemed resigned to that fact. But a good confidence trickster could spin the encounter into a threat to her person if she thought it would help her along.

"I am growing worried about her now," I said. "I hope she ran off to seek another target in another city—another country if she is wise—but we'd better make certain she is well."

Grenville's hand landed on my shoulder. "*You* will not. You will go to Gabriella's wedding breakfast and toast her until you cannot stand. I will go with Vernet and try to clear your name.

I'm certain Mr. Denis has people he can pry from their beds to assist."

"And I," another voice said as Denis gave Grenville a frigid nod.

Moreau had appeared from the crowd to regard Vernet impassively. "I know Lyon," he said. "I can aid in the search."

I was pleased he was willing to help, though I knew that hunting for Signora Ruggeri might also bring Moreau to Madame Paillard's missing letter.

Vernet eyed me severely. "I was instructed to arrest you, Captain. But ..." He spread his hands in resignation. "I must live in this city, among its people. If it became known I removed you from your daughter's wedding, and that daughter has just married a Devere ..."

"Lyon would become too hot to hold you." Fernand Devere had appeared at Vernet's shoulder. "We will watch over Captain Lacey. If he proves to be a mad abductor, we will bring him to you, tied up and ready to surrender."

"I am obliged to you, Fernand," I said dryly. "Take Brewster with you," I told Grenville. "He is excellent at searching. I will join you later."

I truly was anxious for Signora Ruggeri's safety, and indignant that whoever had taken her had decided to blame me. Any other day, I'd insist on rushing off with Vernet, but not this morning.

Today, I wanted to be in Gabriella's presence, to watch my beloved daughter blossom into the woman she was meant to be. I'd too soon have to leave her behind.

I stepped around Vernet, waved a vague salute to the others, and followed Fernand down the village street toward the Auberge farm, where we would celebrate the joining of our families.

———

For a time, I did rejoice. The wedding party had gained the farmhouse as I'd argued with Vernet, where the breakfast had been set up in the garden on this fine day.

Brewster had gone to join Vernet, Grenville, Denis, and Moreau. Before Brewster departed, Gabriella had bestowed a blossom from her bouquet on him. He'd thanked her and tucked it into a buttonhole, his eyes becoming suspiciously moist.

Gabriella now fluttered through the garden like a butterfly, the ribbons on her gown she'd so painstakingly searched the markets for fluttering. She had time for everyone—her half-brothers and half-sisters, her mother and Major Auberge, and all the guests, especially Donata and Marianne, the Devere family, and me.

"I am so very glad I found you again, Father," Gabriella gushed as she took a vacated chair next to me as the feasting wound down. We'd been served a lavish Lyonnais breakfast with plenty of meat and sausage, and wine to wash it all down. "I had both fathers I love at my wedding. I have the best fortune in the world."

She was giddy with joy, her happiness overflowing.

"My fortune is doubly great." I pulled Gabriella into my arms, wishing I could hold her forever. "Thank you for allowing me into your life."

"I would rather have *more* family than less." Gabriella broke the embrace, smiling at me. "An abundance of affection. Is that not better?"

"I suppose it is." I prayed life would not bring her too many disappointments, too many tragedies. I preferred her to believe in the goodness of the world, not its darkness. The opposite of my own path, in fact.

But my path had widened these days, with many forks of possibilities.

When the couple took their leave to walk to their new home, Donata accompanied them, as did the female Deveres, Marianne, and Madame Paillard, who seemed to have struck up a friendship with Donata.

Carlotta declared she'd stay home, as there was so much to do once all the guests departed. I suspected she did not wish to be in Donata's presence any longer than needed.

Gabriella's sisters generously assured their mother they'd remain to help her. They hurried into the house while Carlotta lingered at the garden's gate, shading her eyes to watch Gabriella depart.

"She will never be far," I said, stepping next to her.

Carlotta swung to me, her eyes red-rimmed. "No, she will not. She will never live in England with you."

"I know," I said calmly. Carlotta's anger at me no longer found an answer in mine. "She belongs here. You and Auberge raised a fine young woman."

Carlotta started, as though surprised I'd express such a sentiment. "We did." She eyed me narrowly. "If you expect me to apologize for deserting you all those years ago, I never will. I am not sorry I did so. I traded misery for a chance at peace."

"I was a rotten husband, it is true." I gazed after Gabriella, her step exuberant, as she, surrounded by ladies, disappeared around a bend in the road. "I have learned much since then. I am likely still a poor husband, but my new wife does not care."

"And I should not have cared?" Carlotta demanded.

"You deserved better, and that is what you found. I am glad now, and I'm pleased I can be glad." As Carlotta stared at me, I dared touch her cheek. "*Au revoir,* Carlotta."

Carlotta swallowed, the pretty young woman I'd once fallen for showing briefly in her eyes. "Goodbye, Gabriel."

I nodded at her and turned away, taking my leave and putting the past firmly where it was meant to stay.

———

Denis's hired coach waited at the end of the lane from the Auberge farm. Denis had sent it back for me, the coachman relayed, before he assisted me inside. I told the him where I wished to begin the search and rode back to Lyon in comfort that only Denis could procure.

The coachman let me off before tall gates to the villa that the comte had lent to Signora Ruggeri. It lay on a road that wound northwest of Lyon, in a pretty grove of trees heavy with the green of summer. I'd decided to trace Signora Ruggeri's steps from where she'd last been seen.

When I entered the house, which was a smaller version of the villa Donata had hired, I found Colonel Moreau arguing with the housekeeper.

No one but Moreau was there, and I assumed Brewster had accompanied Denis and Grenville wherever they'd gone. Brewster would be more interested in protecting those two than Moreau, a man he still thought me mad for trusting.

The agitated footman who'd admitted me into the house faded from sight, as though unwilling to join the confrontation.

The housekeeper, a round-bodied woman with gray hair and a soft face, had a stentorian voice that did not go with her appearance. She snapped at Moreau that she had no idea where the signora kept her precious papers.

"That woman was nothing but trouble," she finished. "I hope I never see her again."

"I beg your pardon," I said in French. "Can I help?"

The housekeeper swung around with a start.

Moreau straightened from where he'd leaned to interrogate the woman and regarded me awkwardly. He was clearly hunting for the cache of Gallo's papers, but he must have antagonized the housekeeper instead of gaining her trust.

"Will you allow us a look into her chambers?" I asked the housekeeper, at my most deferential. "She might have left some sign of where she's gone."

"I hope she's cleared off for good," the housekeeper declared. "But yes, search, by all means. If she doesn't come back, I intend to give all her things to the police or the Hôtel Dieu."

Whether the hospital would want Signora Ruggeri's ostentatious clothing was debatable, but I supposed they could sell the gowns for the money places that tended the sick always needed.

This villa was not a large one, but I saw as we followed the housekeeper's directions to Signora Ruggeri's private rooms, it was luxurious. If the bishop who'd lived here had seen to its decor, he had fine taste. The paintings we passed were of secular themes—landscapes and still lifes, not a religious scene in sight. Either the bishop didn't care to be reminded of his profession while at home, or Signora Ruggeri had asked for any religious art to be removed.

Signora Ruggeri's chambers on the light-filled first floor consisted of a large sitting room opening to an equally large dressing room, with a bedroom behind that. A wealth of windows gave a view to the well-tended garden whose flowers bloomed red, gold, and blue in the June sunshine.

Moreau and I, without speaking, began our hunt. I'd come to search for the woman, not whatever she'd hid for Gallo, but I had the feeling that if we found the papers, they would point the way to Signora Ruggeri.

We worked through every table, every cupboard, every niche. We pulled out the drawers from the bureau and writing table and turned them over to see whether anything was hidden on the underside. As I had in Gallo's rooms in La Guillotière, I slid beneath the bed to discover whether anything had been tucked under the mattress.

Moreau, having learned well from Brewster, began to tap the paneling and then to examine the bricks in the fireplace. We took our time to go over every inch of the room, but turned up nothing.

Plenty of Signora Ruggeri's own belongings were still here—gowns, shoes, gloves, hats, ribbons, nightgowns, and slippers—but no papers or books of any kind. The writing table had a few sheets of unused foolscap and a bottle of ink that looked as though it never been opened. Signora Ruggeri wrote to no one, it seemed, but perhaps she'd learned that this was safer.

The fact that her clothes were still here did not make me easy about her fate. Confidence tricksters did sometimes flee in the night with what little they could carry, but still I felt more than a little concern.

"She might have hidden the papers elsewhere in the house," Moreau suggested when we met in the middle of the sitting room, both of us dusty. "As she did when she lived in the Presqu'île."

"I think it unlikely in this one," I answered. "I imagine the housekeeper here kept a sharp eye on Signora Ruggeri whenever she wasn't in her own chamber." I guessed that the housekeeper had worked for the bishop—her resentment of Signora Ruggeri was sharp. "Housekeepers are aware of everything. If Signora Ruggeri had hidden the things in other rooms, she'd be certain to find them. My wife employs a butler rather than a housekeeper at our London abode, but the man can put his finger on anything in the house whenever he wishes, even when I don't realize I need the item in question." Indeed, I was often amazed at Barnstable's percipience.

"True, my own housekeeper knows when I've not eaten or when I've stayed all night with Madame Paillard. *Her* servants don't look after me as well, she claims."

I smiled with him, but my amusement was short-lived. "Coachmen, too, are aware of their employer's comings and goings," I said, as ideas began to churn in my head. "Signora Ruggeri's seems loyal to her. Perhaps she gave him the papers to protect."

"We must ask him," Moreau said with animation.

I agreed, and we went in search of the housekeeper.

"He's gone off," she told us when I inquired if we could speak to the coachman. "He commandeered the bishop's coach when the signora moved in, and now he's left in it to search for her."

"Is he an Englishman?" I asked, wondering if he'd served Signora Ruggeri when she was Imogene Cooke.

"No," the housekeeper answered in puzzlement. "Why should he be? He's from Calais." Her voice held a sneer for those from the far north.

Perhaps hired when Signora Ruggeri first landed in France, which meant he'd have taken her all the way to Padua and then here to Lyon. I recalled him applying the whip without remorse to those who tried to hinder her carriage in the plaza. I could imagine him murdering Gallo to protect her, though he looked a strong enough brute to then heave Gallo's body from the bridge.

How far had Signora Ruggeri trusted him?

"May we see his chamber?" I asked the housekeeper.

She eyed me dubiously. "Why? What's he done?"

"Possibly nothing, Madame," I said. "But again, we might find some sign of where the signora has gone."

"There was nothing untoward between them," the housekeeper said, as though disapproving of my conjectures. "She employed him, and that it all. I'd have known if there were goings-on in the coach house."

About which she'd have quickly told the comte, I had no doubt. Anything to have Signora Ruggeri dismissed.

"Even so, he might have kept her letters or some such."

"Not without my knowing," the housekeeper assured me. "But search if you must."

She called a footman to take us from the villa to the coach house across the yard, which he did with quick deference.

The bishop's own coachman had departed with him, one of the grooms told us when we reached the coach house. He hadn't wanted to stay and drive a tart about.

No carriage occupied the space behind the wide doors, and only one horse remained in the stable, pulling at hay in a desultory way.

The grooms and coachman had quarters above, one open room for the grooms and a small, cramped chamber for the coachman.

"Never said much, the signora's coachman," the groom who guided us up the stairs told us. "A ruffian, he is. He's gentle with the beasts, though. Likes them more than people, I think."

I experienced a sudden dart of sympathy for the coachman. I sometimes felt the same.

The groom shrugged when we said we'd look over the coachman's chamber and left us to it.

The room was tiny and sparse, and we found nothing hidden

in it. The man's change of clothing and a brushed coachman's hat remained, as though he meant to return.

"He could have taken the papers with him when he went out," Moreau suggested as we descended.

I thought it unlikely, but did ask the groom if the coachman had packed a box or valise into the coach before he went.

"None that I saw," the groom said. "I hitched up for him in the yard when he called down for the coach to be made ready. He came barreling down the stairs, climbed straight up to the seat, and off he went. I didn't notice him carrying nothing."

We thanked the groom and departed.

"I think the coachman is genuinely concerned for Signora Ruggeri's safety," I said as we settled into Denis's carriage. "As am I. I hope the others have found her, by now."

"They were heading to the Croix-Rousse when I left them," Moreau said. "Captain Vernet wished to speak to the actors she'd met through your friend Mr. Grenville. She might have gone to them for help, he said."

"And you came here to search for the papers."

"I thought I'd better," Moreau said uncomfortably. "Vernet is being thorough."

I nodded my understanding and bade Denis's coachman to take us back into Lyon.

"Where do you suggest we go now?" Moreau asked as we bumped along the road.

"I am returning to my reflection on housekeepers. They do know everything, as this one did. She was certain the coachman and Signora Ruggeri were *not* having a romantic liaison, and I believe her. Housekeepers know much," I concluded softly. "And they keep the secrets of their employers well."

"Not always," Moreau said. "Servants spread the word faster through this city than the local post."

"The housekeeper here does not hide that she despises Signora Ruggeri," I mused. "Madame Martin, the woman who tends the house in the Presqu'île, was carefully neutral—she must see plenty of tenants come and go. Gallo's landlady—what was her name?"

"Jourdain," Moreau supplied. "She was quite belligerent."

"You bypassed her and picked the lock on Gallo's rooms, did you not?"

Moreau nodded, only slightly ashamed. "She refused to let me in the first time I called. So I lingered until her attention was elsewhere."

"If there *had* been something in Gallo's rooms, I wager Madame Jourdain would have known about it."

"That is possible. However, she did not find the Italian letter or Potier's name."

"Those were very well hidden, but even if she had found them, they'd likely mean nothing to her. She wouldn't have been able to read the letter in its archaic Italian, and if she was not born in Lyon, Potier's name might not have alarmed her either."

"Reasonable," Moreau grunted.

"But suppose Madame Jourdain *can* read in French, or at least she realized that the papers Gallo had collected were valuable. The police would not have searched her chambers, if she even lives in."

"Signora Ruggeri told you she had the letters at her townhouse," Moreau pointed out. "And that they vanished from there."

"I am keeping in mind that Signora Ruggeri lies to make her living. She might have told me the truth, yes. But perhaps she invented the tale to put me off, and the papers never left Gallo's lodgings."

Moreau's brows rose. "Then we return to La Guillotière?"

"I think we should, though it is only one possibility." I tried to make myself think through the problem rationally, but my thoughts continued to tangle up in themselves. "Signora Ruggeri still might have taken them to the townhouse, as she claimed. Madame Martin, another housekeeper who likely knows everything that happens in her abode, might have found them there."

"Signora Ruggeri would not have easily relinquished the papers even if Madame Martin had come upon them," Moreau said with growing impatience. "Besides, we searched that house. Your man, the former thief, searched. We found only the ledger with the names, which had been very well hidden."

"We searched the *house*. Not the housekeeper. Suppose Signora Ruggeri brought Madame Martin into the ring? Needing an accomplice to keep safe the secrets, because Signora Ruggeri was closely watched and plagued by the citizens of Lyon. Perhaps the papers did vanish, but they were taken by Madame Martin, not Gallo."

"That is a grand speculation," Moreau said dubiously.

"I know, but I prefer it to believing Signora Ruggeri sent the letters far out of our reach. If Signora Ruggeri had destroyed the papers, she would have told me, instead of foisting me off with the tale of their disappearance. Plus, we would have found evidence of their destruction. As would the housekeepers."

Moreau went silent, fixing his attention on a point on the carriage wall, similarly to what he'd done in Gallo's rooms, as he thought through what I'd argued. I'd seen the same look when he'd stood over my supine body in Spain, pondering what to do with me.

"*Bien,*" he said after a time. "Let us go speak to Madame Martin at the townhouse."

I TAPPED ON THE ROOF AND DIRECTED THE COACHMAN TO THE house near the plaza in the Presqu'île.

Clouds had begun to gather as we'd searched the villa, and by the time we reached the river, a dark bank of them hovered to the south and east.

Moreau was silent as we crossed the Pont Tilsit and wound

through the city's narrow streets. He was not convinced, as I was growing to be, that Madame Martin or Madame Jourdain had anything to do with the papers.

But I could not believe that either of those ladies had remained ignorant of Gallo's schemes and Signora Ruggeri's part in them. If one of the housekeepers hadn't absconded with the letters themselves, they might very well know what Signora Ruggeri—or Gallo, if he'd stolen them before he'd died—had done with them.

The coachman let us off at the mouth of the lane that led to the townhouse, the coach unable to fit into the narrow artery. We walked from there, the air heavy with the coming storm.

The door to the townhouse stood ajar. Both Moreau and I, with the caution of battle-hardened experience, paused on its doorstep, peering carefully inside.

All was silent. I glimpsed no one flitting through the house and heard nothing.

I pushed open the door with my walking stick, and we very quietly entered.

The house felt empty, stale. The previous night's coolness hadn't permeated it, indicating that all windows were shut, leaving the place stuffy from yesterday afternoon's heat.

Moreau and I proceeded warily, pausing before any open door to scan the chamber within. Drapes were drawn in every ground-floor room or shutters were closed, and no one appeared.

Not until we entered the petite dining room on the first floor did we find signs of the struggle that Captain Vernet had reported.

The carpet was littered with broken glass where a decanter and goblets had fallen from the sideboard. The small, square dining table was askew and its chairs lay on their sides. A silver candelabra sprawled among the debris, a pale cascade of dried candle wax frozen over the chair backs and carpet. A square, muddy boot print, from what a coachman might wear, was evident in the middle of the mess.

My own boot, about the same size, crunched on glass, and a sharp odor of brandy wafted to me as I surveyed the scene.

That someone had fought here was evident, even before I lifted a shard of glass to find it stained with blood.

"This way, I think." Moreau had moved to a panel in the walls that didn't quite fit with the others.

This was a door to the servants' passageways, now unlatched. A small smear of blood stained the molding near it, as though someone had clutched the wall to prevent themselves being pulled or pushed through the opening.

Vernet might have missed it, or perhaps he'd explored and found nothing. He had a note purporting to be from me and a large boot print, which had been enough for him to hurry to waylay me after my daughter's wedding.

Moreau took up a candle that hadn't been crushed or melted and struck a spark to light it. He pulled open the paneling and thrust the candle inside, its flame a small point in the darkness.

We found rough stone walls and a narrow corridor that bent around a corner to descending stairs. These would lead to the ground floor and the kitchen in the rear of the house.

Another bloodstain smeared the wall of the stairwell. I imagined the episode—one person overpowering the other, then dragging her through the servants' passageway and down the stairs to exit without being seen from the street.

We found no remains of candles as we went, nor at the bottom of the staircase, where a door led to a tiny courtyard. Whoever had used the route was so used to it they could navigate it without light.

Had Signora Ruggeri been forced down these stairs? Or had she been the one doing the forcing?

The door was unlatched, the house open for anyone to enter. Moreau pinched out his candle and laid it on a table beside the door before we stepped into the courtyard.

Mud prevailed here, along with broken bottles and boards had been shoved into one corner of the enclosing walls. A gate opposite the door led to a narrow passageway between houses, likely one for the night soil men to use.

A small, thin boy, accompanied by an equally small and thin dog, gaped at us as Moreau and I popped out of the gate. The dog gave a high-pitched yip, but the boy stared mutely, poised to run.

"*Bonjour,*" I said to the lad as cordially as I could. "Do you come down this way often?"

The boy stared at me uncomprehendingly. Moreau, with startling gentleness, went down on one knee and began speaking to him in the city's dialect.

He must have mentioned the dog, because the boy abruptly looked proud and patted his companion. The dog, pleased to be among friends, wagged its tail hard enough to wobble its hindquarters.

Moreau continued the conversation, and the boy answered him readily, though he darted suspicious glances at me.

When the discussion concluded, Moreau handed the lad a coin. The boy grinned as he took it, then he raced back along the passageway, his step light, the dog scampering behind him.

Not until we'd exited the alley to the main street, did Moreau enlighten me.

"He saw Madame Martin come out of the back gate early this morning," Moreau informed me in English. "She was with another woman, who had dark hair and a fine coat. He believed the second woman to be the comte's ladybird, but he hadn't seen her here in a while and couldn't be certain."

"Were they walking calmly or fleeing?" I asked.

"He said Madame Martin was very angry, and the other woman was weeping. Madame Martin dragged the woman along the passageway and out of sight. It was still dark, and he did not see which direction they went."

I stood indecisively on the cobbles, which had warmed on

this summer day, despite the building clouds. The house we'd departed stood calmly behind us, with no sign of the altercation within.

"I will put forth a guess where they've gone," I said. "If I am wrong, we might be too late to save Signora Ruggeri's life."

"We must act in some way," Moreau said. "Shall we fetch the gendarmes?"

"We will help the signora, retrieve your letter, and *then* fetch the gendarmes."

Moreau gave me a nod. "Then lead on. Where to?"

"La Guillotière," I said grimly.

CHAPTER 29

We made for the other side of the city's island in Denis's coach and over the stone bridge to the east bank of the Rhône.

The clouds had coalesced into a solid, dark mass. Lightning flickered within, and I was happy that Gabriella's wedding and party had occurred early in the day. All should be home and snug by the time the storm hit.

No one in La Guillotière seemed to be bothered by the shift in weather. They lingered in the streets and on the bridge or wandered the river's edge. A sharp breeze blew from the clouds, welcome coolness.

Denis's coachman let us off at the end of the bridge, and we again navigated the streets too narrow for the conveyance on foot. Without discussion, we made for the dilapidated boarding house that had lodged Vincenzo Gallo.

As at Madame Martin's, we found the front door open and the place deserted.

We were about to ascend to the rooms above when I heard a faint moan. Moreau heard it too, both of us halting warily.

"Là!" Moreau pointed down the dim corridor behind the stairs.

I headed that way, keeping my footsteps as silent as possible, Moreau following quietly.

Behind a door at the very end of the hall came another groan and then a sigh, as though the person beyond had resigned themselves to their fate.

Finding the door unlocked, I carefully swung it open.

A woman huddled on the bare floor within. Shelves lined the walls around her, filled with foodstuffs, crockery both whole and broken, and piles of cloth that looked fit only for the rag-and-bone man.

The woman did not move when I entered the room, too lost in her own pain. In the little light that came through the doorway, I saw a darker stain on the back of her sand-colored gown.

I limped forward, still guarded. I'd watched a soldier bend over a seemingly wounded compatriot on the battlefield—either to help him or rob him, I was never certain—and the blood-covered man leap up and cut down the other soldier. I hadn't been able to reach the first man before he'd died, but I'd shot his murderer with my carbine.

"Madame?" I touched the woman's shoulder and gently turned her over.

It was Madame Martin. She breathed shallowly, more blood staining her neck.

"Madame, what has happened?"

Madame Martin blinked, frowning as though trying to place me. "She cut me." The words came in a cracked whisper.

"Signora Ruggeri did this?"

"No." Madame Martin took a long breath. "She is mad. She took her. Killed me so she wouldn't have to share the money. Contemptible bitch."

"Tell me who, Madame."

Madame Martin's eyes slid closed. *"Ma sœur."*

"Your sister?" I asked in surprise. "Who is—?"

Madame Martin did not answer, her pain rendering her insensible.

"Is she dead?" Moreau asked, his worry tinged with compassion.

I straightened. "No, but she needs a surgeon."

I seized a few of the cleaner rags from the shelves and pressed them to the cut in her neck. The gash hadn't severed the vessel that would have gushed her life's blood from her, but she'd die without help.

Both of us feared to move her, in case we made the wounds worse, but we found blankets and pillows in other rooms and tucked them around her, rendering her as warm and comfortable as we could.

"We will bring help, Madame," I assured her, though I was uncertain she heard me.

Moreau and I headed out of the house. I scanned the street for a patroller of some kind, but I saw no one. We'd have to cross the bridge again, to alert the gendarmes and find help for Madame Martin.

The first drops of heavy rain began to fall by the time we reached the bridge. I saw, to my dismay, that Denis's coachman and carriage were nowhere in sight.

"Bloody hell," I said, not bothering with French. "I suppose he went to wait out the storm."

"Go back and stay with Madame Martin," Moreau said. "I can reach the gendarmes more quickly."

I saw the sense in this and nodded to him. The cool humidity of the coming storm made my injured knee stiffer, and I'd be slow.

As we turned to take our separate routes, a shriek of terror rose from beneath the bridge.

"Captain! Help me!"

The English words held the unmistakable accent of Manchester. Signora Ruggeri's second cry cut off abruptly, then came splashing.

Moreau and I hastened to the edge of the bridge and peered down the bank to the Rhône. The river was even more swollen today, with more rains in the mountains filling the riverbed. Heavy drops now pattered on the water, quickly wetting the light summer coat I'd donned for the wedding and Moreau's more sturdy jacket.

A small boat rocked on the river's waves below us, the struggles of the two inside making it pitch and roll.

One figure was Signora Ruggeri. Her hair had come down, curtaining her face while she fought with the more robust woman.

Ma sœur, Madame Martin had said.

Her sister, the caretaker of Gallo's rooms, Madame Jourdain.

I'd thought Madame Martin was familiar when I'd first met her, but I simply assumed I'd seen her about in Lyon. I hadn't made the connection with Madame Jourdain, whose face under grizzled hair had been marred by her persistent scowl.

If Madame Jourdain had realized that Gallo was blackmailing the wealthy and prominent of Lyon, she could have contacted her sister, Madame Martin, in the Presqu'île for help. Perhaps she bade Madame Martine suggest to the comte that the townhouse would be a perfect place in which to hide his ladybird. With their eyes on both Gallo and Signora Ruggeri, the two sisters could scheme get their hands on the blackmail money.

Signora Ruggeri had soon begged the comte to give her another home. Because the townhouse was not up to her standards, the world thought. But perhaps Signora Ruggeri realized the danger that both housekeepers posed for her.

Signora Ruggeri had told me at Marianne's soiree that she feared for her life. She'd related this with a melodramatic quaver, so I had not quite believed her, but perhaps she'd been telling the truth.

Her fears were proving true. Madame Jourdain was now doing her best to subdue Signora Ruggeri in a boat on the wild river.

Without a word, Moreau started down the bank. I followed,

shoving my walking stick hard into the slippery earth to keep myself upright.

The bridge towered beside us as I half-slid, half scrambled toward the river. This bridge, whose massive arches spanned the great Rhône, had been built and rebuilt for the last thousand years. Floods had regularly torn it down, but the citizens of Lyon had doggedly replaced it each time. Now it stood solidly, the river forming rapids around its foundations.

The water was high—no cargo ship could have fit beneath the bridge today. The tiny boat Madame Jourdain had commandeered would skim nicely downriver, however. That is, if it didn't overturn and drown both women.

Moreau reached the boat before I did. Signora Ruggeri cried out to him, begging for help.

Madame Jourdain turned a pistol on him.

Moreau backed away, water splashing to his knees, and Madame Jourdain fired.

The fuse of the ancient gun sputtered feebly, and then rain drowned the spark before it could ignite the powder.

Madame Jourdain cursed and flung the pistol into the boat. Signora Ruggeri lunged for it, but I could tell her it would only be useful as a club in this downpour.

Moreau and I rushed the boat, he reaching to seize Madame Jourdain.

I shouted a warning before Madame Jourdain sank her knife into Moreau's arm. He hung on to her, blood running from his sleeve to spatter into the water.

Madame Jourdain fought him, clawing and stabbing, and managed to loosen Moreau's hold.

She leapt from the boat, landing up to her waist in rushing water, but she came on at us, brandishing the knife.

She slipped, fell, and went under.

I plunged my hands into the water where Madame Jourdain had gone down, finding nothing but emptiness. I groped, teetering dangerously myself, sweeping my walking stick through the current to find her. She'd drown in moments, and while I was not fond of the woman, I could not simply dust off my hands and let her die.

Moreau called out. From a few yards downstream, he hauled Madame Jourdain from the water, where she hung from his grip like a waterlogged rat.

Moreau dragged her toward the bank. I waded to them and caught the woman under one of her arms, helping Moreau pull her out of the river. Madame Jourdain hung limply, the knife no longer in her hand.

We dropped her on the bank, where she coughed, still alive. I left her to Moreau while I turned back to pull Signora Ruggeri to safety.

Signora Ruggeri screamed as a wave caught the boat and sent it spinning toward the middle of the river. At the same time, the clouds belched forth torrents of rain, and lightning whitened the sky.

I flung aside my hat, jammed my walking stick into the mud, and dove for the boat, blessing my misspent youth sailing anything navigable in Norfolk. The middle of a tumultuous river during a storm wasn't the same as punting in the Broads, however, and I was no longer a youth.

I stroked for the boat and seized its gunwale before it could careen too far. Signora Ruggeri wept, begging me to take her to shore.

I could stand on my feet in this depth, the water to my chest. It was cold—the river's source was the Alps—though not the deadly cold the water might have in winter.

I gripped the boat's side, but the river fought to wrench it from me. The craft rocked and bucked, tearing my gloves as I tried to keep my hold.

I'd need to climb inside and row, but getting the boat to stay still long enough to heave myself into it was the trouble.

The hand Signora Ruggeri extended to me bounced in and out of reach. I kept dragging the craft forward, trying to reach shallow enough water where Signora Ruggeri and I both could climb to shore.

Moreau had pulled Madame Jourdain higher onto the bank, where she lay prone, hands outstretched in fists. Whether she still lived or not I'd have to worry about later.

No one rushed from above to help us. The storm had finally driven residents indoors, and the sheets of rain, steaming when they hit the cold river, would hide us from any still on the street.

Moreau left Madame Jourdain and splashed out toward the boat, whatever cuts he'd sustained not slowing him. He grabbed at the boat just as the gunwale jerked itself from my hands. Moreau caught the prow and hung on, and I was finally able to claw my way up onto the boat's side.

I'd hoped for a coil of rope with which we could tow the craft to shore, but only a shred of whatever had tied it up in the first place remained. Madame Jourdain must have cut the rope and left it at the pier, in too much of a hurry to haul it in and stow it.

There was one oar and a small tiller. This boat was meant to take a person from one side of the river to the other on a calm day, not fight the overwrought current on a stormy one.

"Hold that," I bellowed at Signora Ruggeri, pointing at the tiller.

She obeyed, climbing the short distance to the stern, her cheeks streaked with rain and tears.

I heaved myself the rest of the way into the craft and took up the oar. With that and Moreau pulling the prow, we managed to take ourselves a bit closer to shore.

Streaks of lightning threaded the sky, bathing us in bright white light. The crack of thunder that followed immediately was deafening.

Signora Ruggeri wailed in fear, but she never let go of the tiller. Inch by inch, we moved toward the bank. I prayed that we could get ourselves out and under shelter before we were all struck by lightning.

A sharp gust lifted the boat, nearly tearing the oar from my hands. At the same time Moreau slipped, and the prow struck him squarely in the face.

His arms went up, and he went down.

"Moreau!" I yelled.

The river swirled where he had been, white foam bubbling in the rain.

"Where is he?" Signora Ruggeri shrieked.

She tried to lean to find him, but I pushed her back down. "Steady it," I commanded.

She wept, but obeyed. She gazed fearfully into the water, hands locked on the rocking tiller.

I reached over the gunwale as far as I dared, breaking the waves with my hands. I shouted, not for Moreau, but for anyone on the bank to help us.

My heart banged in relief when Moreau surfaced about ten feet from me. He tried to gain his footing but was losing the fight with the current.

I desperately rowed toward him. The river pushed us sideways. Signora Ruggeri resolutely held on to the tiller, gaining my respect for her resilience.

Moreau started to go down again. I thrust the oar at him, and he lunged for it, but his hands slid away.

I dropped the oar behind me, braced my feet on the bottom of the boat, and thrust my arms deep into the water. Rain pelted me, soaking my hair and running inside my coat.

I found the thick material of Moreau's jacket, with a warm, living body inside it. I hoisted him upward with all my strength. Signora Ruggeri counterbalanced with her weight and the tiller, keeping us from going over.

Moreau broke the surface, water pouring from his mouth.

The face he turned up to me held not fear, but shock. He'd

expected me to let him drown, perhaps assisting the river in taking him.

I hauled Moreau into the boat, he landing in a wet heap on top of me. He coughed and gasped, while I struggled out from under him and took up the oar.

"Don't you die on me," I snarled at him. "I will *not* live with the guilt of killing the man who once left me for dead. And I *truly* do not want to face Madame Paillard with the news."

Moreau grunted a laugh, then coughed again, spilling foul river water onto the boards.

With our combined weight, the boat sagged lower in the water but was steadier. I rowed as hard as I could, nearly weeping in relief when the boat finally wedged in the shallows of the bank.

I reached for Signora Ruggeri and half lifted, half tossed her over the side, where she landed knee-deep in the river. She wasted no time struggling up onto the muddy shore, then waited as I got Moreau out of the boat.

I wrapped his arm around my shoulders, taking his weight as we climbed to safety. Moreau lost his footing more than once, but we managed to stumble up the bank.

Another bolt of lightning struck, dancing on the top of the bridge.

Signora Ruggeri scurried to us, looped her arm around Moreau's other side, and helped us escape the pull of the river. At the top of the bank, she sagged, but I shouted at her not to stop.

"We need to get under something."

Signora Ruggeri nodded, her eyes fixed in panic.

Above us, Madame Jourdain had managed to gain her feet. She staggered toward the road above, but I let her go. I'd save ourselves first, worry about Madame Jourdain later.

The three of us half hobbled, half ran toward the bridge, ducking into its shadow just as another bolt struck not far from where we'd come ashore. Signora Ruggeri yelped and flung herself to the damp earth.

"I want to go home," she screeched, no longer bothering with French. "I never want to see this bloody country again!"

I barked a laugh as Moreau and I fell beside her, Moreau still coughing.

"I do not disagree," I told her over the rampaging storm. "Where did you learn to handle a boat so well?"

Madame Ruggeri, who at the moment resembled nothing of the Paduan siren she pretended to be, gave me a shrug.

"Me dad ran boats from Manchester to Liverpool. I was on the tiller since I were a wee lass, weren't I?"

"Thank God for that," I said fervently.

Moreau coughed. "I owe you a debt, Madame."

Signora Ruggeri—now plain Imogen Cooke—shrugged again, hugged her knees to her chest, and buried her face in her sodden skirts. She heaved with sobs, but I was too exhausted to comfort her, Moreau, or myself.

Another scream startled us. I crawled to the north edge of our hiding place and scanned the road above the bridge.

I saw Madame Jourdain, moving at a limping run. The coach Denis had hired closed in on her, and from it stepped Captain Vernet. His men came behind on foot, surrounding the woman, who began to fight.

Another coach halted near the first, Signora Ruggeri's ruffian coachman leaping from its box. He caught Madame Jourdain and shook her until the woman ceased her failing.

I dropped back to the stones of the bridge's base. "They've snared our bird. Did *she* murder Gallo? Or was it Madame Martin?"

Signora Ruggeri regarded me limply. "It was Jourdain, the old besom. She boasted that to me, today, when Madame Martin dragged me to her. Madame Jourdain turned on her own sister, can you credit it? And then she tried to do me over when I wouldn't tell her where I'd hidden Vincenzo's papers."

"Where are they?" I asked her tiredly. "You won't be able to use them now."

"Safe." Her lips tightened. "I'll give them to you, don't worry, if you promise to burn the lot of them."

I exchanged a glance with Moreau. "We will," I said.

Thunder rumbled once more, but more distantly, no longer over our heads. I climbed wearily to my feet.

"Well, *mes amis*," I said. "Shall we retreat somewhere drier before we catch our deaths?"

I held out my hand to Signora Ruggeri, who let me lift and steady her. I extended the other to Moreau, who grasped it firmly as he rose.

He gave me a nod, and we limped back into the open. The rain slackened as abruptly as it had started as we emerged from under the bridge.

I saw, standing upright in the riverbed, its goose-head handle breaking the river's waves, my walking stick, the one Donata had given me several years ago. I'd realized, shortly before then, that I loved her.

I burst into laughter and caught it up.

I leaned heavily on the walking stick—the old friend that had been my prop for years—and hobbled with my new friends up the remainder of the bank.

We reached the top and surrendered to the ministrations of the gendarmes who'd run to meet us. The coachman dropped Madame Jourdain unceremoniously and turned to Signora Ruggeri, his craggy face softening in relief. He had his own coat off and wrapped around Signora Ruggeri before Moreau and I reached the street.

Around them all came the unmistakable form of Brewster, who began cursing at me the moment he was in earshot.

CHAPTER 30

Imanaged—by sheer good fortune or the grace of God —to avoid catching too much of a chill in the events at the river.

Or possibly, it was the blankets Brewster wrapped me in and the brandy he poured down my throat once he'd bundled me into Denis's carriage. He got me home without Captain Vernet waylaying me, and left me with Bartholomew, who stripped me of my wet clothes, plunged me into a hot bath, and then shoveled me directly into bed.

Moreau did not fare as well. I heard, via a letter from Madame Paillard, that the poor fellow, whom we'd conveyed to her home in the Presqu'île, was quite ill. He had swallowed a quantity of river water, which at that point was none too clean, and had to contend with the cuts Madame Jourdain had inflicted on him.

As neither Donata nor Brewster would let me out of bed for the next several days, despite my insistence, I could only wish the man well.

A more pleasant aspect of my confinement was that Gabriella came to dote on me.

She arrived the day after my adventure, flushed and beautiful in her new matronly attire, to bring me a thick, very tasty soup. I did not at all like to think about what had put the pinkness in her cheeks or the flutter in her laugh. I would need to avoid Emile for a time.

Grenville had also caught the sniffles as he'd walked about in the rain, but he'd been well enough to visit me and explain how they'd come to be there to capture Madame Jourdain.

When Denis's coachman had left Moreau and me in La Guillotière, the man had decided to report our whereabouts to Denis. He'd found Denis in his agent's office on the plaza, Brewster and Grenville with him, where they'd paused in their search to wait out the rain. Once the man had explained that we'd rushed from the townhouse to La Guillotière, Grenville had insisted on sending for the gendarmes.

Denis and Brewster had proceeded to the bridge in the coach, but had to wait under shelter on the island side of the Rhône because of the storm. Once the rain and lightning began to ease, they'd crossed, sweeping up Vernet along the way, to find us climbing out of the water, and Madame Jourdain trying to flee.

Madame Jourdain had been arrested for Gallo's murder and waited in the cells of the gendarmerie for her hearing before a magistrate. The gendarmes had found Madame Martin where I'd told Vernet she would be. Her wounds were being tended, and she'd live, but she too was under arrest for assaulting and abducting Signora Ruggeri.

Signora Ruggeri's protective coachman had bundled her away somewhere, Grenville knew not where. Out of reach of Vernet, we both assumed.

Grenville ended his visit with well wishes from Marianne, and I took the opportunity to congratulate him on his upcoming offspring. Grenville thanked me with a mixture of pride and trepidation.

A few after this, I at last convinced Donata to allow me to go downstairs to the library.

I was penning a reply to another letter from Madame Paillard, which gave me the welcome news that Moreau had turned for the better, when Bartholomew announced that I had a visitor.

"Who is it?" I asked without looking up. If it was no one I wished to see, I could feign illness to avoid the encounter.

"It's that actress," Bartholomew replied. "Signora Ruggeri." He held out her engraved card.

I raised my brows, laid aside my pen, took up the card, and followed him to the sitting room.

I noted when I entered that Signora Ruggeri had dressed plainly, in a narrow gown of dull brown without much ornamentation. She appeared subdued, as though she used the ensemble to avoid attention.

Signora Ruggeri surged to her feet when I entered. "Captain Lacey." She bobbed a stiff curtsy. "I heard you were unwell."

I bowed in return. "Only mildly. You seem to have fared better than I or Moreau did."

She shrugged. "My coachman got me to a warm place quickly enough. Besides, I rarely take ill."

"Yes, you told me you were used to boats and water. I suppose you gain a hardiness from them."

"Possibly." Signora Ruggeri lifted her chin. "I am returning to England."

"To Manchester?"

"Mayhap. I met an actor-manager at Mrs. Grenville's soiree who has offered me a place in his company. Mrs. Grenville put in a good word for me."

"Did she?" I wondered if Marianne had done so from sympathy or from recognition of Signora Ruggeri's talent. After all, she'd fooled an entire city for a time into believing she was someone she was not. "I am glad for you."

"No more Signora Ruggeri from Padua." She spoke the words in her florid Italian accent, then dropped it. "Miss Cooke I will be again."

"Who knows what Miss Cooke might become?" I said. "You have much of your life ahead to find out."

Signora Ruggeri appeared more resigned than excited about that prospect. "I must thank you and Colonel Moreau, twice—once for rescuing me from that awful river and then for convincing Captain Vernet that I had nothing to do with Vincenzo's death."

"You did not," I said with conviction. "As you told me, that was all Madame Jourdain."

"Poor Vincenzo." Signora Ruggeri sank to the chair I gestured her to and laid her gloved hands in her lap. "He came after me that night at the comtesse's chateau, because he was certain I had betrayed him. I'd taken all the papers out of his reach, you see."

"Ah." I sank down, easing my sore knee. "I had suspected something of the sort. But you were really keeping them from Madame Jourdain and Madame Martin."

A nod. "Madame Jourdain had become too interested in what we'd collected. Gallo was the one who'd suggested the townhouse in the Presqu'île—he said because its housekeeper would let him in to see me when the comte wasn't there. She was Madame Jourdain's sister and would understand. It was not difficult for me to persuade the comte to let me live there."

The comte had been so infatuated with Signora Ruggeri at that point, that he'd have given her anything she asked.

"But you became suspicious of Madame Martin?"

"Almost at once. I had taken the ledger we used to tot up the figures of those who'd paid. I'd hidden it in the parlor where I met those who called to hand over their money, but I found Madame Martin leafing through it one day. She at first scolded me for my sordidness then offered to assist in our venture. For a share of the profit, of course. Eventually, she began to threaten me. She told me she'd have her sister find the papers Vincenzo had hidden in the La Guillotière house and simply take over our business if I did not capitulate."

"Then you convinced the comte to move you yet again."

"I did. I know I incurred the wrath of everyone in Lyon, but I was less afraid of them than Madame Martin. I didn't dare sleep at night when she stayed in the house, and I was highly nervous. Once I settled into the villa, I went back to La Guillotière, waited until everyone was out, then crept in and took the papers."

"But you left the ledger behind in the townhouse."

Signora Ruggeri shook her head. "There were too many servants packing up my things when I left for me to fetch the ledger. I'd hoped to return to the house when Madame Martin was out, but I had no opportunity. The day I tried, a mob waylaid me in the square." She shivered.

"I recall." So, I had been correct that she'd been to the townhouse that morning, though I'd been slightly wrong about the reason.

"I stored Gallo's papers for a time at the villa," Signora Ruggeri continued. "But I was still afraid. One of the maids at the villa said she was cousin to Madame Martin and Madame Jourdain. She dropped the remark in an offhand way, and she might have simply been passing the time of day, but I feared she meant to aid them. So, I needed a better hiding place."

My eyes widened as I thought through all the places she could have deposited them. "Do not tell me you took them to the comtesse's chateau."

Another nod, but this time a smile danced on Signora Ruggeri's lips. "No one would ever gain entry there without the comtesse's permission. It was a bold plan, I know, but I felt I had no choice. The comte had told me with pride about the old house and the tunnels beneath. I went around the back of the chateau while all the comtesse's guests were pouring in the front and hid the box."

"And then kicked up a row at the front door, demanding the comte admit you," I said, "I was there that night. It was quite a performance."

Signora Ruggeri flushed. "My plan was for the comte to let me in, if only to make me be quiet. Then I would slip down to the tunnels, retrieve the box, hide it, then pretend to retreat to my own house in shame." She sighed. "But the comte was not at home, and the comtesse, to my amazement, took me in. She was kind to me, and the kindness was not feigned." Signora Ruggeri's voice held respect. "I've never met a woman like her. The comte does not deserve her." She finished with conviction.

"I agree with you. Were you able to retrieve the box from the tunnels?"

"I did. I took it to the dressing room of the bedchamber given me. They supposed I'd slept late—an indolent woman—but really I was thoroughly hiding the papers."

"The only paper you did not have was the Italian letter you stole from the comte."

Signora Ruggeri smiled again. "You know much, Captain. Vincenzo had hidden *that* so well I could not find it. I assumed he'd let me have it when I negotiated a good price from the comte."

"You also gave Gallo the name of Lucien Potier."

Her smile vanished. "Yes, but I soon learned that even saying the name earned one censure and even threats. We never did discover why."

"The man was more hated even than you and Gallo," I said, but I gentled my voice. "Wise of you to not pursue that avenue."

"I believe so," Signora Ruggeri agreed. Tears moistened her eyes. "I was dazed when I heard that Vincenzo had been killed. I hadn't loved him in a long while—we were partners in business only once we arrived in Lyon—but I'd known him for years, and at one time, we'd been very close."

"Madame Jourdain has confessed to Vernet that she murdered him," I said.

"So I have learned." Signora Ruggeri heaved a heavier sigh. "She came after him that night, she told me, believing that he knew where I'd taken the papers. According to her, Vincenzo claimed—rightly—that he had no idea where the letters had gone, and wouldn't tell her even when he was dying. She simply left him there and stamped home. She was a madwoman, and her sister wasn't much better."

I nodded. "Madame Jourdain struck down Madame Martin as well."

"Yes, it was terrifying. The two of them were going to make me tell them where the papers were, but then they got into a quarrel as to who would take the lion's share of the profits. I tried to get away while they were fighting, but Madame Jourdain caught me. She took me to that boat …" True fear entered her voice. "She planned to take me downriver where she could kill me if I wouldn't tell her. She'd have killed me anyway." She shuddered. "I can only thank you once more, Captain."

"You can reward me for my valor by letting me have those papers," I said pointedly.

"I brought them." Signora Ruggeri regarded me tiredly. "I went to the comtesse, told her everything, and asked for them. She offered to burn the lot herself, but I didn't trust that someone in her house wouldn't try to make use of them. I trust *you*, Captain, to release the people we held in thrall. I am ashamed, but when one is desperate, one so easily resorts to villainy."

Her entreaty, made while she gazed intensely at me with liquid brown eyes, helped me understand how she'd ensnared the comte, Gallo, and any other man who'd crossed her path. My heart wanted to warm with her flattery, but my common sense reminded me that she was indeed a gifted actress.

"I will destroy the letters, of course," I said. "Never fear. The ledger as well. My man has hidden that somewhere, but I trust him to unearth it for me again." I hoped Brewster hadn't literally buried it, but I honestly had no idea what he'd done.

Signora Ruggeri rose. "Then I will leave you to it. I give you my word that every single thing Vincenzo and I collected is in that box. I never want to see those papers again."

Her disgust made me believe her. How long Signora Ruggeri would remain on the path of righteousness, I could not tell, but her true terror on the river would likely make her step back from crime for a while.

"Is your coachman going with you?" I asked her.

A flush stained her cheeks. "He is. Dumont has been with me from the beginning of my journey and has become a loyal friend. I believe he is sweet on me, poor man, but I will treat him kindly."

I was not certain whether she had true fondness for Dumont or simply saw his usefulness, but her eyes did soften when she spoke of him.

"Be well, Miss Cooke." I took her hands, dared to kiss her cheeks in the French fashion, and then released her.

Signora Ruggeri studied me closely for an alarming moment, as though assessing what sort of protector I'd be, then she shook her head.

"I will try, Captain Lacey. Good-bye."

"Godspeed."

Signora Ruggeri bathed me in one more smile, then turned and glided through the door Bartholomew opened for her, as though on cue. A perfect exit.

I heard Bartholomew direct her down the hall and then front door open and shut. After a few moments, carriage wheels grated on the graveled drive, and Signora Ruggeri was gone.

Bartholomew returned presently with coffee for me, followed by his brother, Matthias, a signal that Grenville had returned. Matthias bore a large box with a stout lock.

"She left this for you, Captain," Bartholomew said as Matthias set the box squarely on an empty table in the corner of the room. "Oh, and this too."

With a grin, Bartholomew produced a key from his pocket and laid it on my open palm.

CHAPTER 31

Grenville, Donata, and I spent the rest of the afternoon sorting through the papers and letters, cross-referencing them with the ledger Brewster brought out of hiding.

Brewster helped Matthias build a large bonfire in the garden, and we burned the entire contents of the box, save for Madame Paillard's letter. That, I would return to her personally.

I opened her letter only enough to ascertain that it was the one she sought, then I folded it again and wrapped it in another paper. Though I was curious, it was Madame Paillard's secret. It would be up to her to tell me what the letter contained, if she wished.

We decided to take the ledger to the comtesse and let her inform those inside it that they no longer had to fear. They would have more confidence in her, I concluded, not the interfering foreigners.

A few days later, I tucked Madame Paillard's letter into my pocket and made my way to the Presqu'île and her cozy home.

Moreau was with her. His face was pale and drawn, but when he shook my hand when I was shown into the sitting room, his grip was strong.

Madame Paillard drew me down to kiss my cheeks and then warmly embraced me.

"You are much welcome here, Captain." She kissed me again before releasing me. "You have done me so many good deeds that I can never repay you."

I cleared my throat, uncomfortable with her adulation. "I have done very little, I assure you, Madame."

"Very little." Madame Paillard's laughter tinkled as she led me to a sofa. "The English are famous for pushing away praise. Saving my Nico's life and sending him home to me was not *little*."

Moreau, who appeared as embarrassed by her gushing as I was, gave me a nod. "I owe you a great debt."

"You did catch the grippe, which I'm certain was humbling enough," I told him. "Consider it a debt paid."

I knew Moreau would not agree, but he nodded again, limping slightly as he resumed his chair near the fire. Still healing from Madame Jourdain's knife, I assumed.

I drew the letter from my coat pocket and held it out. "Madame, your correspondence. As it was private, I did not read it."

Madame Paillard stilled a moment before she took the letter from me warily, as though it might turn and bite her.

She unfolded the pages and skimmed the words, her cheeks burning a sudden, dark red. Then she marched to the tiny fire that crackled on the hearth, thrust the letter into the flames, and jabbed the paper with a poker until it had quite burned to ash.

Moreau and I watched her in silence. Madame Paillard stabbed the embers a few more times, then she straightened, gazed at the hearth a moment, and calmly returned the poker to its place.

She turned back to us and let out a sigh. "There. That is done. Would you like coffee, Captain Lacey? Perhaps some more of my cook's excellent pastries?"

———

THE REST OF MY VISIT WITH MOREAU AND MADAME PAILLARD was congenial, she laughing and jesting with a lightness of heart.

We avoided discussing the case of poor Gallo, who'd paid the ultimate price for his scheming and intimidation, and Signora Ruggeri, who'd nearly paid it as well.

As the afternoon waned, I took my leave, explaining that we would depart for England in a few days.

Madame Paillard once more showered me with kisses and thanks, encouraging me and also Donata to write and to visit whenever we had the mind to.

Moreau walked out with me, he too now leaning on a walking stick. Bartholomew had cleaned and polished mine after its time in the river, and its wood and brass gleamed like new.

"Lacey." Moreau faced me on the doorstep. "You have done me many a good turn since you arrived in Lyon, and this after I had done you only a terrible one. If we had known each other before the war, I might have called you friend."

"Then it would have been awkward when we met in the woods in Spain," I said in a light voice. "You'd might have felt obliged to kill me to prove your loyalty to France."

He answered my feeble humor with a faint smile. "I am glad it did not have to come to that. But now, I *would* like to call you friend. I will not force you to think of me as such in return."

"Nonsense." I held out my hand. "As I have said many a time now, encounters in war are different from encounters in peace. I am pleased to consider you a friend, Moreau."

He hesitated, then clasped my hand, his grip even more certain than before. "Be well, *mon ami.*"

He then towed me a step forward and kissed me on both cheeks without shame. Though I could not bring myself to return the gesture, I wrung his hand harder, appreciating his sentiment.

"*Au revoir,* Colonel," I said to him when we released each other. "I will write, as Madame Paillard requested."

"*Au revoir,* Captain. *Bon voyage.*"

We studied each other for a moment longer, two gentlemen regarding each other stoically in the street.

I gave him a nod, which he returned, then I turned and strode away, my walking stick ringing on pavement that returned the heat of the summer sun.

Brewster fell into step with me when I reached the end of the lane. "I'll miss their cook, I will."

"We might return one day, Brewster."

"Huh. Not if that trip is like this one. You do have a way of finding trouble, guv."

"I find as much at home, so where I am scarcely matters, does it?"

Brewster only grunted in return. "You finished cozying up to your old enemy?"

"Enemies no longer, I am pleased to say."

Brewster shook his head as we made our way to the plaza. "I've given up trying to understand you. I think I never will."

"Never mind, Brewster. Let us have a cup of wine and ease our cares, shall we?"

"As long as it's ale instead, I'll not argue."

We turned for Beaumont's tavern, I determined to enjoy my last repasts there.

———

THE NEXT MORNING, WHEN I WALKED DOWN THE HILL TO Beaumont's for my coffee and breakfast, I found Fernand Devere waiting for me.

He rose from my usual table when I entered, then stood

silently until I took a seat. Beaumont brought me coffee and plunked down a plate of meat and bread, plus another coffee for Fernand.

"Please, eat." Fernand waved at my food. "There is no reason to speak of business when one can enjoy a meal."

While I approved of this philosophy, it was a bit unnerving to consume my breakfast while Fernand sipped coffee and watched me.

Even so, I decided to take my time over the excellent sausages and fresh bread, savoring the simple but delicious fare. I wondered if I could prevail upon Donata's already excellent cook to find food like this in London.

Once I'd finished and drained a second cup of coffee, Fernand stood. "Will you walk with me, Captain?"

"Of course." I dabbed my mouth on my handkerchief, as Beaumont did not supply linens, and drew out coin to leave for my meal.

Fernand stopped me, explaining he'd already paid for it. I gave him my thanks and the inhabitants of the shop a nod of farewell, and followed Fernand out.

Not surprisingly, he led me to the wide space of the plaza. A market thrived there that morning, vendors peddling bright summer strawberries and other fruits, deep green vegetables, pastries glistening with sugar, piles of meat, and strings of sausages, both fresh and dried. They shouted their bargains, and wives and servants argued with them over prices.

Fernand led me past all this to a relatively calm space in the middle of the square. His belligerence had lessened signifi-cantly, and he appeared more sad than angry.

"Captain, I owe you an apology," he began, keeping to English. "I have treated you abominably. We thought—"

"No need to explain," I said quickly. "It is understandable. I arrived to poke up something that should have been left in the past. I am certain that you feared the worst."

"We did." Fernand drew a breath. "I did not trust you, Lacey. Emile did, but the lad can be naive."

"Do not be too hard on him," I said with sudden fondness for my new son-in-law. "There is nothing wrong with seeing the good in people. I am happy my daughter found such a gentle and honest man to be her husband."

Fernand sent me a wry glance. "Perhaps Emile is a little *too* honest. By the bye, it was not he who convinced me I should come and speak to you today, but your daughter. Gabriella explained to me what an honorable man you were and how she'd come to trust you with her life—which you indeed saved on one occasion. It seems you are prone to such things."

I shrugged, discomfited. "Perhaps I am determined for others to have a fair chance."

"If you like. She also assured me that for any secrets the family has, you are not the one who will betray them."

"That depends." I kept my voice mild. "If any harm comes to Gabriella, or even *appears* to come to Gabriella, you can be certain that I will act against the person who threatens her. Not with knowledge of past misdeeds, but with a more savage solution. I'm certain you understand that. You feel the same about your own family."

"I do," Fernand acknowledged. "Believe me, Lacey, Gabriella has nothing to fear from us. We will protect her as fiercely as you would yourself. Auberge is the same."

"He is." I could not deny that Auberge had kept Gabriella safe all the years she'd spent apart from me. "Will you at least satisfy my curiosity about Potier? I have heard the true tale of his death from the comtesse, but she claims she knows nothing of what happened after you took him away. Perhaps it was wiser of her to close her eyes at that point."

"Indeed, she told us of your conversation, and it is true we never spoke of it after that day. As you no doubt have guessed, the furnaces in our foundry burn hot. We destroyed every piece of the man and all we found on him. The ashes were fed to the river. Emile's father said prayers for him, and he has lit a candle for Potier at the village church ever since. I have told Auguste such things are a waste of time on so a vile person, but Emile inherited his honesty and compassion directly from his father." Fernand shook his head as he finished.

"Your faith teaches you that the Lord saves sinners," I said.

"It also teaches that those who do great evil are damned. I certainly do not want to meet Potier in heaven, if I, indeed, am admitted." Fernand shrugged. "I might have to drink with him in hell, instead."

"You acted to aid a woman of great valor, who saved many more from death. I'm certain there will be forgiveness for that."

"Perhaps." Fernand did not sound convinced. "We try not to dwell on the past, which is why you frightened us, Lacey. The past was so very ugly. But our city and our family has survived much and will continue to do so."

"I have no doubt." I clapped Fernand on the shoulder. "I am grateful that my daughter is in good hands. I wanted to be certain, you see."

"I do not blame you." Fernand stepped away but clasped my hand strongly, much as Moreau had. "We will look after her, I promise you. She will be the happiest woman in France."

"See that she is."

I firmed my handshake, and Fernand winced before flashing me his rare smile.

"When next I journey to England on the ironworks' business, may I call on you?" he asked when I released him.

"I would be offended if you did not," I answered with sincerity. "We will be honored to receive you. Brewster will point us to the best alehouse in London, and we will toast each other until we can no longer stand."

"An agreeable idea." Fernand made me a polite bow. "May you have a safe journey home."

"I intend to," I replied. "Thank you, Devere."

———

THE MOST DIFFICULT PART OF DEPARTING LYON WAS LEAVING Gabriella. Donata and I called upon her and Emile in their new home on the road between the ironworks and the Auberge farm the day before we went. It was a pretty cottage, with a fine garden that Gabriella already enjoyed tending.

We spent the afternoon being shown over the house and then reposing in the shady garden, consuming rich coffee and tiny cakes, made by a cook who fussed around Gabriella in a motherly fashion. Brewster had accompanied us, and Gabriella insisted on him joining us to partake of ale and all he wished to eat.

She would be well set up here, I realized. Emile already doted on his new wife, obeying her every wish. Gabriella might become spoiled by his deference, and I fervently hoped she would be.

I shook Emile's hand when we departed, while Donata embraced Gabriella, not without tears. Then I pulled Gabriella into my arms and held her hard.

"Do not forget us," I whispered. "When a very English rain falls here, think of me, shivering in London's cold and damp."

Gabriella laughed, though her voice was thick. "I would never forget you, Father. We will come to visit, I promise you. You must not fear about that."

She held my hands as we came out of the embrace and peered at me with confidence. Emile, behind her, nodded.

She had honor, I knew. I'd seen it. Gabriella also possessed steely determination, and I decided to believe her vow.

I bent close again. "I love you so very much, my daughter."

"And I you, Father." Gabriella kissed my cheek. "Always."

I finally managed to make myself release her, laughing as Gabriella flung her arms around a startled Brewster and bussed him on the cheek.

"That is for your Em," she said.

Brewster grinned, pleased. "Along with all them other gifts you're making me take her."

"She deserves it, Mr. Brewster," Gabriella said.

"She does that. Keep well, Miss Lacey—no, I mean Mrs. Devere, don't I?"

Gabriella flushed. She reached for Emile's hand, and he took it with a glance so loving it made my breath catch.

Donata and I returned to the carriage for the ride back to the villa, Brewster on his perch behind it, where we'd finish our packing to leave on the morrow. Denis had offered his very luxurious carriage for our long trek to Calais—with a stop in Paris so Donata could shop. I knew Denis offered it for Donata's comfort, not mine, but I thanked him for it.

Denis had his de' Medici letter, but he'd expressed his intent to remain in Lyon a few more days, pursuing other business. I decided not to inquire what business, not that he'd have imparted an answer to me if I'd asked.

Grenville and Marianne also planned to linger, staying with Marianne's friends for a time. I looked forward to the reunion of us all in London.

For now, Donata and I would go to Oxfordshire, to spend the rest of June in the soft air of the countryside.

I wiped my eyes as we rolled from Gabriella's home, she and Emile waving us off with great enthusiasm.

"I am sad to leave her," I said as Donata snuggled next to me. "But very glad we shall see Peter and Anne at journey's end. My heart has been empty without them."

"You are a fond papa." Donata patted my arm. "But I agree. I long to hug the both of them and not let go."

"We will have to let them go at some time," I said with resignation. "They will grow up, marry, and leave the nest."

"And have children of their own," Donata reminded me. "Heavens, we'll be overrun with babes. Let us enjoy the quiet while we can."

I kissed her hair. "As long as I can enjoy it with you."

Donata raised her head, eyeing me with the sparkle I'd fallen for years ago. "You are so very flattering, Gabriel. We will certainly bask in our quiet time together."

She gave me a very promising kiss, then settled against me for the ride into Lyon and up the hill to our temporary home, which would now hold many a fine memory.

AUTHOR'S NOTE

Thank you for reading! I hope you enjoyed this jaunt to France with Captain Lacey and family for his daughter's wedding.

As I researched for this book, I uncovered many fascinating facets of the city of Lyon and its long and eventful history. I barely touched on the events of the French Revolution and its aftermath, which were complex and devastating. There is now a monument in Lyon to those who fell during the reprisals after the siege, acknowledging that part of their history.

My research was complicated by the fact that many of the buildings, streets, and bridges were different during the English Regency period, and it took much digging to find what was where at the time of Lacey's visit. Much changed later in the nineteenth century, until most of the bridges and quays there today were put into place. Any errors I have made with roads, place names, and buildings I can only apologize for, as I went with the materials and maps I could find.

Captain Lacey and family return to England once again to solve mysteries in forthcoming books. The captain has more friends and family to assist and many more stories to tell.

HISTORICAL MYSTERIES
BY ASHLEY GARDNER

Robert Archer Paranormal Mysteries

A Matter of Honor

A Matter at New Year's

Leonidas the Gladiator Mysteries

Blood of a Gladiator

Blood Debts

A Gladiator's Tale

The Ring that Caesar Wore

Saturnalian Gifts

Brother at Arms

Captain Lacey Regency Mysteries

The Hanover Square Affair

A Regimental Murder

The Glass House

The Sudbury School Murders

The Necklace Affair

A Body in Berkeley Square

A Covent Garden Mystery

A Death in Norfolk

A Disappearance in Drury Lane

Murder in Grosvenor Square

The Thames River Murders

The Alexandria Affair

A Mystery at Carlton House

Murder in St. Giles

Death at Brighton Pavilion

The Custom House Murders

Murder in the Eternal City

A Darkness in Seven Dials

Murder on the Rhône

The Gentleman's Walking Stick

(short stories: in print in

The Necklace Affair and Other Stories)

Kat Holloway "Below Stairs" **Victorian Mysteries**

(writing as Jennifer Ashley)

A Soupçon of Poison

Death Below Stairs

Scandal Above Stairs

Death in Kew Gardens

Murder in the East End

Death at the Crystal Palace

The Secret of Bow Lane

The Price of Lemon Cake

(novella)

Mrs. Holloway's Christmas Pudding

(holiday novella)

Speculations in Sin

A Measure of Menace

(novella)

A Moveable Feast

(novella)

A Silence in Belgrave Square

Murder in Blackfriars

Mystery Anthologies

Past Crimes

Crimes of Christmas Past

ABOUT THE AUTHOR

USA Today Bestselling author Ashley Gardner is a pseudonym for *New York Times* bestselling author Jennifer Ashley. Under both names—and a third, Allyson James—Ashley has written more than 120 published novels and novellas in mystery, romance, fantasy, and historical fiction. Ashley's books have been translated into more than a dozen different languages and have earned starred reviews in *Publisher's Weekly* and *Booklist.* When she isn't writing, she indulges her love for history by researching and building miniature houses and furniture from many periods, and playing classical guitar and piano.

More about Ashley Gardner's mysteries can be found at the website: www.gardnermysteries.com. Stay up to date on new releases by joining her email alerts here: http://eepurl.com/5n7rz

Follow Ashley Gardner
www.gardnermysteries.com

www.ingramcontent.com/pod-product-compliance
Lightning Source LLC
Chambersburg PA
CBHW030858060726
47591CB00005B/1330